Under The African Sun

Gail Gilbride

CACTUS RAIN
PUBLISHING

Arizona USA

Published by Cactus Rain Publishing, LLC
San Tan Valley, Arizona, USA
www.CactusRainPublishing.com

ISBN 978-0-9962812-5-6

Cover Design by Cactus Rain Publishing, LLC
Certified Proofreader Anita Beery, www.AnitaBeery.com

Published December 1, 2016
Published in the United States of America

DEDICATION

In memory of Jimmy James
...and Rhodes University
1976.

ACKNOWLEDGEMENT

My eternal gratitude to Nadine Laman and her dream team at Cactus Rain Publishing for believing in my story and gently nudging me in the right direction.

My heartfelt thank you to Dr Jo-Anne Richards and Richard Beynon for their amazing mentorship programme at: www.allaboutwritingcourses.com.

To my family, friends and readers, thank you for your endless patience, support and encouragement. I am lucky to have you in my life!

Under The African Sun

Gail Gilbride

Chapter One
October 1976, Cape Town.

The mug shattered as it hit the tiles. Hot coffee splattered over her toes, and she turned up the volume to hear the rest of the seven o'clock news.

"... Ongeluk. Meneer Christopher Jarvis ... kritiese toestand ... Pretoria Noord hospitaal. Geen ander passesiers ..."

"Debs, you look like you've seen a ghost. Are you okay?"

Julia grabbed her arm and Deborah slid onto a barstool. She was aware of Bob's wet nose on her leg, and of Julia pushing him away.

"You're shivering. Tell me, for God's sake!"

"Chris has been in an accident!"

"What's happened?" Julia was leaning over her, her dark eyes scanning for clues.

"Pretoria Noord hospital. I need to phone."

The floors groaned as Julia ran. She had the ward matron on the line in what seemed like a second.

"Come quickly, Debs."

Deborah grabbed the receiver. "Mr Christopher Jarvis. Yes." She held the phone so that Julia could hear, too. "Is it possible to speak to him?"

Her hand went to her mouth. She tried to absorb the matron's words. "Mr Jarvis is not conscious. He is in a critical condition in the Intensive Care Unit."

The phone clanged against the wall and she slid to the floor. No, she couldn't do this. She couldn't collapse. She didn't have the luxury. She had to fight for him, for both of them. She turned on to her hands and knees and pushed herself upright. She staggered to the bedroom and dragged her suitcase from under the bed, tugging drawers open and throwing clothes into it.

"Debs?"

"I must go to him. I have to get to Pretoria."

Julia's hand reached out to her, but she pushed it away and ran past her. The retching didn't stop, even when her stomach was completely empty.

Julia's voice sliced through the running water. "… on standby for the next available flight? Perfect."

Deborah's hand shook. She lit a cigarette and accepted the steaming mug from Julia. The first sip choked her.

"Pack. I'll take you as soon as you're ready."

The doorbell rang insistently. She leant her head against the doorframe, listening to Julia's footsteps and her struggle with the brass knob. It seemed absurd that people were still doing ordinary things. She couldn't pack. It seemed irrelevant. What did it matter what she wore?

"Yes?"

Aimlessly, she followed Julia into the passage. The door was slightly ajar.

"I'm Katie, Chris' assistant. I need to speak to Deborah, it's very important."

"This is not a good time."

"Please."

The door creaked open. Deborah took another deep drag of her cigarette and turned to face the plump, raven-haired woman who was staring at her intently.

"Can I come in?"

The woman was already halfway down the passage. Deborah stared at her. She didn't want delays. Not now. Chris was injured and she should be with him.

"I'm Katie, Chris' research assistant."

Deborah looked at her blankly. She couldn't fathom why she was there. The silence hung until Katie added, "We need to speak."

She searched for a response. Julia looked up from her fabric collage and indicated the barstool.

The woman kept her dark eyes on Deborah. Scooping her long hair into a makeshift bun, she settled on the stool. Deborah took out another cigarette, and Katie produced a light before she could rummage for one.

"I thought it best to meet now, and not at his bedside."

Deborah felt her cheeks heat. Who did this woman think she was? What was this all about?

Katie leant towards her and spoke again. "Chris spoke about you a lot."

Deborah noticed the woman's long leather boots. Muddied Boots.

Julia was frowning. "Listen, I think you should—"

But Katie got in first. "The hospital has put Chris on the critical list. I'm flying to Pretoria this weekend … to see him. Perhaps you want to make plans for next."

Deborah held onto the kitchen counter. It wasn't possible. She must have misunderstood. "Why are *you* flying up to see him? He's not in any condition to—" This woman was behaving as if she were his … The penny finally dropped. She opened her mouth to talk, but a strange noise came from somewhere deep inside her. She needed to breathe and made her way to the back door. The blast of fresh air was welcome. Reluctantly, she turned back to face Katie.

Chris' assistant, or whatever the hell she was, stared, intense brown eyes boring into Deborah. She rose and held out a card. When Deborah didn't move, she flapped it at her, indicating that she take it.

"Here's my name and number, in case you need it."

They *were* riding boots, definitely. She watched the woman drop the card on the counter. She tried to say something, but no words came.

"It wasn't Chris' fault. I—"

Deborah shook her head and held up her hand to stop the words. "No. No, don't—" She couldn't hear this. It wasn't possible. Chris loved *her*, Deborah. He'd said so the night before he left. He'd promised a future together. He'd, he would never have … Why would he have done this to her? Surely she would have seen the signs?

Julia stood and took a step closer to the intruder. "I think we should let Deborah finish packing now, if you don't mind." She walked firmly from the room and Deborah heard the front door open. Her voice floated back to them, disembodied, "We're also about to leave, so you really should go."

At last, the woman dragged her eyes from Deborah's face. "Of course. Yes, of course. I'm just on my way."

Katie stubbed out her cigarette, gathered her velvet hold-all and made her way to the door. She stopped at the entrance and turned to face Deborah. "Oh, and I don't mean to alarm you, but this might not have been an ordinary car accident."

Deborah put her hand to her throat.

"Look, there's no proof, but it seems as if the steering wheel jammed, somehow."

Her voice came back instantly as panic took over. "How do you know this? Why would you know all this? Are you—?"

"I love him, that's all."

Deborah took a few steps towards her. She wanted to grab her shoulders and shake them, tear at her hair, scratch her eyes out. How dare she? She stopped and simply stared at her in disbelief.

Katie hesitated for a moment and then said, "I'll change my flight for next weekend."

○ ○ ○

Chapter Two
January 1976, Pretoria.

"One bag, Pix. We're camping."

Deborah looked at her pile of clothing skeptically.

"Halve it."

She took a shirt and two sundresses off the top reluctantly and put them back in her cupboard. Chris threw her cigarettes in the bin and held out her bikini.

"You might need that."

Deborah rescued the cigarettes and put them in her handbag as Chris folded the tent meticulously. When he had all the bits and pieces counted and in the bag, he tied it to the bottom of his rucksack.

"Give me your sleeping bag." He shook his head and grinned, then unrolled it and rolled it into a tight, perfect bundle, which he strapped to his, above the tent.

"Where's your ID book? You're going to need that."

Deborah rummaged through the desk drawer and was relieved to see its dark green cover under a pile of papers.

"Breakfast's ready. Coffee?"

Mum laid out the cups, as the ground beans filtered into the pot. Chris took a deep breath and inhaled the aroma. "I'm in heaven."

Her mum glanced up at him and almost smiled. She seemed to be warming to him a bit. He packed the Volvo and then strode back.

"Thank you very much for having me stay."

She hesitated and looked up nervously. "Please bring my precious daughter back safely. Yes, I know you don't think she needs looking after, but humour me."

He held the passenger door open.

"She's quite capable, and it's important she stand up against—"

"Chris," Deborah caught his arm and frowned at him. "Mum, I'll be fine. Don't worry."

But her mum wasn't to be fobbed off so easily. She kept her eyes on Chris. "Stand up against what? What do you mean?"

"Nothing, Mum. He just means that we need to travel in Africa and experience this continent. That's all."

ooo

The engine started with a splutter, and Deborah turned to wave as they drove around the circular driveway and began their long journey. Clipped hedges were slowly replaced by long grass and thorn trees. She found herself dozing off and then suddenly jerking awake.

"You okay?" Chris was wiping her cheek with his finger. "He's in a better place now, Pix."

She closed her eyes again.

"Sleep. It'll do you good. I'll wake you when we get there."

Alice Cooper's "Only Women Bleed" played in the tape deck, as Mbabane came into view. Chris mouthed the words and tapped the rhythm. It was growing dark. The bus stops were crowded. She spotted more than one live chicken tucked under an arm. Goats wandered the streets and bicycles zigzagged around their car. People queued for the late bus home, baskets laden with goods, balanced expertly on their heads. A portrait of King Sobhuza II appeared in every shop window, and there seemed to be a woman dressed in a sparkly, slinky, black outfit on every street corner.

"Why are there so many women dressed up like that?"

Chris laughed and patted her leg. "Ladies of the night. They're a tourist attraction here."

Deborah turned her face to the window. She felt like an idiot. Why did she never think for half a second before opening her mouth? She should have guessed that. Once they were through the town, Chris found the campsite and pulled up under a tree, some distance from the other campers. "Shouldn't we move farther down, where the other tents are?"

Chris shook his head. "I prefer to be a bit separate."

Deborah didn't like arguing, but she couldn't help worrying.

"But we're out of the fenced area."

He squinted at her in the gloom and grinned. Holding out the first peg, he scrambled for the hammer with his other hand.

"Hold the peg firmly."

Deborah bit her tongue for a moment and then said, "I'm not comfortable about being out of the campsite. I feel—"

Chris' shoulders tensed and he cut her off sharply. "Pix, you're being neurotic now. We'll be fine just here."

"But I—"

"Oh, for God's sake. If you're going to go on and on about this, we might as well pack up."

Deborah swallowed hard. Chris was right. She was scared of everything. She had to control this. She was being irrational. The last thing she wanted was to spoil this special time. She took a deep breath.

"Okay. Maybe I am being a bit neurotic."

Chris' shoulders dropped and he smiled at her. "Trust me?"

She nodded and put her hand out for the next peg. When they'd finished, he unzipped the entrance and held it open for her. "Home sweet home."

Chris unrolled the sleeping bags and zipped them together. He stripped down to his boxers, and Deborah stepped out of her jeans.

"You should never have given up dancing, you know that? Those legs belong on the stage."

She grinned up at him. "I wasn't that good. PACT wouldn't have taken me."

He patted her thigh and she punched his arm in return.

"I've seen all the newspaper cuttings. You left them lying around in the spare room."

"No, I didn't."

Daddy. He'd packed The Magpies' cutting in his hospital bag. He must have left the rest on the desk. She swallowed awkwardly. Chris pulled her out of the tent once more and folded her in his arms. He gazed up at the stars.

"Look up at the night sky, Pix. What do you see?"

She tilted her head back on his chest. "Stars. Lots of stars." Perhaps Dad was in amongst them. She closed her eyes and swallowed.

"Find the Milky Way now. Can you make it out?" He guided her head with a hand and pointed with his other. "And look, there's Orion's Belt. See, the buckle and then the belt. Three bright stars, really."

"Wow. That's amazing."

Both arms cloaked her and they stood like that, in silence. Eventually, Chris spoke again. "Our fates are already written in the stars. You and me, we were destined to meet."

"We're destined to be together. We're soul mates," she added.

"Maybe we came from different planets, though."

She stretched her arms around his neck. "We didn't."

The crescent moon disappeared behind a cloud, and the air grew nippy. Chris took her hand and drew her into the tent. He shone a torch to check for spiders and then secured their makeshift home with an extra peg. He slid in beside her and adjusted her head on his chest.

"Who are you meeting up with tomorrow?"

Chris traced her collarbone with his fingers. "Just some colleagues from the university here."

Deborah leant on her elbow to raise herself a little. "Can I sit in on your discussions?"

His fingers moved down to her belly button and he circled it slowly. "I don't think so, Pix. It's all pretty confidential stuff. When the time is right, I'll let you know."

She slid away and folded her arms across her chest. Okay, so she hadn't gone on to Masters, but still, she wasn't an imbecile. He also had the annoying habit of reading her mind.

"I know you were involved at Varsity. But this is no longer student politics."

She turned her head away and chose not to reply. There was no point.

"Okay, look. The schooling system's reaching boiling point. The government is talking about enforcing Afrikaans as a medium of instruction for certain subjects. The whole Bantu Education thing is a major bone of contention. It has to go, Pix. It's completely insane. Anyway, a small circle of academics, myself included, is involved in talks about this. More than that, I'm not in a position to tell you."

She frowned as he pulled her closer.

"Of course I'm interested. I want to know. I—"

"I'm trying to protect you, Pix. Can't you understand? It is better for you not to know too much."

She wriggled away, but he reached out for her again.

"As soon as the talks are over, I'm all yours. We can do anything you'd like. I promise."

She allowed his kiss, before wrapping her arms tightly around his neck. "I'd like—"

The words were muffled by his mouth, and she relinquished her future desires, which now drifted into insignificance.

The wind flapped against the sides, but the tent was securely hammered in and hardly moved. Deborah was aware of Chris' deeper breathing as he drifted and she felt herself sinking into sleep.

The sound of ripping penetrated her dream. Her eyes opened slowly, but the noise continued. She sat bolt upright. It was coming from inside the tent. A curved silver blade appeared through the tear, and a man's crouched silhouette was visible against the canvas.

She couldn't breathe. She froze in terror and her eyes stayed glued to the apparition. She touched Chris' shoulder carefully, put a finger on his lips and pointed at the cut, which was growing by the second.

One foot entered the tent through the tear. In a few seconds the intruder would be inside. The panga was clearly visible, and each second passed in slow motion. Through the rip, a light shone farther down the campsite. The camp guard must be on a routine check.

Deborah prayed desperately for him to turn the flashlight their way. Instead it turned farther to the left. In another second, they could be dead. A leg entered through the cut, just as the guard's flashlight finally swung their way, lighting the figure that loomed over them. The panga withdrew instantly, and Deborah listened as the intruder's feet pounded back into the forest behind them.

Chris grabbed her hand and tugged her urgently to the car. Locking her door, he scrambled into the driver's seat. Her body shook uncontrollably, and he held her tightly.

"You were really brave, Pixie. I'm proud of you."

They lay there in the darkness until, gradually, the sky turned red and the first rays of sun appeared. "Let's pack quickly."

Chris gave the ripped tent a quick shake, folded it and put it in the boot. "There's a Southern Sun on the hill. We'll book there for tonight."

Now that they were packed and on their way, Deborah felt resentful. Chris should have taken her fears more seriously. She hadn't been wrong to feel unsure about their camping spot. She hoped he'd apologise, but it didn't seem likely, and it wouldn't be a good idea to bring up the subject again. He'd think she was saying I told you so, and they'd just end up having an argument. She turned her face to the window and watched the sheep grazing the scanty grass at the side of the road.

Eventually the words just popped out of her mouth, "We should have camped in the secure area."

Chris grated the gears as he jerked the car into third.

"Shouldn't we go straight to a police station?"

"No." Chris was concentrating on the road ahead.

"But surely—"

He cut her off abruptly. "I don't want to get involved with the police here. You should understand that."

She watched his eyes flash angrily and inhaled deeply. A brood of red hens dashed across the road and goats sauntered the verge. Dust rose around the car. In the field alongside, a lamb tried to suckle from her mother's empty teats.

Chris' hand reached out for hers. "The guy was just being opportunistic. It was nothing sinister, Pix."

She remembered the steely glint of the panga through the canvas and shivered.

"There's a lovely pool up at the hotel. You can swim and soak up some sun tomorrow while I'm at my meeting. We could even have a look at the casino when I get back."

She'd never been to a casino. It might be exciting. Not that she had anything suitable to wear. "I wouldn't mind the casino."

"Consider it a date."

She adjusted her seat so that she could lie back. The green hills rolled by as the Volvo wound its way upwards to the hotel. The glint of the panga receded in her mind.

"Don't say anything to your mum about last night."

"I know."
Defiantly, she lit a cigarette.

○ ○ ○

Chapter Three

"I'll come back for a few days in winter. I promise."

Her mum nodded. She was biting her lip. "That's a deal then. I'll sponsor the train tickets."

Deborah swung her suitcase up and then pulled herself onto the steps. She hoped to have the compartment to herself, but that was unlikely this time of the year. Mum was waiting at the window and she pushed it right down.

"Eat properly. Not too many takeaways. And write to me, will you?"

"I will, Mum. I will."

Guilt washed over her as she remembered all the times she'd meant to write. She settled back onto the hard green leather to watch the outer suburbs drift by. Just as she was spreading herself out, an elderly lady appeared.

"Ek was in die verkeerde plek," she said by way of explanation. Deborah quickly shifted her belongings off the spare seat as her companion squeezed herself through the doorway.

"Hello, I'm Deborah."

Her companion smiled gratefully. "Elsa. Tannie Elsa. Was that your ma at the window?"

Deborah nodded.

"Pa didn't come, too?"

She hesitated for a moment before answering. "My father passed away, a few weeks ago."

Tannie Elsa grabbed Deborah's hand. "I'm very sorry."

The first dinner gong sounded, and Deborah stood to go as the woman shook her head and opened her cooler bag.

"Kom eet saam met my. I've got more than enough food."

Deborah would have preferred not to, but a plate was already being prepared for her and she sat down again. Warm vetkoek, sweet pumpkin fritters and a bean salad were placed in front of her.

"Gemmerbier?" Tannie Elsa was already pouring her a glass.

"Thank you very much." She put her hand out to take the knife and fork wrapped in a yellow napkin, and her hand was enfolded for a moment.

"You miss him."

Deborah felt her throat choke up. She didn't want to speak about this, but her companion waited for a reply. "He was our rock."

Tannie Elsa leant towards her and met her eyes. "Jy moet bid. Prayer is very powerful, you know."

Deborah tried not to look away from the woman's intense eyes.

"You'll never be alone. God is altyd daar."

She bit into the vetkoek and the warm, spicy mincemeat lifted her spirits a little. She wanted to believe that God was always there, but it didn't feel like it. Her companion seemed to sense her doubt.

"My kind, dit is alles in God se hande. You must believe that. I'll pray for you."

Deborah felt comforted by the offer. Her prayers wouldn't go amiss. A whole new year awaited her in Cape Town, and she could do with God watching over her.

ooo

The sun was streaming through the window when Cape Town Station crept into view, and the steam train screeched to a halt. Baggage men were already manoeuvring huge black trolleys along the platform, ready to transport heavy suitcases to taxis outside. People waved and hugged their loved ones. She scanned the crowd anxiously until she spotted Chris. He strode towards her and his blue eyes surveyed the crowd. A faded blue t-shirt stretched across his chest, and a darker blue sweater was tied loosely around his neck. His mouth pursed in concentration and then relaxed as he saw her. She waved and struggled past fellow passengers to reach the door.

"Pass your suitcase through the window," he shouted.

She heaved it up onto the seat and then balanced it on the basin before she managed to push it halfway.

"I've got it. You can let go now."

Deborah squeezed past passengers in the narrow passage and reached the doorway. She was in his arms in a second and he lifted her off her feet. When her All Stars touched the ground again, he whispered into her hair.

"At last you're back."

She kissed his cheek. "I missed you every single day."

Chris picked up her case, declined the offer of the baggage ride and took Deborah's hand in his. "I'm parked just outside."

As they walked along the platform, Deborah remembered how much she loved this city.

"A peach for my peach," a young hawker called out to her. "Strawberries for her beautiful hair," he shouted to Chris. When they walked on, he called after them, "Don't be so stingy, meneer."

Chris laughed as he ruffled Deborah's hair. "Strawberry head."

A cloth settled over Table Mountain. Deborah rubbed her shoulders as the southeaster threatened to sweep her off her feet. She took Chris' arm quickly and he opened the passenger door. Her hair had blown all over her face, and she tried to push it back so that she could see in front of her.

"Baby, I Love Your Way" filled the car and Chris reached to turn it up.

"I'll take you back to the cottage tomorrow morning. But tonight you're coming home with me."

The festive lights above Adderley Street lit the sky, and angels flew above them. The company Gardens up ahead were teeming with people, and she resolved to take a walk through the rose garden as soon as possible. As they reached the top of Kloof Nek, she watched the cable car bringing down its load of tourists. The road wound down and hugged the coast, with Camps Bay, Bakoven, the Twelve Apostles appearing on the left. Clouds were forming. White horses galloped along the sea and a cargo ship hugged the horizon. Seagulls screeched and dive-bombed for fish, as waves broke and then moved swiftly between the rocks below. Llandudno came into view, and Deborah stretched her neck to see the surfers taking a wave.

"You okay?"

Chris rubbed her cheek and she leant into his hand. "Yes. As long as you'll be with me forever."

He put his hand back on the wheel and tapped a rhythm. "I'll give you up for music and the free electric band," he sang.

"You wouldn't really, hey?" She punched him harder than she'd intended.

"What's with this 'forever' stuff? You're sounding a bit heavy. Lighten up, girl." He picked up the lyrics again.

The valley of Hout Bay came into view as they passed The Suikerbossie restaurant. Chris turned left into Valley Road, and Deborah saw horses appearing on either side of her. Huge chocolate brown stallions grazed next to dappled ponies. A black stallion reared and whinnied, before he trotted over to a little group gathered at the fence. Towards the end of the long road, Chris stopped to open a wooden gate at the entrance to a large Cape Dutch manor.

"You've moved here now?"

"Over there."

He pointed to a little cottage in the corner of the property, far from the main house. The Volvo juddered to a stop as he pulled onto the grass.

"We've just run out of petrol," he said cheerfully.

He held the cottage door open, and she stepped onto the terra cotta tiles of a cosy lounge. A fireplace caught her attention straight away, and she noticed the cones in a basket, all ready for the next Cape winter.

"The bedroom is through the arch." Chris put her suitcase down next to the neatly made mattress on the floor. "Welcome to my abode."

He held out his hand to her and led her out into the back garden. "Meet my new best friend, Hercules."

She put her hand out tentatively, and Chris guided it onto Hercules's velvet nose. "Don't be afraid. He won't hurt you."

The stallion's chocolate eyes met her gaze. He was magnificent and she stared at his dark, glistening coat and powerful muscles. A white star on his forehead added an angelic touch, and she felt herself melting in his commanding presence.

"How long is forever, anyway?" Chris hooked his thumb into the top of her jeans.

The winding road to Rondebosch left Deborah feeling queasy.

"Good luck, Pix." Chris pecked her on the cheek and pulled away before she reached the gate. Bob's tail wagged wildly and he barked until she stopped to hug him. She wiggled the door handle until the key clicked, then dragged her case to the small bedroom and unpacked. A bunch of Shasta daisies were reflected in the mirror. Julia's touch! She couldn't wait to see her that evening.

The clock struck eight. Oh hell, she hadn't realised it had gotten so late. If she hurried, she could make the next train to town.

"Sorry, boy," she shouted over her shoulder as she sprinted out and towards the station.

Deborah squeezed in as soon as the train doors opened and balanced herself against the edge of a seat. People surged onto the train at every stop, and by the time they reached Cape Town, she knew how sardines felt. The doors opened and the packed occupants burst free, swarming in all directions. She wove her way through the crowds and turned into Adderley Street. The "Cape Doctor" had turned it into a wind tunnel, and her skirt instantly whipped itself around her head. She struggled to smooth it down and had to cling to the hem for the rest of the walk. This could qualify as a real black southeaster. She pushed into the wind for another two blocks, before Newspaper House came into view.

The sound of speeding typewriters was overwhelming. Coffee and cigarettes filled the air, and no one looked up when she entered. Ginger tapped on his mug with a pen. "Everyone, this is Deborah Morley. She's our new intern and will be part of the newsroom from now on. Show her the ropes. Be nice."

A few heads lifted, grinned at her and then bent over again. Ginger steered her to a spare desk and pulled the chair out.

"Right. The 'bergies' in the Gardens. Find out who they are and why they're there, how long they've been living like this, how they survive. You'll work with Annie for a few weeks. She'll show you the ropes."

Deborah watched his long legs zigzag between the desks. Chairs scratched across the wooden floor as journalists moved to accommodate him. When he got to the other side of the room, he turned and pointed to the coffee table, which sagged a little from the weight of mugs, Nescafe bottles, special teas, milk jugs and sugar bowls.

"Help yourself," he suggested, before disappearing behind his desk.

She accepted a cigarette from Annie and smiled.

"Nervous?"

"Terrified, actually."

Annie rearranged her spiky fringe and adjusted her glasses. "You'll be fine."

A tall, freckly young man pushed a strand of his unruly blonde curls out of his eyes, before he stretched a hand out to her.

"Charlie. Welcome to the madhouse."

"The political reporter," Annie whispered in her ear as she grabbed her arm and steered her around the desks.

"Politics was one of my majors," Deborah said hopefully.

"That so?"

"Yes, but I don't think I could write about it."

Charlie raised an eyebrow and then turned back to his typewriter. She felt her ears heat up as Annie pulled her along.

"This is Vusi, over there Johnno, Lesley behind the counter, Tom at the window, June, Nigel and Steven. Don't worry about remembering everyone's names today."

Deborah returned the "hellos" and took the pile of papers Annie held out to her.

"Start reading. This afternoon we'll go into the Gardens and find a bergie or two to interview."

She tried not to be distracted by the earnest conversation Immediately behind her. Charlie was briefing someone about an assassination that had just happened. She couldn't make out exactly what they were saying, but she felt the intensity. She forced herself to concentrate on the notes in front of her.

○○○

Deborah elbowed her way through the crowd. A ponytailed student spilt beer on Deborah's shoulder and apologised. As she squeezed between two burly rugby players she recognised a few girls from Varsity days and waved. The Pig was swarming with young bodies. Deborah squinted to find him. A hand waved above the heads and Chris stood up, causing a familiar lurch in her stomach. People turned and she noted the looks of amusement when he whirled her into a bear hug.

"Working girl now."

She matched his smile.

"I've got you a shandy, Pix."

He squeezed over to make room on the bench, and she swung her leg over next to him. Rodriguez crooned, "I wonder how many times you've had sex and I wonder if you …" and some of the rugger bugger crowd raised their beers in unison, before they banged them down on the wooden table. Chris sipped and frowned when Deborah lit a cigarette.

"I thought you were going to give it up?"

Deborah shrugged her shoulders. "I will soon."

"You know what they say about kissing a smoker?" he whispered into her hair. She put it out in the aluminium frog.

"Share some chips?"

She was suddenly ravenous. The day had whizzed by, and she hadn't given any thought to food.

The waiter put four pints down at the next table. Chris took another sip. He always had only the one.

"So a journo, hey?" He punched her on the arm as she took a gulp of her drink.

"An intern still," she corrected. He gave one of his infectious laughs, which always made her smile.

"What are you going to be writing about?"

"Bergies."

She could feel Chris' amusement as he wound his fingers through her hair. She felt a familiar warmth seep into her body.

"Chris, someone important was assassinated this morning. Someone called Albert."

His face changed in an instant, and she found herself wishing she hadn't mentioned this. "Albert Jennings," he whispered.

She shifted uncomfortably on the bench and waited for the rebuke.

"Don't you know who he is, Deborah?"

She hesitated before meeting his eyes. She had heard of Jennings but didn't know exactly what he was involved in.

"Sometimes I can hardly believe you majored in pol—"

An anxious bubble was now forming in her gut. She needed to turn the clock back quickly. "Stop it, Chris. What does it matter? At least I want to know, that's why I asked you."

When there was no response, she touched his cheek. "Please. Give me a break. It was my first day, after all."

His arm went around her waist and she moved closer to him again. "Sorry, Pix. He was a colleague. I'm just upset."

○○○

Deborah leant against the door to push it open. Bob raced out to chase the hadedas off the little patch of grass. He lifted his leg on the rosebush and gave the birds one more warning bark before following her inside. His tail slapped her on the legs and he wove around her, almost tripping her.

"Bob, bugger off now." Deborah pushed his wet nose away. Julia was already home and spicy smells wafted down the passage.

"Hmmm. What's for supper?" She watched her friend stirring the cast iron pot and adding copious amounts of red wine.

"Pasta à la Julia."

"Can't wait."

She kept quiet about the plate of chips she'd just shared. Oh well, it wasn't often she got to have two dinners.

She dropped into the brown sofa and put her feet up on the coffee table. Chipped pink nail polish caught her eye, and she made a mental note to redo them.

"How was your first day, Debs?"

"Good."

"That's it? Good?"

Deborah yawned and plumped the cushions. "It was great. I loved it. I'm going to love being a journalist. Yours?"

"So-so." Deborah waited for the rest. "Can't get the right fabrics for my client. Bit frustrating, but I'll get there eventually."

"What are you looking for? Blue velvet and silk again?"

"Raw silk, shades of blue, for a fancy twenty-first. She wants an 'out of space' theme. Difficult to source the material for a start."

"I would offer my services, but wouldn't know the difference between raw and ordinary silk if it bit me on the bum."

She watched Julia's face break into a wry grin. Then she folded the serviettes carefully and laid them next to the knives.

"Chris not coming?"

She shook her head and reached for the plates. "Gone to a colleague for a working supper."

"Male or female?"

Deborah flicked the dishtowel at Julia's arm. "I don't know, Jules. I didn't ask him."

"Well, you should!"

"He'd tell me if it was important."

The pasta suddenly got a vigorous stir. Julia seemed to hesitate then blurted, "I worry about you. You're naïve sometimes."

"I'm not."

"Yes, Debs. You are. Everyone loves you for it. But I think you should ask Chris more …"

Deborah reached for the wine glasses. She didn't really want to talk about this. Chris would tell her if he needed to. It obviously wasn't a big deal.

"How long have you two been dating now?" She sliced the fresh baguette thinly and arranged it on a narrow board.

"Four years." She closed one eye to fill the salt cellar and then leant forward to reach for the pepper.

"Four years! Where's that engagement ring? C'mon, girl. Give him a bit of a nudge. You should, you know."

Deborah scooped up the spilt salt and tossed it over her left shoulder. Then she took out the dead flowers and manoeuvred the vase under the cold tap. She rearranged the still okay ones and swung the vase so that the crack faced the sink.

"How's that supper coming along, Jules? I'm starving."

○ ○ ○

Chapter Four
February 1976

"Bye, Bye, Miss American Pie" blared down the road. Deborah moved the curtains to see where the racket was coming from and shook her head.

A bakkie mounted the pavement and stalled. Camouflage jeans emerged and the door slammed. Bob barked wildly as the old bell jingled. Deborah opened the door.

Boetie ducked his head, flung her over his shoulder and then strode to the kitchen, paying no attention to Bob, who was attacking his ankles. The sofa squeaked like a trapped mouse as she landed on it.

"Tea, sleeping beauty?"

Deborah laughed. This guy was something else. If it had been anyone else, she'd have been cross.

"I'm not five years old and stuck up a tree. I'm all grown up, you know."

He ducked and the cushion whizzed past him.

"You're also a bit heavier. I hadn't thought of that."

Deborah reached for a cigarette.

"Where's the Lady Julia?"

"Sailing. It's Saturday, remember? The day Julia sails and I sleep in, if it's not dancing day. What are you hanging around here for, anyway?"

"Fixed your neighbour's wiring. At least she was pleased to see me."

"Well, you know what they say about lonely ladies who call in the tall, dark, sexy neighbourhood electrician, especially on a weekend."

"At your service, princess."

Boetie picked up her ballet shoes from the carpet and put his hands in them. He did a finger dance, before placing them on Deborah's feet.

"That's kind of you."

"What is?"

"You know. The free lessons for those Gugs kids. Really nice."

Deborah shrugged and looked down. She didn't feel she needed the praise. She loved the classes. It just felt good to be able to offer the kids a taste of ballet. And of course she also got to dance a bit.

"Do you girls own a proper tea pot?" Boetie was already opening cupboard doors when she pointed to the shelf above the sink. He switched the kettle on and swished the dishcloth, matador-style, before Bob, who turned in a quick circle, laid down and fell asleep. Boetie turned and draped the dishcloth tenderly over Deborah's face.

"Boetie!" She threw it off impatiently and lunged at him. He jumped out of her way.

"What, princess?"

She put a hand to her forehead. His antics were fast becoming a little tedious.

"You can't just barge in here, throw me over your shoulder like a bag of potatoes and then take over our kitchen."

"I just did."

She tucked one leg under her and blew on the tea. He was annoyingly cheerful, but she couldn't help being amused. "You are incorrigible."

Boetie did a rabbit-like wiggle of his nose. "Incorrigible. Big words for the journalist, hmm?"

"Don't be stupid, Boetie."

He wasn't put off by her reprimand. On the contrary, it seemed to spur him on. "Ah ha. So now I'm the village idiot."

She shook her hair back from her face and took a big gulp of her cooling tea. He was getting ready for some sparring, and his rugby thighs spread out as he leant over his mug.

"Shift up, Debs." He shifted her closer to the edge of the sofa. "So?"

She indicated "what" with her hands.

"So tell me about the newsroom. How was your first day?" Deborah put her mug down and lit a cigarette before turning to face him full on.

"It was terrifying. I met all the people in the newsroom and I don't remember a single name. My fingers froze on the typewriter and I couldn't think of anything to type. I'm never ever going back and ..."

Boetie chipped in before she could think up any more to say. "You liked it, jou stoute ding."

A laugh bubbled out of her and she stopped pretending. "Yes. I loved it."

Boetie jumped up, drew a tape from his shirt pocket and jammed it into the deck. He stretched his arms out, and when she didn't respond, pulled her to her feet.

"You should be dancing." Ge Korsten's "Liefling" vibrated the floor. "Show me what you teach the kids."

She shook her head at him.

"Ag, c'mon meisie. Just one of the steps. Please." His frown deepened as he tried to follow her.

"Right foot out, in, back. Left foot back. Right front, left front, skip, click together. Point those toes."

"I've got it," he shouted, and Debs allowed him a few more turns around the room before she pushed him back.

"I've just woken up, Boetie. It's too early for sakkie-sakkie." She turned the music down and wilted into the sofa again.

"Nou's jy a 'wet blanket.'"

Ge's voice tapered off gradually and Boetie sang along. Pouring himself more tea, he settled in the armchair.

"So what's your first story, then?"

Deborah hesitated before she answered. She'd seen Chris' reaction. "The Gardens' bergies ..."

Boetie raised a dark eyebrow and cocked his head. "Hmmm. You must let me read it when it's finished, hey?"

"I'm hoping to shadow Charlie, the political reporter. He's investigating the Jennings murder."

It was like flicking a switch. The flippant mood dissolved instantly. "Jennings? Are you serious?"

Deborah didn't offer an answer.

"Ag nee man."

She put out her cigarette and emptied the ashtray in the bin. If she'd thought about it, she could have predicted this reaction.

"Debs?" She could feel his emotions intensifying.

"What? You want me to write about koeksuster recipes?"

Boetie shook a finger, but a smile was already creeping into the corners of his mouth. She returned it.

"I did study politics."

"This is dangerous territory. Really. I'm just worried about you. You don't know what these people …"

She looked out of the window at the hadedas. Why did everyone think she was such an incompetent? Out of the corner of her eye, she watched Boetie pace. The floors vibrated under his army boots. He started to say something and then stopped when the phone rang.

Debs ran to answer it. "I'm having tea with Boetie. He popped by. Don't be silly. We're just friends."

She listened to Chris' excuse for the night and bit her scraggily nail off. "… need to work … research assistant can only help tonight …"

This was becoming a pattern, much as she was trying to deny it. She plunged in before she could change her mind. "Is your research assistant a girl?"

It was blurted out and she held the phone away from her ear as Chris exploded. "What a ridiculous question. You're being really silly … immature."

The receiver went down gently and she met Boetie's eyes. He shook his head at her.

"That Chris is another story. I don't know why you hang in there. I'm pretty sure this phone is tapped because of—"

The shrill ring drowned out his next words and he picked up the phone immediately. "To Deborah? Afraid not. She just left with a rugby player. Yes, I'll tell her …"

Deborah grappled with Boetie and managed to grab the phone out of his hand. "Sorry."

She expected Chris to be annoyed, and his reply took her by surprise.

"I see he's still the funny guy, hey?"

Her toe circled the cushion as she waited for the apology. He always did, in some way or another, and he knew she'd never resist him. "How about a ride on Noordhoek Beach, early tomorrow morning?"

It took her a moment to gather her thoughts. "I've never ridden a horse, Chris."

"Always a first time."

Debs nodded into the receiver.

"He can't see you," Boetie mouthed and crossed his eyes at her.

Chris didn't wait for her reply. "I'll pick you up at seven."

Boetie was drawing hearts in the air and pretending to swoon. Deborah turned her back so she wouldn't laugh.

"I love you, too."

She started to pick up the mugs and run the water in the sink. She knew he loved her. It was just that sometimes …

"Okay, okay, I'm leaving." Boetie shrugged in defeat, pecked her on the cheek and flicked his tape out of the deck. "I can find my way out. Don't worry about me."

The front door creaked open, and, just before it closed, he threw in a parting shot. "That poephol doesn't deserve you, you know."

She submerged her hands in the warm soapy water and winced as the front door slammed.

ooo

"Put your foot in my hand, Pix."

"But you can't hold me …"

She grabbed the saddle beneath her to steady herself before attempting to stroke the horse's mane. Chris had her reins in his hands.

"Cuddle her. She loves that."

Deborah leant forward, rubbed her face against the horse's soft, piebald mane and then wrapped her arms around her powerful neck. Chris seemed to be whispering in her ear. She crunched the carrot noisily and sniffed his palm for more.

"She's called Sea Breeze. Talk to her."

Deborah had never talked to a horse before. She kept stroking her mane while Chris adjusted her posture and tightened the stirrups over her takkies.

"Knees tightly against her. That's it. You're looking good."

He mounted Hercules effortlessly and clicked his tongue.

25

"I've got your reins for now. We'll see how you go first, and then I'll hand them to you."

Hercules walked ahead and Sea Breeze followed. Deborah breathed deeply. She wiggled into the saddle and tried to grip with her knees. She could sense that Sea Breeze wanted to be right next to her friend, and if he behaved, she would. Her mouth felt dry and she tightened her grip on the saddle.

"Keep the knees tightly against her."

They waded into the surf, and salty spray shot up into her face. Hercules circled her, and she put a hand on his velvety nose. His hot breath tickled her palm. Seagulls screeched ahead and dive-bombed for fish. Thin wispy clouds drifted across the sky as the waves whooshed and broke, bubbling and foaming on the sand.

Chris scooped up a white shell with his crop. He rinsed the sand off it, pressed his lips against it and then pressed it into her hand. Deborah held the cool shell tightly for a moment and then pushed it down into her pocket.

"Take the reins now. We're going into a slow trot. Just follow Hercules."

Chris clicked his heels against the huge stallion and whispered a command. Sea Breeze whinnied and Deborah gently pulled the reins so that they fell into line.

She mimicked Chris' slow up and down movement and tightened her bottom and knees. A bubble of excitement rose in her chest. She was riding a creamy piebald horse on the most beautiful beach in the world. Her hair swept across her face and she blew it out of her eyes. Chris' familiar back and long legs bopped up and down in front of her. If she were dreaming, she would hope never to wake.

"Whoa boy."

Chris slowed them to a walk and turned just as Deborah felt her grin reaching her ears.

"Swing both legs over to this side. That's it."

Both sets of reins hung loosely in Chris' one hand while he whisked her off Sea Breeze's back with the other.

"I'm impressed. Really."

As he looped both reins over a rock and pulled them tighter, she moved closer and smelt the salt on his t-shirt.

"You have extraordinary eyes, Pix. Sometimes they're emerald green, and today they're as azure as the sky. I've never seen a pair like this on anyone else."

He pulled her down onto the sand next to him and kissed her until she had to pull away for breath. Sand and sea salt mingled on her tongue as she reached for him again and again. Sea Breeze nuzzled Hercules, and their thick tails flicked away a few flies.

The northwester came up and the waves crashed onto the shore, bringing little jelly bluebottles onto the sand. She leant against him and looked up at his face. It was rare to see him so carefree, and she put her hand up to stroke his "bok-baard."

Then he was on his feet and adjusting Hercules' saddle.

"Hold Sea Breeze. Here."

Chris turned Hercules, hoisted himself into the saddle and raced off down the beach. Deborah scrambled to stand and grasp Sea Breeze's reins. Hercules moved from a fast canter to a gallop across the beach. Chris' straight back was leaning forward and his knees gripped tightly. Horse and man swiftly faded into the mist, and the sound of muffled hooves gradually disappeared. She was uncertain now. She wished she could turn the clock back just those few minutes. Why had he suddenly raced off?

Deborah was relieved when they came back into focus. The gallop slowed to a trot and Chris' t-shirt clung to his wet chest, glistening in the soft light. Hercules turned towards Sea Breeze. Chris patted and stroked the snorting horse, whispering into his ear. Sea Breeze whinnied in protest, and her ears perked up to welcome her warrior. Chris flopped down next to Deborah and wiped his face on her t-shirt.

"Hey!"

He pushed his head into her stomach, and she rolled away so that his face dropped into the sand beside her.

He spat the sand out fiercely and then tackled her. "Don't you roll away from me, girl."

He was on top of her, pinning her down with his knees, tickling her until the beach echoed with her laughter and she pleaded with him to stop.

"Say sorry."

"I'm sorry."

"Say sorry, Chris."

"Chris …" She was winded by the time he released her and dropped her head into his lap. He tucked her hair behind her ears. Then he rubbed her back roughly. His light mood seemed to have dissipated.

"I wish we were in a small village and you were the girl next door. We could court and then get married."

Deborah sat up and looked at him quizzically. "I can be the girl next door. We can get mar—"

Chris shook his head quickly. What did he mean? Why would he say that? She felt confused, and suddenly she knew that there was a lot more to this.

"Chris?"

"I wish life was that simple, Deborah. But it just isn't. We're living in dangerous times, in a country torn apart by politics, and I'm slap-bang in the middle of it."

He held out his hand to pull her up. He gently disengaged her before lifting her onto Sea Breeze's back and patted her on the cheek.

"Let's just live for today. Today you are the girl next door. You're my Pixie girl."

She tilted her head at him and wriggled into the saddle. "What just happened, Chris?"

He tightened the stirrups, handed her the reins and turned Hercules around.

○○○

Deborah struggled with the key, managed to turn the creaky knob and dashed to pick up the phone. Chris patted the barking Bob, picked up her bag and followed her into the cottage.

"Hello. Yes, it's Deborah."

She mouthed a sorry to Chris and gestured at the sofa.

"It'll be ready for Monday morning. First thing, I know. No, I won't. I'm a hard-working intern. How could I fail to be? I'm trained by the best, aren't I? Okay then. I'll be in early, early. You too. Bye."

She took the offered wine glass and noticed Chris' pursed lips. "That was my boss, Ginger."

"I gathered as much."

She sat in the armchair and leant towards Chris. "Why are you being all strange now?"

There was the hint of a smile. "Not at all, Pix." His face tensed up again and he looked down at his watch.

"Chris?"

"You seem very sparky when you talk to your boss."

"I'm not all sparky!"

"Yes. You are. You never talk to me like that."

Deborah got up and moved towards the sofa. Was it possible Chris was a little jealous? She could hardly believe that. He knew how she felt about him. Still, his reaction was …

Chris was up and putting his beer bottle in the sink. "I need to get going now."

"Aw. Really?"

"A research meeting."

She wanted to ask who he was meeting. Was his research assistant a girl or not? Why was it all so secret? She studied his clenched jaw and glazed eyes. They didn't tell her anything. Her eyes searched his as he pecked her on the cheek, squeezed her shoulder and then strode down the passage. She waved from the gate but Chris had already turned the corner, without a backward glance.

○○○

"A good start, Deborah."

Ginger waved her first story under her nose. Annie raised a thumb, and her silver-starred nail sparkled in the light.

"Now a follow-up. Could some families be traced? Dig into their former lives. Could some of these bergies have had careers in a previous life?"

She scribbled down Ginger's suggestions as he spoke.

"Uhmm ..."

Ginger waited for her to continue.

"Would it be possible for me to also shadow someone on the Jennings story?"

Ginger twiddled his moustache.

"Why particularly that story?"

"I'm interested in it."

He studied her. "You know a lot about Jennings, or are you just interested in politics, generally?"

Deborah met his gaze. "Politics, whatever's happening right now. I'm curious about people."

Ginger tapped a pencil against her chair as he summed her up. "Let me give it some thought, okay?"

"I don't want to be in the way." She stepped back and adjusted her notes.

"Coffee, Debs? "Annie was lighting a cigarette and spilling milk as she did so.

"Please."

"How was your weekend? Chris pitch?"

"Great. Yes. Yours?" Deborah took a gulp of her coffee and glanced at her notes.

"Charlie Parker's with the usual crowd. A blast. Tequila flowing, dancing till late, late …"

Ginger was standing at his desk, indicating his watch. Deborah patted Annie's arm and jerked her head in his direction.

"We'd better get onto it." She slid into her chair and added to the cacophony in the room.

"Meeting at five." Ginger's voice rose above the steady click-click. Shoot. She'd have to miss her beer with Chris.

As the newsroom emptied, he gestured to Deborah to stay behind. She took out her notebook, but he waved it away.

"Would you be interested in coming paddling on Saturday?"

She was a bit taken aback. It was her Saturday for the dancing class. But she supposed she could swop it for the following week, just this once.

"A group of us are doing the Berg River together. You'll have the chance to meet some of the team outside of the newsroom."

She didn't know anything about canoeing, either, and stalled for time.

"Double canoes. You won't have to handle one on your own, if that's what's worrying you."

Her New Year's resolution was to seize all opportunities which came her way. Here was one, staring her in the face.

○○○

The Berg River was pumping. Ginger was shouting over the rush of the rapids, organising partners for the narrow canoes lined up on the bank. Charlie made his way over to her. Deborah hoped she'd be partnered with him, or at least someone else a little experienced. Her stomach stirred, and she wasn't sure whether she was feeling really excited or just nervous.

"I'm Charlie, in case you didn't remember everyone's name." He seemed much friendlier today and she smiled warmly. "I believe you have an interest in politics?"

"Well, it was one of my majors, but I ..."

"Okay." He tipped his canoe the right way up. "Perhaps you'd be interested in tagging along with me, sometime next week. I could do with an extra helper."

Deborah felt her cheeks heat up and she blurted, "I'd love to."

"Great. We'll chat about it Monday then. It's Deborah, isn't it?"

She watched him put on his life jacket, before he pushed his canoe into the shallows. Annie had walked up quietly, nudged her in the side and was now nodding her head knowingly. She was hoping Charlie didn't have a paddling partner yet, when Ginger's voice boomed from the bank.

"Girl with the purple fringe can come with me."

Annie shrugged and idled her way towards Ginger's canoe. Charlie turned to Deborah, and she moved forward to claim her place. She took the life jacket from him and stepped a little shakily into the back of the canoe.

"Front, Deborah. Unless you want to steer?"

She shook her head, picked up her paddle to follow his demo and listened intently to the do's and don'ts in the river. While she was tying her splash cover tightly, Charlie slid into the back and patted her on the shoulder.

"You paddle, I steer. Got it?"

Deborah felt her throat tighten.

"Dip in on the left. Now right. Left. Right. That's it. Slowly, slowly. Keep a steady rhythm."

They were gliding slowly. Deborah wiggled her hips down and pushed her feet against each side. She felt the canoe moving effortlessly down the river. Tall grasses hugged the banks, and a few white-eyes swooped in and out of them along the way. A hawk free-wheeled on its mighty wingspan, and clouds floated in the azure sky. Deborah shifted her hips to make sure she was stabilized and then slipped into Charlie's easy rhythm.

Her breathing slowed and her shoulders relaxed as she listened to the river sounds. "I can do this," she whispered to herself. Charlie pointed out the weavers' nests and the angry wives rejecting their husbands' poor efforts. A fish slapped the water next to her, and dragonflies hovered over the long grasses. The river was rich with life, everywhere she looked. Deborah turned her face up to the sun and felt its warmth on her cheeks.

She was lulled into a dreamy state and was just beginning to think it was really quite easy, when Charlie changed pace. The water grew steadily louder and the gentle swishing sound was being drowned out by loud rumbling. Her reflexes heightened instinctively. She followed Charlie's lead and lifted her paddle out of the water.

"Rapid up ahead, girl."

Her breath was coming in shorter bursts.

"We'll approach slowly. When I shout paddle, you do that. Okay?"

He patted her shoulder and then dipped his paddle in the water. Waves chopped against the boat and she adjusted her balance.

"We're approaching it now." Charlie pushed back with his paddle, and the canoe moved sideways.

"Paddle hard now. Ease a little. Harder again."

She could feel Charlie steering them and she paddled as hard as she could.

"Good girl. You're doing well."

Her heart was beating wildly, and the rush of adrenaline made her giddy with excitement. They were almost through.

"Dig left, Deborah. Left!"

The canoe tipped in a split second. The river took her, bumping over rocks, tumbling her over and through the tangly reeds. She gulped water and tried to stop herself by grabbing at rocks and bits of grass. She no longer knew which way was up. The water was relentless, and she felt herself being swept away.

"Grab the reeds. Both hands!"

She heard his voice as she came up for air. She lunged and managed to hold on, her feet frantically treading water. The river was determined to take her with it. Her knuckles strained with the effort, but she forced herself to hold tighter.

Charlie was wading towards her. He held the canoe with one hand and stretched the other out to her. "Grab my hand."

"I can't."

"You can. Let go with one hand and grab me."

She took a deep gulp of air and lunged towards him.

"Now let go of the reeds."

She hesitated for a moment and then released the clump.

"I've got you."

Charlie held her tightly around the waist and manoeuvred her onto a nearby rock. She hugged her knees and dropped her head onto them.

"I'm sorry," she spluttered, between gasps of breath.

"You were great. No need to apologise."

She shook her head. "I couldn't do it."

"Nonsense. You did well."

It took all her will power to get back into the canoe. The first few strokes felt shaky, and she forced her breathing to steady. But soon the gentle rhythm kicked in, and she felt herself in sync with Charlie. Her shoulders felt surprisingly strong, and she dipped her paddle in a little deeper. The pull felt good and a semblance of control replaced the butterflies.

By the time Charlie indicated the bank and began steering the canoe towards it, she was relaxed. She rested her paddle across the boat and stepped into the muddy water to help pull the canoe up, as if she'd done this all her life.

"Bit more. Okay."

Annie was strolling over to meet them. "About time, you guys. What the hell happened? Still some cold beers and sarmies left, if you hurry." she shouted.

Deborah was about to follow, when she felt herself being pulled back by her soggy t-shirt.

"You can do anything you set your mind to, blue-eyed girl."

She looked at Charlie enquiringly.

"I truly believe that."

She fought back a grin as her stomach did a startling lurch.

"Do you have a dry t-shirt? Change into it then."

Deborah felt her blush move up to her ears. Oh my goodness. She probably looked like a drowned rat.

○○○

Deborah dropped her soggy clothes on the floor of the shower, before she collapsed onto the sofa.

"How was the river?" Julie shouted from behind her purring sewing machine, as her expert hands slid the silk along gently. The sapphire evening dress was taking shape.

"Amazing. Phew."

"You look exhausted."

"I am. Supper and bed for me."

"Did you meet some more of the newsroom crowd?"

Deborah slid herself upright. "I met quite a few, including Charlie, the political reporter. He's invited me to tag along next week. I'm so excited!"

"Is he the one who wrote the Jennings story yesterday?"

Deborah nodded. "I think there'll be a follow-up next week. I'm not sure I'd be any good, but hopefully he'll let me help with research or something."

"Way to go! That's great news for you."

The doorbell rang and Deborah struggled to heaved herself up to answer it.

"Ta ra!" Boetie stood in the doorway, holding up packets of fish and chips. "I brought enough for the three of us. Presume that's okay?"

"Thanks. That's amazing."

Deborah frowned as she tore open the newspaper on a cutting board. Boetie's emphasis on "the three of us" bothered her.

"Help yourselves, meisies."

"And?" Boetie tore at his fish with his fingers and devoured a mouthful before he turned towards Deborah.

"It was great. Exciting. There was a super crowd."

"What was it like? Did you manage all the paddling? Weren't you nervous?"

Julia constructed elaborate little towers of fish and chips with her fork as Deborah spoke. She didn't want to tell them about tipping the canoe. It was embarrassing. She'd skip over that part and tell them all about the bird life along the banks.

"I fell out in a rapid."

The laughter triggered Bob's barking, and the phone rang on cue. Boetie rolled his eyes as Deborah went to pick it up.

"Yes. It was great. Well, I was about to phone you in a few minutes. Okay. Why don't you come around now? Oh. But I'd like to see you. Tomorrow then. The Pig at six. Love—"

The phone was dead before she could finish her sentence, and Boetie was crumpling up the oily newspaper. A moment ago he'd seemed settled in for a long visit, and now it was as if his balloon had popped and the air was whizzing out.

"Stay for a bit. Why the rush?"

Deborah took the crumpled ball of paper from his hand.

"Places to go, people to see," he mumbled while washing his hands and then picking up his jacket.

○ ○ ○

Chapter Five

"Your tea, lazy bum."

Deborah made room for the steaming mug on her bedside table. She slid herself up to a sitting position and took her first sip.

"Sit, Jules."

Julia shook her head and hovered in the doorway. "I must finish my letter to Pierre. He should have arrived in Paris by now."

Deborah sat up properly. "You're missing him already."

Julia hung onto the doorframe.

"Do you want to talk about it?"

"Nope."

"Sure?" Deborah tilted her head encouragingly, but her friend shrugged and retreated into the passage.

A train rumbled past, the signal for her to carry her mug to the shower. As she was wrapping herself in a towel, she heard Chris' voice from the kitchen, and a ripple of excitement ran through her. She dashed back to her room, tripped over yesterday's jeans, pulled them on and gave her hair a haphazard rub with the towel. Glancing over her shoulder, she caught sight of her reflection and paused, stepping back to apply a hurried lick of mascara.

He was leaning against the counter, chatting to Julia, who was sewing pearly beads onto a bodice. Deborah slipped up behind him to cover his eyes with her palms. He grabbed them and leant forward, balancing her weight on his back.

"You want to join us for a walk up Constantia Nek, Julia?"

Julia seemed to concentrate fixedly on her sewing. Deborah waited for her to look up, but she replied, without making any eye contact.

"No thanks, Chris. I've got things to do around here."

Deborah hesitated for an awkward second and looked back at Chris, who shrugged his shoulders at her.

"See you later, then," she ventured as she backed away and followed Chris to the door.

ooo

Chris' long strides forced Deborah to speed up behind him. Bob took off into the forest, looped back to check if they were still coming and sped off again. Sunlight dappled through the trees, and the mossy smell of autumn leaves filled her nostrils. Early hikers mumbled, "Morning," already making their way back to the car park, dogs sniffing their legs as they passed. The leafy suburbs below came to life gradually, and Deborah inhaled the earthy smell of fungi. She considered picking some, but never quite trusted her judgement on which was safe to eat.

"Do you know which are edible?"

Chris shook his head and smiled. "I only know we probably shouldn't pick the magic ones."

She examined a pine cone instead, shaking out the nuts hidden deep between the fronds. "Want some pine nuts?"

He didn't slacken his pace, but glanced over his shoulder at her. "Keep me some."

Chris disappeared from sight as she tried to ease out the last few. Dry twigs snapped under her takkies, and as she rounded the corner, water burbled through a series of rounded rocks. Chris was already perched on a log.

"Open the rucksack."

She loosened the string to find a neatly packed parcel of food and two appletisers. Chris disentangled his legs and handed her a bottle. Then he unwrapped the silver paper to reveal fresh baguettes.

Deborah reached for one as she glanced at him. He was gazing into the water. She looked away as she bit ruminatively into ripe tomato mingled with soft cheese, crisp lettuce and cucumber. She would've liked to ask him about last night, about why he had sounded so offish. No. She couldn't spoil this. Maybe this was his way of saying "sorry?" It would be churlish not to accept it the way he intended, wouldn't it? They sat there for a while, not speaking, until Bob barked, as if to chivvy them along.

"Shift that butt. Bob wants to walk." Chris swung the rucksack onto one shoulder and took her hand to pull her up. She managed to keep up with his pace and chatted about her job, Ginger, her new friend Annie, and Julia's new house rules.

She stopped to tie her shoelace, half expecting Chris to stride ahead, but he stopped, and then edged closer. About to stand again, she felt a handful of twigs slide under her t-shirt and Chris raced away. She chased him and he crisscrossed the path to escape her. Eventually he turned and caught her. He shook out her t-shirt and brushed the twigs out with his hand. Then he sat on a rock and pulled her down with him. Deborah rummaged in her pocket for a hair band, pushed her wild mop out of her eyes and caught it all up into a ponytail.

A Labrador and her silver-haired owner passed them, and the elderly man tipped his hat.

"Lucky to be young and in love!" he whispered, as he passed them.

"Yes." Chris squeezed the breath out of Deborah.

They sat like that without speaking until Deborah felt restless and a little stifled. Pulling herself free, she took the lead, Chris following just behind her.

"Let's pretend we live here and never ever have to go back to our lives down below there." He pointed down at the manicured lawns and grey slated roofs.

"What do you mean? We do live here," Deborah whispered.

Chris shook his head. He hesitated, as though grappling with something. "Pix, I may need to go away again soon."

She slid a hand across her eyes and braced herself for the rest. This wasn't going to be what she wanted to hear.

"Albert Jennings' assassination has changed things … it's more important than ever to keep under the radar."

She reached for his hand, but he lifted it to indicate, "Wait."

"I won't always be able to tell you where I'm going … for your own safety."

She took a breath as his face stiffened and turned impassive. She wanted to argue, but stopped. That familiar look meant "out of bounds." She turned from him and walked on slowly. Suddenly he grabbed her from behind and tickled her until she had to laugh. The sparkle was back in his eyes.

"You're right. We do live here. You're a pixie in the forest, put here to lead me forever astray."

Deborah walked backwards so she could look him in the eyes as they spoke.

"And you are?"

"I'm the king of the forest. You have to obey my every command. If you don't, you get punished."

She threw the last of her pine nuts at him as she sped up a little.

"You're so going to get punished now."

She skipped backwards and kept herself just out of reach.

Chris stretched out to try and grab her. "You're going to fall."

She shook her head. When the rock tripped her up, he caught her, but she slid from his grip, turned and raced him to the car, Bob overtaking her en route.

He panted up to her. "I think I'm addicted to you."

She looked up at him and then made herself grin. "Me, too. I mean, I'm addicted to you, too."

When they reached the cottage, Chris stopped and kept the engine turning over.

"Aren't you coming in?"

"Got work to do."

There was urgency in his parting kiss, before he stretched over suddenly to open her door.

○○○

It was unusually quiet and it took her a moment to notice Julia sitting on the back step.

"You okay?"

Jules nodded. "Just thinking ..."

"About?" Deborah squeezed in next to her friend.

"Pierre. I haven't heard from him since he arrived in Paris."

She nodded in sympathy. Long-distance relationships were always complicated. She'd had two years of that with Chris and thanked her lucky stars that they were in one place again.

"Is he the ONE, Jules?"

She noticed that Julia didn't deny this immediately. Her friend was usually pretty uncompromising when it came to men. If they didn't come up to par, she retreated faster than you could flutter an eyelid.

"I'm sure Pierre will phone. Once he's settled in, he'll phone."

"He could've taken the contract, though, couldn't he? Alliance was desperate for him to stay." Julia's hands hung limply between her knees.

Deborah gently bumped her shoulder. "Everyone needs to go home sometimes, Jules. You know that. He was pretty stuck on you."

Julia turned to look at her and Deborah nodded emphatically, and then placed both hands on the step to push herself upright. As she turned the kettle on, the phone rang. Deborah threw Jules a look and reached for it, in that moment fully expecting to hear the French operator. A funny ticking sound echoed in the background.

"No one there. Boetie always says this phone is tapped. Do you think he just might be right?"

Julia shrugged and began stacking cups in the sink. "Do you collect cups, Debs? I found a whole installation in your room. Why would anyone want to tap our phone?"

"Sorry." Deborah smiled. She could think of a reason, but she couldn't say. She had only the vaguest inkling of what Chris was involved in, but it was best for all of them if she kept it to herself. She didn't want to worry Julia more than she already was.

"Oh, before I forget," Julia raised her voice above the water, "your cousin phoned. You should call him back. He sounded upset."

ooo

"… Cuz?" Deborah listened intently as her cousin broke the news. "I can't believe it. So, so sorry."

She checked the time and took a deep breath. "I'll be there by this evening. I'll let you know as soon as I arrive. Love you."

Deborah put the phone down and covered her face with her hands.

"Debs?"

She sat down on the floor as the salty tears dripped into her mouth. "Uncle Jay's died, an aneurism."

Julia knelt down and put her arms around her.

"I can't imagine life without him."

The smell of dishwashing liquid mingled with rose moisturiser. It was oddly comforting.

"I always seem to lose the men I love deeply."

"What do you mean?"

Deborah pushed herself up to reach her cigarettes, lit one and took a deep drag. "First Dad. Now Uncle Jay."

Julia's forehead creased as she shook her head. "Don't think like that. Lots of wonderful things happen to you, too."

She shook her head. "I feel as if tragedy is always waiting in the wings."

Julia stood up and walked to the window. "Come on now. You've had a big blow. This is grief talking."

She tried not to say it, but the words slipped out. "I wouldn't survive if something happened to Chris."

Julia's jaw clenched and her voice rose an octave. "Stop it. Don't even say something like that! Nothing is going to happen to him. And anyway, you're a young woman. A strong young woman, though you don't always realise it. You can survive a helluva lot more than you think. I'm really sorry about your Uncle Jay, but stop being ridiculous."

Julia abruptly let her go and returned to the sink where she clattered pans and shoved them into a drawer.

ooo

Chris opened the passenger door for her and then put her suitcase into the boot. As he turned onto the N2 towards the airport, he rubbed Deborah's knee. "I know how important he was to you. I'm sorry."

She blew into her soggy tissue and felt around her bag for a fresh one. "He said you were leading me down the garden path."

Chris laughed. "Am I?"

The wind rattled the car window, and she rolled it up tightly to keep out the fishy air. Bits of paper and plastic were blown across the road, and Chris swerved to avoid a pedestrian dodging between the cars.

"Crazy man!"

"Chris?"

She waited for him to turn towards her. "Remember the sangoma on your farm?" He nodded. "He said your life would be very interesting, but—"

Chris interrupted her before she could go further. "What are you going on about? You don't seriously believe any of that stuff, do you?" He reached across and pinched her cheek. "You're just really sad. Don't spiral down into a dark hole now. C'mon."

Her mood lifted a little, despite herself.

"That's better. Uncle Jay wouldn't want you to be so sad. He'd want you to crack open a beer. Celebrate his life."

She lowered her head. "I love you, Chris."

"Love you, too."

She could feel her heart beating against her chest. She didn't know if she could express what she was feeling, but she had to try. It was suddenly imperative that he knew. Her mouth felt dry and she licked her lips before the words formed.

"I've loved you from the moment you stepped through the res door, all those years ago. I knew then that we … You felt it, too. I know you did. I would not survive …"

"Hush now, my darling."

Chris squeezed her leg and she lay back a little. The turnoff for the airport was just ahead. He sped up. When he spoke his voice was gentle. "You'll have to jump and run when we get there."

Chris hauled her suitcase from the boot and held it out.

"Phone as soon as you can."

She was already half-running when she looked back and mouthed, "I am the girl next door, Chris."

She turned back one last time, just before she reached the terminal doors. He was still standing in the same spot, as though he'd been turned to stone.

○○○

It was Boetie and Julia who picked her up on her return. Deborah saw them as she walked through the glass doors. They were waving and Bob was straining on his lead. She dropped her bag to embrace them.

"How was the funeral?" Julia held onto her arm. "Are you okay? I thought of you all weekend."

Boetie dropped the overnight bag in the back and opened the passenger door for Julia and Deborah.

"I still can't believe he's really gone." Table Mountain stretched out before them, and the cloudy tablecloth crept over it. A slight breeze picked up and Deborah rubbed her shoulders.

"Lots of people?"

Boetie was turning onto the highway.

"It's a little stone church, you know? But it was packed. My uncle was the life and soul of the party, even at his own funeral."

Deborah felt her eyes moistening, and she focussed on the passing fynbos for a while. They took the Rondebosch turnoff. The common was teeming with dogs and joggers. Elderly ladies stopped for a quick chat, while Labradors pulled at their leads.

Boetie stopped at the Silwood bakery. She looked at him questioningly.

"Fresh croissants. It's that donnerse Frenchman's influence,"

"Pierre. His name is Pierre, Boetie."

Chris was sitting outside the cottage. He stood up as they turned into the road. "Himself has arrived, I see."

Deborah clutched Boetie's arm. "Don't be like that."

"He shouldn't be like that, not me. I've a good mind to tell him a thing or two, if you'd—"

She jumped out as soon as the bakkie mounted the kerb.

ooo

Boetie arranged the croissants in a basket and unwrapped his freshly baked banana bread. Deborah peered into the tinfoil.

"Wow, Boetie. You're becoming so domesticated."

"Ja well. Maybe the way to a woman's heart is through her stomach."

"Isn't that the other way round, Boet?" Julia loved to be right about matters of language.

"Lady Julia, not in my case, it seems." Boetie donned an apron, cut the bread, smeared spread butter on the slices and offered them around.

Julia lifted her slice, and then dropped it again without tasting it. Not like her at all. She had two bright spots of colour on her cheeks, as though she had a fever.

"Jules, are you—"

Julia spoke at the same moment. "This might not be the best timing … sorry, Debs … but I have an announcement to make."

She wiped her fingers carefully on a tissue then looked around. "Pierre popped the question this morning!"

"From Paris?"

Boetie turned from the table, grabbed Julia and dipped her back in a tango flourish.

Deborah tried to take Chris' hand, but he drew it back and fumbled for something in his pocket.

"Congratulations, Julia," he mumbled.

"Oh yay, I knew he was stuck on you, you old idiot ..." Deborah slapped her friend on the arm, before she hugged her.

Julia produced a chilled bottle of champagne as Deborah and Boetie fussed around her. Chris hung back from the circle a little. He busied himself with opening the bottle and then carefully filled four flutes.

"To Lady Julia and her invisible Frenchman," Boetie quipped.

Glasses clinked as Deborah and Boetie fired questions.

"So tell. When's the wedding?"

"Where will it be?"

"Who's coming?"

"Hold on, Debs. I need to ask you something first."

Deborah sucked her breath in and glanced at Chris, but he was suddenly clearing the plates and running water in the sink. Julia was holding her hand tightly.

"Deborah, would you do me the honour of being my bridesmaid?"

She gasped in delight and flung her arms around her friend. "I'd love to."

Boetie refilled the glasses and lifted an eyebrow when Chris covered his with his hand. Deborah eyed him nervously. She knew what he was about to say.

"I should be on my way. Still got some research to finish."

When they reached the Volvo she hesitated before she put her hand on his arm. "What's wrong, Chris?"

He turned away from her and then suddenly swung to face her, eyes flaring angrily.

"I know what you want, Deborah. You want this engagement thing, too. This is all so bourgeois, so white picket fence. You should know by now that this is not what I'm into. Our country is on its knees. We're in the middle of a massive struggle. Teachers and pupils are up in arms. And it doesn't stop about the Afrikaans issue in the schools. This Minister of so-called "Bantu Affairs" is a flippin' lunatic man. There's going to be rioting any day. And you, you who majored in politics, are more interested in engagement parties and white weddings and—"

Deborah felt the knife in her stomach. Her mouth dried up. Her eyes pricked and she pressed them back with her palms. "I never said a word, Chris."

He shrugged her hand off. "You didn't have to."

She pushed the gate open, went into her room and flung herself face down on her bed. The breeze moved the curtains a little, and as the light faded, she became aware of Boetie's presence in the doorway.

"And this just after your uncle's died. Hy's 'n poephol man. You deserve better, Debs."

He pulled her door closed behind him as he left.

○○○

Chapter Six
16 June 1976

"I'll phone when I get to Pretoria," Deborah called, as the train pulled out.

Julia cupped her hands to form a loudspeaker. "Love to your mum."

Deborah pulled her legs up and arranged her woollen wrap over her. It looked like she was alone this time. She found her bookmark and settled into *Tess of the d'Urbervilles*. Chris always rolled his eyes at her choice of reading, but Thomas Hardy was still her secret delight, particularly Tess. She saw herself reflected in Tess and totally related to her destiny.

The bearded Indian man, who had the incongruous title of "the bedding boy," rattled her compartment door later in the afternoon. When the first dinner gong sounded, she made her way to the dining cart. She admired the heavy silver cutlery as she tucked in to the roast beef and Yorkshire pudding.

She watched the landscape change gradually and hoped she'd still be awake to see the Karoo materialising. By the time the waiter arrived with a bowl of hot toffee pudding and homemade custard, Deborah was feeling mellow and contented. She accepted the coffee, mostly because of the solid silver coffee pot and matching milk jug.

When they had finally grown up, she'd serve meals like this to Chris, in their own home. During those long years apart, she'd pictured them like that. But now it seemed less certain. She took the last sip of her wine. It tasted warm and slightly sour.

ooo

Deborah woke to the rhythmic click-clack of the train on the tracks. There was something soothing about trains that made her sleep like a baby. She pulled up the stiff blind and looked out at the Highveld. The smell of burnt grass filled her nostrils, and she could already feel the sun breaking through the bitterly cold night. The familiar rattle of the door handle made her jump up to meet the pre-breakfast round.

"Coffee and a rusk, please."

She wrapped her hands around the Styrofoam and sipped the piping hot liquid. The train ground to a halt unexpectedly. Strange. There was no station nearby. People were opening their doors, and excited voices drifted down the passage. There was a buzz outside. She pulled her tracksuit on and stepped into the passage. Men were doing something to the tracks, and the train staff seemed to be rushing around nervously.

"What's happening?"

The "bedding boy" smiled unconvincingly at her. "Moenie worrie nie, Nooi."

She looked around for someone else to ask. A brawny conductor was walking towards her, and she stepped towards him.

"Can you tell me what's happening?"

He hesitated and then said, "We're re-routing via Germiston. Trouble in Soweto this morning. Nothing to worry about. We'll get you to Pretoria."

Deborah stepped back into her carriage. Trouble in Soweto? What kind of trouble? There had been a lot of newsroom buzz about the whole Afrikaans issue in the black schools. Chris was right. You couldn't force people to learn in the language of the masters. There was bound to be trouble. Rioting. Her stomach did a lurch. She put the rusk down and pulled her door open. Snippets of passing remarks confirmed her suspicions.

"Blerrie skool kinders ..."

"They should be learning, not running around the streets ..."

"Die polisie moet geen nonsense vat nie."

By the time the train reached Pretoria Station, Deborah was packed and waiting to alight. Her mum was on the platform, holding a bunch of flowers. She rushed towards Deborah and hugged her tightly.

"I was so worried about you, Cookie. There's been some—"

Deborah cut her off. "Mum, can we get home as quickly as possible? I need to get hold of Chris."

She tried not to snap at her mum's chatter. Usually she loved to hear all the stories from home, but it all seemed so irrelevant now. She wondered how Chris would be part of all this. She looked out of the window at the winter landscape. It was stark and icy cold, but blue sky was breaking through the clouds, and soon the day would warm up.

"I know you like to see everyone when you visit, so I've invited the whole family for a braai on Sunday. I got some nice lamb chops from Piet's butcher. And farm boerewors. Milly brought us some, when she visited last week. We'll get the fresh rolls on Sunday morning. Just remind me, Cookie."

Deborah nodded distractedly. When they pulled up next to the huge oak tree, she ran to unlock the front door.

"I'll come back for my case in a minute," she called over her shoulder. The phone was already ringing off the hook when she reached it.

"Chris. Thank goodness it's you. I've just arrived … was just about to …"

She could hear him breathing loudly. "I was really worried about you, Pix. Glad you're safe."

Her hand went to her mouth as she listened to his next words. "A school child, Hector Pieterson, has been shot and killed in Soweto. Many others injured. There'll be hundreds more. It's started. This is our worst nightmare and there's no going back now."

○○○

It was all over the front page of the local newspaper by that evening. Deborah scoured each article. It seemed unreal. Pupils and teachers had met at Orlando Stadium to protest against being taught in Afrikaans. Chris had said this would happen.

"Senzeni na" (What have we done), they chanted. Placards screamed, "Amandla Awethu" (Power to the people) and "Away with Afrikaans."

Deborah put her hand over her mouth as she stared at the picture of twelve-year-old Hector Pieterson, dying in his friend's arms. His sister, Antoinette, ran beside them, screaming in horror. The picture needed no explanation. "Unrest in Soweto," police officials said. "An uprising," the journalist wrote. Soweto was in flames and people had died. Children had died.

She read Desmond Tutu's words, "Unless something drastic is done very soon, bloodshed and violence are going to happen in South Africa." He'd said that a month earlier. Clearly, no one had taken any notice.

"Are you coming to help me, Cookie?"

"In a minute, Mum." She folded the newspaper and made her way to the kitchen.

"You okay?"

"I'm fine. Just …" She pulled out a chopping board and began to dice the carrots.

"You don't look fine. What's the matter?"

Her mum was never fooled. She lined up two carrots and pressed down hard with the knife. She felt a sharp sting in her finger. Blood welled and dripped onto the chopping board.

"Put it in your mouth quickly."

Her mum reached to open the tap and guided Deborah's hand under it. Then she mopped it dry and reached into the cupboard for a plaster. She frowned as she wrapped it around Deborah's finger as though it required the utmost precision.

"I'm upset about the Soweto thing."

"I know, Cookie."

She allowed herself to be enveloped in her mum's embrace for a few seconds before she pulled away and returned to her chopping. Why would the police fire live ammunition at schoolchildren? Surely they could have stopped the protest some other way? She couldn't let go of the image of Hector Pieterson's little sister screaming and running for help. But no one could help him now. Or any of them. It was too late. A line had been crossed, which could never be uncrossed. Nothing would ever be the same.

"Don't forget the onions."

She pulled the bag closer and eased two through the orange netting.

"Hopefully this will be the end of the trouble now." Her mum was still frowning, eyes darting across her face as though trying to decipher something which had been scrawled there in a foreign language.

"No, Mum. It's only just started. This is definitely the beginning."

Mum flipped the chopped onions into the pot and closed the back door. Lightning was already flashing across the sky, and the first drops of rain landed on the stoep. She started at the first clap of thunder, despite the fact that she had known it would come. "What do you mean, Cookie?"

"I mean things are about to get hectic." She turned up the gas and gave the pot a vigorous stir. A sip of Mum's Shiraz slid down her throat, and she didn't refuse the refill held out to her.

"I'd, I would like to know what you think, Cookie. I like to know how you see things. But, please tell me you're not going to put yourself in danger? I … I know it's important to you, but I do worry, you know."

"I'll be fine, Mum, you don't have to worry." Deborah took a gulp of her wine. Then she laid the table and folded serviettes into neat triangles, the way her mom liked them.

It seemed absurd to be carrying out such banal tasks when their world was imploding around them. But she had her mom to worry about. Deborah was all she had left. She couldn't allow her to worry needlessly.

This was what Chris didn't always understand about her. She and he believed in the same things. For him, though, belief was not enough. He was focussed. More than focussed. He was fixated on the cause he had aligned himself with. He would carry out what he thought was right, no matter whose needs stood in his way. Even hers.

She couldn't do that. The people she loved would always come before principle. She couldn't help it.

She hesitated a moment, then reached for the good cutlery. Absurd it might be, but her mum had Deborah with her so seldom, she wasn't going to spoil what little time they had together. They could talk about it all after supper.

Chris' words echoed in her head. This was their worst nightmare. There was no going back now. The dogs of war had been released, and their country was in for a turbulent ride.

But for now, she pushed the horror aside and lit the candles on the table.

ooo

Her long weekend in Pretoria seemed like another lifetime, once Deborah was back at her desk in the newsroom.

Typewriters clicked furiously, and the ping of carriages punctuated the nippy air. Rain pelted against the windows and umbrellas dripped water in the corner of the newsroom. Deborah smelt the posy of wild flowers on her desk and looked around for Annie, but she wasn't at her desk. She pulled her wrap around her and read through what she had typed.

A bergie who goes by the name of George said he used to have a family; a wife and two children. Booze ended all that, and after losing his job, he began living in the Gardens. Hmmm. Maybe she should change "living" to just "sleeping on a bench." She pencilled in her correction and then sighed as she slipped carbon between three sheets of newsprint pad and rolled them into her typewriter. Pity she'd only gotten 58% for typing. She felt a tap on her shoulder and turned to face her boss.

Ginger thrust the newspaper under her nose and patted her back. "Sharing a by-line on the first bergies story. Here's looking at you, kid!"

"Let's see, let's see." Annie seemed to appear from nowhere, and her silver pirate ring dug into Deborah as she peered over her shoulder. Deborah felt a rush of excitement. She wanted to let out a loud "yay!" Instead, she nodded and beamed.

"First of many," her friend enthused.

"Thanks."

"No dilly-dallying now. When you've finished the bergie and his dog, you can shadow Charlie on the B J story. So get cracking."

"Okay, Boss."

Annie moved back to her desk and hammered away at her typewriter for a bit. A few minutes later, she caught Deborah's eye. "Pretoria go okay?"

Deborah nodded. "Thanks for the flowers. Really sweet of you."

Annie gave her a thumbs up. "It's a once-off hey."

Deborah turned back to her story and began tweaking her sentences. The bergie and his beloved dog. She needed to go back to the Gardens with a photographer and somehow persuade her bergie to talk to her.

"How do I get my bergie to talk to me?" she asked, of no one in particular.

"Invite him for dinner," a colleague quipped from farther down the room. The ring sounded louder than usual, and Deborah laughed at Annie's clown face as she answered the phone.

"Wrong extension. But I'll put you through to her." She jerked her finger towards Deborah's phone and waited before she slammed hers down.

Chris' voice was softer than usual. "Pix, I've never really apologised for my outburst."

Deborah waited for him to explain.

"You know. Just before you went to Pretoria … the whole anti-wedding thing? I'm really sorry. I've got too much stuff darting around in my head. I didn't mean to hurt you."

She held the phone away from her ear and felt a lump form in her throat.

"Pixie?"

"I'm here."

"Can I make it up to you?"

She hesitated, before she replied, "I suppose so."

"The Pig, after the weekend? I'll be back by Monday. We can grab a bite as well, if you like."

She cleared her throat.

"Pix?"

"Okay."

He'd forgotten about the Hermanus weekend. She might have known he would. She wished she could just say no to him. She wanted to be angry, to shout and scream at him, tell him how much he'd hurt her. But she couldn't. His voice melted away all the things she'd wanted to blurt out. That one niggly thing at the back of her mind pushed its way forward.

"Chris?"

"What?"

"Is your research assistant a girl?"

There was a long silence on the other end before he answered. "Yes. She's a girl."

Deborah blew out. She wanted to ask what her name was, whether she was really only his assistant, and if he was keen on her …

"Is she pretty?" It just sort of popped out of her mouth.

"Deborah!"

She waited for the rest, the anger, the remonstration. Chris' voice sounded strange now.

"You have your own prettiness. You know that."

She didn't. He'd never said so. She waited for him to break the silence.

"See you on Monday then."

She slid the phone back onto the holder and went to fetch herself some coffee.

"You look weird. You okay?" Annie was peering at her over her glasses.

"Fine."

She sipped her coffee and re-read her story for the hundredth time. Out of the corner of her eye, she could see Ginger pacing the room, and she concentrated on her typing.

ooo

"Are you packed, Debs? We're leaving in five."

Deborah threw her bikini and a towel into the overnight bag. Spring was still a long way off, but if there was a beach and sea, she swam.

"Mermaid genes," Boetie always said.

Fresh undies, a t-shirt, shorts, a hairbrush, toothbrush, toothpaste. Julia was already hooting. She looked around her room quickly, grabbed her box of cigarettes and made her way to the car.

Cape Town gradually faded into the distance, and Deborah watched the fynbos take over. City life gave way to clear blue sky and wide stretches of untouched vegetation.

Sir Lowry's Pass opened up the vista, and the Blue Mountains framed the edges of the patchwork landscape below. Tall pine trees clustered together to form impenetrable lengths of forest, which quickly opened up to rolling green stretches. Soon they were heading up Houw Hoek pass, and Deborah anticipated the drop into majestic landscape, just before Julia took the Kleinmond/Hermanus turnoff. The Blue Mountains and clear sky were reflected in the lagoon as they wound their way towards the sea. The long road past Onrus and then Hawston and then the outskirts of Hermanus were up ahead now. It was a majestic introduction, and she leant out of the window to breathe in the salty sea air. The quaint little shops on the Main Road whizzed past in a flash, and soon she was counting the houses along the seafront. Suddenly they were pulling up outside the Beechleys' holiday home.

"We can toss a coin for the main bedroom."

"Heads or tails?" Julia called, as she twirled it into the air.

"Tails," Deborah shouted and put her foot over it, before anyone could cheat. Julia kicked her foot off it and swooped it up.

"It's your lucky day," she announced, as Deborah caught her flying tog bag before it hit the ground. She raced off to claim "her room" and was arranging her bits and pieces in the bathroom when she heard Julia's shout.

"We're going for a run before it gets dark. Come!"

The pathway zigzagged between the rocks and wound itself all the way down to the little beach below. Deborah breathed in the salty air and felt her lungs expanding as they jogged. By the time they reached the beach, her heart was pounding, and she stripped down to her panties before diving into the turbulent waves. Bob was paddling furiously to keep up with her, and he whined when she dived under a wave and swam farther out. She lay on her back and floated, letting the waves bob her up and down. She leant her head back to dunk her face right into the water. The salty taste made her feel squeaky clean. Seaweed wrapped itself around her waist and she pushed it away. She body-surfed the next wave and was about to dive in once again, when she saw Julia waving a towel at her.

"We still need to get a fish for tonight. The visitors will be here soon." Deborah waded through the swell and seized the towel. She pushed Bob away with her foot as he shook water on her.

"What visitors?"

"I invited Boetie and his electrician crowd. Oh, and Charlie, your political reporter."

"What? How come?" She hopped on one leg and then the other to pull her shorts up.

"He phoned when you were out ..."

She looked closely at Julia, but her expression was unreadable. "What are you up to?"

"Oh, don't be silly. He was just so chatty that before I knew it, I'd invited him along. I thought I'd keep it as a surprise."

Boetie, Joubert and Piet had the fire roaring by the time they jogged to the house. Red and yellow flames licked against the dark blue sky. The sun had melted into the horizon, and rosy streaks painted the blue. A squawking seagull flew past their heads, and Cape white-eyes announced the sunset from the bushes.

Charlie came striding across the lawn, holding out a beer for each of them. "I took up your kind offer." He adjusted his glasses and winked at Deborah. "Besides, I wanted to see what Deborah got up to outside the newsroom."

Julia was holding a red roman by the tail and wielding a sharp knife, which she offered to Deborah. "You need to descale this, before we stick it on the fire."

She followed her friend to the kitchen and got stuck into scraping the scales off over a piece of newspaper.

"That's a messy job." Charlie laid out fresh paper and folded up the full ones as she worked. Julia was slicing lemon wedges, and Boetie's friends were chopping tomatoes, onions, carrots, avo and cucumbers.

"Don't forget to crumble the feta over the top." She handed the bottle of olives to Charlie, who twisted the lid off in one turn.

The smell of warm baguette filled the kitchen as Julia opened the oven door and Boetie called, "Another few minutes and this fish is braai-ed."

The table on the lawn was filled with food. Charlie poured the wooded Chardonnay into cold wine glasses and then lit the candles. "Cheers!"

Julia handed plates around. "Help yourselves to everything else. The fish can be served straight off the braai."

"This is a feast of note. Thank you."

Charlie lifted his glass to Julia and she leant over to clink it. The sea air always seemed to make people hungry, and Deborah watched her friends dishing up second helpings. She leant back in her chair and looked up at the evening star. Soon more stars dotted the deepening sky. She hugged her knees and smiled when Boetie brought out his guitar.

"Sugarman" lingered over them, and she envied Boetie's fingers strumming effortlessly over the strings. When he started making up words to the song, she made a ball of her serviette and threw it at him. "That's rather rude, isn't it?" Charlie's finger wagged at her and she felt an uninvited hotness at her cheeks.

This would be heaven, if only Chris were here. It was safer for her not to know where he was, he'd said. Secret talks, probably. She knew enough to know that there was a whole underground, growing stronger as the government got more and more inflexible. It was scary enough that Chris was involved. She needed to be outside of it, to be his anchor in the mainstream. But the secrecy was becoming increasingly unbearable. She was balancing two lives precariously, and she wasn't sure how much longer her strength would last. She shoved her thoughts to the back of her mind and hugged her knees.

"Earth to Deborah. Are you still with us?" Julia's voice penetrated the fog and Deborah smiled gratefully at her. What would she do without her friends? Boetie was watching her closely.

"So how come 'himself' couldn't come on the weekend?" Boetie balanced his guitar on his lap.

"I think he had to go away for some work thing."

He screwed up his face and mumbled, "More important, I suppose."

"Well, it's his loss. We're not missing him, anyway." Julia winked at Boetie and reached for a marshmallow. Deborah knew she was being baited, but she couldn't stop herself from rising.

"Speak for yourself." She turned to Boetie. She needed music to drown this conversation. "Play some more, Boetie. Please."

Charlie leant forward in his chair. "So who is this 'himself,' anyway? Why haven't I heard about him?"

Deborah was desperate to change the topic. The last thing she needed was curiosity about Chris' whereabouts. Not that she knew, anyway. "He's my boyfriend. He's away at the moment. It's no big deal."

Charlie's eyes lingered, and she imagined him mulling over this snippet of information.

"What kind of work thing would he be involved in, then?" he said finally.

Boetie jumped at the opportunity.

"He's one of those academic types, you know. He's probably stirring up a revolution somewhere."

Charlie rubbed his chin. "The Internal Security Act is not something to mess around with. I presume he is fully aware of its power."

Boetie leant forward in his seat. "So you're pretty clued up on all these things, I suppose."

"Have to be if I want to keep my job. I'm also not too keen on getting banned."

Boetie strummed as he laughed a little too loudly and some of the group joined in. Deborah could feel her shoulders stiffening, and she tried to pretend she found the joke funny. Charlie was still looking at her, as if he was waiting for her to say something. Instead she flashed him half a smile and then badgered Boetie again. "Play some more Rodriguez."

"Okay. But only if you'll dance for us."

She felt her ears giving her away and brushed him off quickly. "Ag, Boetie, don't be silly."

Boetie glanced at Charlie before he added, "You know she's quite a dancer, hey?"

Charlie raised an eyebrow. "I'm beginning to realise there's a whole lot I don't know about this elusive redhead."

Boetie tuned his guitar and moved his chair a little closer to Charlie. "So what's your story then? No squeeze?"

Charlie roared with laughter as he put some more wood on the fire. "Haven't heard that expression in yonks! I left my girlfriend behind when I was promoted to Cape Town. She's in Durbs. I'm planning to have one in every port, though."

His eyes twinkled in the dim light and rested on Deborah for a moment. She shifted uncomfortably and rearranged the blanket around herself, as she shot Boetie a pleading look. When he started strumming again and "I wonder" drifted into the night air, she lit a cigarette and blew a huge smoke ring into the air.

○○○

Waves broke gently. Bob settled into the curve of her back and moved as she tossed and turned. Chris was on the other end of the beach. She could feel him communicating with her. "I love you," drifted through the mist. A shadowy figure was hovering next to him, engulfing him.

"Walk towards me …"

He stepped forwards, but the silhouette pulled him back.

"Chris!" she shouted urgently.
He slowly retreated into the rocks.
"No! Chris, I'm here …"

"Debs!" Julia was shaking her shoulder. "Your tea. We're leaving in half an hour."

The hot liquid drowned the last of the shadow and she made her way to the bathroom. As she brushed her teeth half-heartedly, she looked out of the window onto the calm water. Something surged out of the sea. Something huge, it was a whale! Couldn't have been. She raced downstairs and was about to blurt it out, but then considered what a fool she'd look if it wasn't true. But they were all already standing on the wall, peering out to sea. It really was a whale—her first whale! Charlie pulled her up and handed her the binoculars. He guided her view with his finger and there it was, breaching once more.

"So cool, man." Boetie shook his head in disbelief. "Ouens, kom. Gou! We won't be seeing another whale anytime soon."

Boetie sprung onto the wall and put his hand out to pull his friends up. The mist lingered over the bay and waves crashed into the rocks. The whale breached again, as if to assure the audience that it was out there. There was another world under the huge ocean, one that wasn't affected by dangerous politics and man-made conflicts. It was somehow comforting. The sheer beauty of her surroundings overwhelmed Deborah; and for a few moments, she was embraced by the sea air, the mist over the jagged rocks and the whale's mysterious call, reminding her that she was part of all this.

Everyone dawdled for a while longer, before the inevitable packing up began. As the sky continued to lighten and orange appeared just above the horizon, the cars pulled away one by one, and Julia locked the front door.

"'Till next time," Deborah called as she blew a kiss towards the ocean and the whale blowing out in the distance. The turquoise Mazda rolled off the gravel pathway, and Julia slid into first gear.

Chapter Seven

"Drinks after work today?"

Deborah shook her head. "Not today, thanks."

Annie drew her eyebrows together and faked a deep frown. "Fobbing me off, hey?"

She pulled her tie-dyed t-shirt back over her belly button and watched Deborah's cheeks redden. "Sorry, I need to visit Hercules."

In unison, her colleagues sang, "Who the hell is Hercules?"

She laughed and sipped her coffee. When she looked up, the faces around her still looked expectant. "Okay, okay. He's a stallion." Amused nods and knowing looks made her ears rosy. "He's a horse, guys. Chris' horse."

The laughter made her crack a smile and she shook her head. Why did she get teased so much? She seemed to be the favourite target. Charlie dropped a copy of his Vorster story on her desk. He winked at her and whispered, "As you requested," before he made his way to Ginger's desk. She skimmed it before finishing her own story and shook her head in amazement. She'd never be that good. Perhaps she wasn't really cut out to be a political reporter.

When she had checked her article on the bergie and his beloved dog for the hundredth time, she made her way to Ginger's desk. His forehead creased as he read it.

"This is a bit bland, Deborah. Find out more about the owner. Paint a picture of 'a day in the life of.' People want to know what it takes to be a bergie dog owner. What do they eat, where do they sleep, how did he get to own the dog?"

Deborah felt mortified. She'd known that her mind wasn't totally on her work, but hadn't realised it was showing so badly. Her visit to the stables was slipping away.

"Tomorrow morning first thing, girl."

"Phew! Thank goodness."

"Thanks."

She backed away, and when she reached her desk, Ginger called out, "You can write well. Do it."

○○○

The stables were fifteen minutes from the bus stop, if she kept a good pace. It was still light, so she'd be able to have a short visit before the sun set. She quickened her steps and turned into the farm entrance. She jogged over the long stretch of lawn and reached Hercules' stable.

Prins was brushing him. Hercules' chocolate coat gleamed. He neighed and nudged her arm until she produced the carrot from behind her back. His velvety nose tickled her palm, and she rubbed her face on his soft snout, inhaling his horsey smell.

"Your master will probably be back tomorrow, boy." She patted his neck.

The feeling of eyes on her made her turn to Prins.

"Don't you want to ride him?"

She shook her head and took the brush he offered her. She groomed Hercules' mane and then swept it back across his sleek coat. He lowered his head as she massaged the muscles down his back and legs. She brushed the tangles out of his tail until it looked silky. When she looked up, Prins met her eyes again.

"The other lady rides him." He was tossing the straw and filling the feeding trough.

Deborah felt her muscles stiffen. "What other lady, Prins?"

Prins looked startled. He hesitated before he answered. "Dis niks, nooi. Vergeet dit." He dug into the straw and turned it over.

"No, Prins. What other lady?"

Prins looked uncomfortable, as if he'd said too much. He tried to make light of it. "Other ladies also visit Hercules. He's a ladies' man, mos!"

Deborah didn't smile. Prins patted Hercules on the neck and looked up at him. "Hey Hercules? You're mos a popular boytjie, ne?"

The sky was turning orange, and a slight chill made Deborah button her jersey. She turned towards the gate. "Thanks, Prins."

An almost apologetic look crept onto his face. It seemed he wanted to say something more, but then thought better of it. "Dis niks, nooi. Come again soon."

She felt his eyes on her back as she jogged to the entrance. The unease in her stomach had heightened, and she was eager to get back to the cottage. A sprint got her to the stop just as the bus pulled up. As they turned the corner, Llandudno came into view, and the sun formed a fried egg on the horizon. The sea had calmed into a lake, and a shimmer of orange hovered over it. Seagulls swooped for their last catch and the salty air got chillier. Bakoven misted over, and as the bus reached the top of Kloofnek, the last cable car for the day was slowly making its way down.

Deborah spotted the turquoise Mazda as the bus turned into Adderley Street, and she was the first one off. Julia was halfway out of the window, waving madly.

"Thanks for fetching me, Jules. I owe you one."

Her friend pushed the passenger door open. "Jump. That cold glass of Chardonnay is waiting."

Julia pulled away from the kerb and sped off towards the southern suburbs. "So? How was the mighty Hercules?"

Deborah fiddled with her safety belt and finally got it unravelled. "I'm not the only girl visiting him." She turned her face to the open window and let the fresh breeze blow her hair over it.

"What do you mean?"

She shrugged an answer and concentrated on the green lawns whizzing by. "You tell me."

She rummaged for her box of cigarettes, lit two and passed Julia one.

ooo

Annie held the lift for her as she ran the last stretch. She pressed "3" and the doors closed slowly. They had both arrived early today, which was a miracle.

"How was your visit to the stallion?"

Deborah laughed. "It was okay."

Her friend gave her an enquiring look, but she didn't bite. Ginger looked up and waved as they made their way to the board.

Deborah scanned the news diary and felt a tingle of disappointment when she saw her stories for the day: Another bergie follow-up, a dog show. Shadowing Charlie? Her spirits lifted immediately. Annie noted her assignments, and Deborah picked up the other newspapers to make sure she hadn't missed anything important. The Jennings follow-up was uppermost in her mind this morning. She didn't spot anything and was about to go to her desk when Annie pulled her back.

"Coffee?"

"Please."

She offered Annie a cigarette, and they walked out onto the balcony to enjoy the five minutes of quiet before the newsroom burst into life. Annie didn't offer any small talk and seemed to be waiting for her to start a conversation. Eventually Deborah broke the silence.

"How would you know if your boyfriend was seeing someone else?"

Annie didn't answer at first and then offered, "I think there are some signs. Usually."

Deborah felt Annie's eyes searching hers. Then she asked, "Why, Debs? Surely you don't think Chris is having an affair?"

Deborah shook her head. "No. I don't know. I just don't know what to think."

Annie put her hands on her hips and narrowed her eyes.

"It's just that … he's been acting quite strangely lately. And the groom at the stable let something slip yesterday."

"Like what?"

Deborah hesitated and then blurted it out. "There's some other girl visiting Hercules, when Chris is away."

"Who?"

"I don't know. That's just it."

Annie grimaced and then asked, "What's your gut feel? I'd say you should take note of that."

Deborah did have a gut feel. She felt completely confused. One minute Chris clearly still loved her. The next he seemed to be on a different planet. "I don't have a clue."

Annie seemed hesitant to comment. Eventually she said what she'd obviously been mulling over for a while. "Where does Chris go to every other weekend, and why doesn't he take you along?"

"Work stuff." Deborah felt her mouth dry up. She stubbed her cigarette out quickly and nodded towards the newsroom. "We'd better get in there."

○○○

Charlie's old Kadett nipped through lines of traffic, and soon they were on the Stellenbosch road. The scenery changed and the urban sprawl was gradually replaced by rows and rows of vineyards, dormant now, except for a few fresh buds, waiting for spring to open them. A few sheep grazed on the lush grass, and the winter rains had deepened the green.

"Um, where exactly are we going?" Deborah felt foolish asking when they were probably halfway there already.

Charlie's easy laughter put her at ease. "We're going to cover Vorster's speech, in Stellenbosch."

The Eerste River was swelling, and the stone bridge crossing it was flanked by weeping willows dipping their branches into the water.

"A listen and learn exercise, you know," he added as an afterthought.

Deborah tried not to look as excited as she really was. "What's he like?"

"Vorster? B J?" He paused a moment. "He's formidable. He's powerful, highly respected by his party, an arch-conservative and very, very dangerous for our country."

Deborah pictured the big man in her head. Her eyebrows lifted as she listened intently.

"Vorster is interesting. He's probably a God-fearing man who thinks he's taking the country down the right path, but he's also delusional. He cannot see that the tide is changing and that he needs to shift, if he wants to stay in power. He's holding onto apartheid as if all our lives depended on it."

"Do you admire him?" She regretted this remark as soon as it was out of her mouth and winced when Charlie swerved to avoid a rock.

"What? Are you crazy?"

"I just wondered what you—"

"No. No, I don't admire him. I think he's just as bad as Verwoerd was, and that's saying something. But we need to take heed of what he is saying. Careful notes."

Deborah nodded into the windscreen as Charlie took a deep breath and steered the conversation into shallower waters.

"I told the boss you'd get colour and reactions, so keep your eyes and ears open. It's amazing what you can pick up by simply observing."

He gave her a reassuring wink as he changed into fourth gear again. The long road leading up to the Lanzerac Hotel made Deborah feel a little underdressed, but Annie always said that's how journalists were meant to dress. Nonetheless, she was relieved that she'd worn a floaty floral top over her jeans today. She stepped out onto a red carpet leading up to the grand lobby.

The bar was filled with political reporters from all the country's newspapers. They seemed so very much at home, swopping tales of the stories they'd covered, and she was glad to accept the Campari and orange juice Charlie held out to her. She could do with some Dutch courage.

"It is alcoholic," he cautioned.

"Duh. I am over eighteen," she reminded him, although she felt about fifteen at that precise moment. Blast. A wave of shyness swept over her, and she felt herself revert to the convent girl she'd taken such pains to shake off. She stuck closely behind Charlie and he grinned at her.

"Stick with me, kid. I'll make you famous!"

An old fireplace glowed in the corner, and huge logs warmed the room. Wingback chairs looked so inviting that she wished she could saunter over and ease herself into one of them. Charlie offered her a cocktail sausage and put her half-emptied glass on the counter.

"Come on. I want to be near the front."

The conference room doors were still closed, but Charlie quietly opened one and guided her to the middle seats in the front row. His notepad and pen were open, and he was already scribbling things in shorthand. The room was filling up now and the Prime Minister entered, bodyguards scanning the room on both sides. Deborah watched him as he strode ahead, not looking left or right. Suddenly he paused, right next to where they were sitting, and tipped his hat at Charlie.

"You're a dangerous man, Mr Jones."

"So are you, sir."

Deborah was aghast. Did this just really happen? This was the most exciting thing she'd ever experienced. Here she was, a bushy-tailed intern, witnessing a conversation between the Prime Minister of the country and Charlie, a political journalist. Jeepers. How influential was Charlie, exactly? And why would Vorster think he was dangerous? She was going to read every word he wrote from now on. She sneaked a glance at Charlie, as a newfound admiration sprang up in her. He was quite "the man."

Vorster's talk was passionate and angry. His finger wagged at the audience as he emphasised his points. Schoolchildren should be at school and not roaming the streets with placards. His government would not be intimidated. They would not tolerate a lack of discipline … Law and order would be maintained at all costs. Orders had been given to make sure of this. The Minister of Police would keep a tight rein on any suspicious gatherings.

Charlie scribbled furiously. Deborah looked around at the audience and noticed that they were nodding their heads in agreement with everything he said. The Captains of Industry were impressed. She was excited to be at the talk, but horrified, too. To her, the man was sinister and heartless. Schoolchildren had been shot at and hundreds of people had died. The 16th of June was still reverberating and things had gotten worse, not better. Unrest was sweeping the country, and here Vorster was spouting forth his government's propaganda. A quick glance at Charlie made her feel a little more at ease, for he, too, was frowning as he wrote, and his face was beginning to get a set, uncompromising look about it.

ooo

Chris would have considered this story irrelevant. But it wasn't. So many people were affected by what the government did and said. She felt the huge importance of their presence here, especially Charlie's. Admiration overwhelmed her now, and she watched him absorbing everything he needed for a counterattack.

Charlie didn't look up for a second. As the speech drew to a close and the audience began clapping, he was up and squeezing through the side door. She sprang up to follow and spotted him at the end of the passage, in the only tickey box available.

"Hello Lizzie. Ready? Okay, here goes."

Charlie rattled off a perfect intro and then rapidly shuffled through his notes as he dictated his whole story over the phone. He didn't hesitate for a second and barely needed his notes.

"... Vorster unsympathetic to the schoolchildren ... no compromise on the Afrikaans issue ... no signs of the government negotiating with protesters ... resisting all attempts at reform ... lacks a sense of urgency ... country faces a turbulent future."

His voice was steady and his language impeccable. He tapered off, thanked Lizzie and closed his notebook. The other journalists were now leaving the venue, and some made their way to the tickey box Charlie had just vacated. It was at that precise moment that Deborah realised she'd never ever be as good as he was.

"See you guys in the bar."

A bespectacled and bearded journalist patted Charlie on the back. "Hey, Charlie."

From farther down the bar, someone shouted, "Good to see you, Mr Brown."

A lanky journalist with a Malmesbury bray called out, "Who's the chick? Buy her some proper earrings with your next million-dollar paycheck."

Deborah fingered her seashell earrings. Chris had found the shells on Scarborough Beach and painstakingly crafted them into earrings. He'd had to be really careful not to break them, drilling a tiny hole in each.

"Ignore him. He's an asshole," Charlie whispered. He pulled out a barstool for her and ordered a Boschendal Chardonnay.

A basket of freshly baked bread, chicken liver pate, snoek pate, slivers of rare beef, a selection of mustards and a bunch of huge green grapes appeared on the counter. Charlie handed her a serviette and a side plate.

"Help yourself. You must be hungry."

Deborah spread a thick layer of the liver pate on a slice of bread. The logs glowed in the hearth, throwing a gentle light on the massive Persian carpet. The hotel cat looped around the legs of a couple of journalists standing in a corner, hoping to be picked up. She called it softly and lifted it onto her lap, where it curled up and purred like a tractor.

Charlie smiled and shook his head at her, before he was caught up in a discussion on BJ and the country's future. She noticed that he didn't give away the angle of the story he had just dictated.

"What do you think, Deborah?"

She was warmed by the fact that Charlie was drawing her in.

"I think schoolchildren are the future of the country and should be protected, not shot at. I'm horrified by the government's heartlessness."

Heads nodded and a few surprised glances came her way before the conversation was taken elsewhere, and she slipped into the background again.

Charlie shifted his barstool slightly, so that he could face her. She asked the question she'd been dying to ask. "Charlie, do you have any idea who killed Albert Jennings?"

He put his glass down carefully. "There are lots of theories about it. But the short answer is no. No, I don't know who took him out. I'd love to find out, though."

Deborah could feel him summing her up, trying to read her. She turned her eyes towards the fire.

"So you'd like to be reporting this kind of stuff one day?"

She considered her answer carefully. "To be honest, no."

He looked taken aback. "But I thought you were interested in politics. You studied it, right?"

Deborah shifted awkwardly. "I am. I did."

His quizzical look made her laugh. "I am interested in it, but I'm not sure I want to write about it." Charlie waited for her to go on. "I can't explain this very well. I care about everything that is going on politically, but I think I write better about other stuff."

"Like?" Charlie was looking at her intensely.

"Like ordinary lives around us. Ordinary stories about people, social events, charities, fashion. Does that sound really shallow?"

Charlie guffawed. "Not at all. I'd hardly call you shallow. Not by any stretch of the imagination."

He rubbed his chin, watching her silently, and then suddenly changed tack. "So tell me about this elusive boyfriend."

Deborah's instincts warned her to be on guard. "Nothing much to tell, really."

"How does he get to keep a plum like you, when he's so scarce?"

She laughed. "How about you? You could tell me about your girlfriend."

It was Charlie's turn to laugh. "Not so fast, young lady. You're dealing with a seasoned hack here."

"I'm all ears—"

○ ○ ○

Chapter Eight

"What do you think, Debs?"

Julia shifted Bob and pulled her legs under her. She was holding up a sketch of a Juliette gown with a long train. Deborah sipped her morning tea and focussed on the dress. It hugged the body tightly, until the waist. Then it tapered into a diamond and flared from just below the hips, where it cascaded to the floor in a full, flowing skirt. The train hung straight down the back from a beaded cap.

"Stunning!"

Julia's face lit up and she scooped her silky mane into a makeshift bun. "You really like it?"

"Love, love, love it." Deborah took the sketch to have a closer look. "What colour?"

"White. You'll also be in white."

She traced her finger along the top. "What comes here? It's quite a high neck."

"Lace. Lace from the chest up and also on the arms."

Now she noticed that the diamond shape was repeated at the chest, and a little cleavage was revealed before the lace took over.

"This is so beautiful, Julia. You've outdone yourself."

Julia beamed and produced a bag of samples, which she laid out on top of the duvet. Chantilly lace, raw beaded silk, satin ribbons, all in an eggshell white. A huge apricot sash was the last item to be laid out carefully.

"Who's that for?"

"You, silly. That's your sash."

Deborah sat up properly and ran her finger over the satin. "Funny. Chris hates this colour."

"And that's important because?"

Deborah winced at Julia's barb. She wished she could rewind for a second and recall the comment. She watched her friend taking a deliberate breath before she spoke again. "Do you want to see your dress now?"

The fabric started just above the chest and flared from under the breasts to just below the knee. A sash was tied under the empire line and ended in a huge, beautiful bow at the back.

"Bare shoulders?"

Julia nodded. "I want to show off your figure. That's also why it ends just below the knee … and of course so that you don't look like the bride. Debs? You okay?"

Her throat tightened and she swallowed quickly. "I love it. All of it. It's divine."

Julia scooped up the fabric and the sketches and unwrapped her legs.

"I'll make us some more tea. We still need to discuss shoes, hair and flowers. Oh, and perfume. I want us to wear Youth Dew."

She heard Julia switching the kettle on and putting mugs on the counter. "Is there anything you haven't remembered?" she yelled in the direction of the kitchen.

"Stockings," came her disembodied voice. "We need Grecian blonde sheer."

"What's left for me to think of?" What did her mum always say when it came to family weddings? "Okay, I'll do the borrowed and blue thing."

She joined Julia in the kitchen and poured the tea while Julia shoved Bob from his spot and made space for them to sit.

Julia waited for a moment before she asked, "Why were you sad a moment ago?"

"I wasn't really."

Julia cocked her head.

"Okay a little. I'm happy for you. Really, really happy. It's just that—"

"Don't spend your whole life waiting for Chris. Give him a kick up the backside, Debs. I've a good mind to—"

"No! Don't say anything. I'm warning you, Jules. Don't say a word to him. He's different. He doesn't think like us. His mind is on other things."

"Damn right he's different. He's lucky to have someone like you. I don't think he realises how lucky."

Deborah took her friend's hand. "Don't. Let's not spoil this. It's so special, and the dresses are going to be exquisite. We're going to be beautiful."

Julia took a deep breath. "We are. Pierre is going to have his socks blown off."

"Who's his best man, by the way?"

"His brother. He's flying over specially. He'll be your groom's man. Chris will probably be away as usual, so—"

"I hope he won't."

Deborah couldn't help feeling that Julia hoped he would.

○○○

Bob barked before the doorbell tinkled. There was no time to change out of pyjamas, but Deborah sneaked into the bathroom to brush her teeth at least.

"Nice surprise!"

Chris pecked her on the cheek and perched on the edge of the couch while she popped some bread into the toaster.

"Coffee?"

"Thanks, Debs. I'll have a little."

He didn't use his usual nickname for her. Funny that. "Are we still on for tonight?"

He hesitated for just a moment. "About that. I'm going to have to postpone for another time. Okay?"

It wasn't okay. She swallowed hard and stirred the milk into his coffee. Then she rummaged through the pantry for some rusks and carefully laid a few out on a plate. She put them down in front of him and sipped her own coffee without looking up.

"There's a research function I need to go to. I've been asked to present, at the last minute. I can't get out of it."

Why couldn't he just invite her along? She'd gone with him a couple of months back. She dunked a rusk and held her hand under it, so as not to slosh damp crumbs all over the counter. His frown burnt into the top of her head.

"I wish you wouldn't do that." The irritation was unmistakable and she couldn't keep the hurt from her face.

"I can't just not go to this. I'm part of the research team. Jeez, Debs. Be reasonable!"

"I haven't said a thing."

He shook his head and glowered. "I know what you want to say. It's written all over your face."

She bit her lip and turned her face to the window.

"And now you're sulking." He made a move towards her. "We can go for dinner and a movie next Wednesday night?"

She nodded. Oh my goodness, why didn't she say something? She wanted to shout at him. Ask him why he didn't invite her. Tell him how she really felt. She opened her mouth to argue with him, but blurted, "Is your research assistant going?"

Chris slammed his mug on the counter and grabbed his jacket. "If you're going to start on this again, I'm leaving."

"I could go with you to the function."

Chris looked as if he was struggling to control his temper. He took a deep breath and put his hands on her shoulders. "Partners are not invited. I can't take you. You wouldn't find it interesting, anyway."

She looked at him in amazement. Why on earth would she not find it interesting? There were no words. He was being cruel and she didn't understand why. She shrugged his hands off and took the mugs to the sink.

The warm water was comforting. She jerked her head away before he could kiss the top of it and kept her eyes on the soapy mugs. He was backing off down the passage now, trying to make eye contact.

"I'll phone to confirm Wednesday. We can go somewhere special, if you like."

The front door closed gently and she heard the Volvo splutter into life. She wanted to run after him. Have it all out. Get to the bottom of whatever was going on. But she stood, glued to the sink. She felt her stomach churn miserably.

"Debs?" Julia was watching her intently from the passage. "Let's have a girl's day out. Grab your bag. I'll start the car."

○ ○ ○

The Rock café was fully booked. Julia and Debs perched at the bar and sipped their cold white wine until a table became available. Deborah couldn't remember when she'd last eaten. She would do that, when she was stressed. Most people ate to comfort themselves. She seemed to go off food and get thinner and thinner. The crowd was comforting, and Deborah looked around at the happy faces. Everyone seemed to be having such fun.

"I gave it up for music and the free electric band." Some of the crowd were singing along. It was one of Chris' favourite songs and he always joined in. It gave her a funny feeling, as if the universe was trying to tell her something. A waiter indicated that their table was ready.

Julia slid into her chair, just as someone else reached the table. "Sorry. This one's ours."

A waiter appeared and Deborah glanced at Julia, who nodded.

"Two sirloin steaks, with chips and salad. Medium-rare. No sauce."

Julia lit two cigarettes and passed one to her friend. Deborah took a long drag and blew out a huge puff of smoke.

"You look better already."

She smiled and settled back in her seat.

"What's up with you and Chris, anyway?"

Deborah shrugged her shoulders. "I don't know. I really don't know what's going on."

Julia nodded and waited for her to carry on talking.

"Something's changed between us. I don't know how, but it has. I'd do anything to turn it around, but I don't know what happened. I'm not making any sense, am I?"

"You're making sense." Julia hadn't taken her eyes off her.

"Chris is going to a research thing tonight."

"And?"

"And, I'm not invited."

Julia nodded and took a drag of her cigarette before she stubbed it out. "Is the mysterious assistant going?"

"I think so." She nodded miserably and turned her face to the window.

"Did you ask him why you couldn't?"

"Yes! Yes, I asked him why I couldn't come. I asked if the research girl was going. I showed him I was upset. I did all of it. And now it's worse than ever. I don't know what to do, Jules!"

"Break up with him."

Had Julia gone mad? "What?"

"You heard what I said. Break it off. Tell him to go to hell."

She didn't answer. She unfolded her serviette and sipped her wine. Julia's hand touched her arm, but Deborah didn't look up. All her energy seemed to have drained away and she was powerless.

"I can't."

Julia lifted an eyebrow. "He's treating you like crap."

The steaks arrived before she could reply, and Julia filled her wine glass.

"Bon appetit, my friend."

"To you, too."

Deborah could feel her appetite reviving. She ate hungrily and saved the chips for last, so that she could eat them with her hands, one by one.

"I love you, Debs. It's hard to sit back and watch you getting hurt. If you'd let me, I'd give Chris such a piece of my mind."

Deborah was about to launch into another speech about why she shouldn't when Julia raised her hand.

"But I won't, because I know you don't want me to."

"Thanks."

"Why do you love him so much?"

Deborah took a deep breath. "I know it doesn't make any sense, but I just know he's the ONE. He's a part of me. Dumping him would be like cutting off one of my own limbs. The first time I saw him I just knew; he's my soul mate."

Julia watched her friend's brow crease. She nodded slowly, before she asked, "Do you think he feels the same way?"

"I know he does. That's why this just doesn't make any sense."

"Do you think that maybe he's just not ready for a real commitment?"

Julia was watching her carefully now, and she allowed the words to sink in for a moment. "I don't know what to think."

"He's a man, Debs. Men have egos. Maybe this assistant girl fancies him big time. He could be immensely flattered by the attention."

She dipped her chip into a blob of tomato sauce and bit a piece off it. "You're being too nice. You should shout and scream. Make a scene. Don't make it so easy for him."

Her friend's face developed the wicked look she put on when she was scheming. "Light bulb moment."

"What?"

"Let's treat ourselves to Irish coffee and I'll reveal my plan."

○○○

The eleven o'clock news began, and Julia switched it off before it intruded. The car turned into their road and she spotted a tall silhouette at the gate.

"Speak of the devil," Julia whispered loudly.

"Shoosh."

Deborah was pulling at her door handle before the car even drew to a halt. "Chris! I didn't expect to see you."

He didn't come towards her, but smiled sheepishly. "Can I come in for coffee?"

He seemed distracted. Something had happened.

She nodded.

"I'm going to sneak off to bed. Lock up, Debs." Julia glanced at Chris and made her way down the passage.

Deborah wanted to ask a million questions. Who was there, why he had come here afterwards—

"How was your function?"

Chris couldn't meet her eyes. "Fine."

She resisted the burning urge to ask about his assistant. A lingering resentment gnawed at her, and she had to force herself not to blurt out something caustic.

He seemed trance-like. She sensed that he didn't want to talk. He reached out for his steaming mug and she cupped her own. They sipped in awkward silence until Chris almost whispered, "Can I sleep here tonight, Pix?"

"Okay."

He held the covers for her when she joined him in the bedroom; but when she tried to wrap her arms around his neck he shook his head, turned her onto her side and spooned into her back. They both lay awake for a long time, and only when she felt his body relax against hers and his breathing ease into sleep, did she allow herself to drift off.

○○○

As the sun's rays streaked across Deborah's pillow, the southeaster was already blowing the curtains out of the window.

Bob was chasing the birds when the early train rumbled past. She barely felt the vibrations from the floor. She'd need to buck up a bit, to make the next train. Julia was padding around the kitchen, packing away cups and plates. The kettle whistled insistently. She got up as quietly as she could and made her way to the kitchen.

"Everything okay?" Julia popped two more pieces of bread into the toaster.

"Fine, fine." Deborah spooned coffee into mugs and stretched over Julia for the milk. "Chat later," she said over her shoulder as she balanced the tray.

She settled back into the bed and watched Chris toss and turn. He mumbled in his sleep and his shoulders hunched against his ears. This was so unlike him. He was really agitated. She just knew something bad had happened last night, but she had a sinking feeling he wasn't going to tell her about it. She waited for his eyes to open, then handed him his mug. "You okay?"

He squinted at her, sat up, and took a sip of coffee. "I'll be fine."

He still seemed strange, far away. "Did something happen to you last night?"

He smoothed his hair. "I don't want to talk about it, Pix."

She'd known he'd be secretive. Damn. She put her piece of toast down. "I'm worried about you. It's unfair not to talk to me."

Chris drank the last of his coffee. He didn't look at her as he said, "I was taken in for questioning by the security police."

A shudder moved down her back. She'd had a feeling it was something like this. This was the nightmare she feared the most. That he might one day simply disappear into detention without trial, without access to her or anyone in the outside world.

"What did they do to you? Did they hurt you?"

He ran his fingers through his hair. "They bombarded me with questions. Random, mind-blowingly stupid ones. When I wouldn't answer, they left me in the cell and locked the door."

"Oh God, Chris, that's awful. It must've been terrifying." Deborah tried to rub his back, but he wriggled away from her. "For how long? How long did they leave you for?" She twisted her hands into each other.

He didn't answer. He wasn't going to talk to her. Her clock ticked loudly on the bedside table. "I don't know. They took my watch, so I couldn't tell."

"And then? What happened when they came back?"

He shook his head.

Maybe she should just leave him for a bit. The coffee mugs rattled as she settled them back on the tray.

"They carried a big bucket of water into the cell. Then they repeated the questions, again and again."

He was struggling with himself. She watched him press his palms into his eyes, and her heart skipped a beat. She'd never ever seen him like this. She put the tray down and sat next to him. This time he didn't move away from her.

"When I wouldn't answer, they pushed my head into the bucket of water. Again and again. Each time they held it down longer."

He didn't resist her hand on his. Her voice sounded like someone else's when she spoke again. "What happened then?"

He buried his head in his hands. Deborah circled his back with her hand and waited for him to go on.

"The last time they dunked me, I must have passed out. I woke up alone, in a pool of my own vomit."

She was confused. Chris had never harmed anyone. He had said over and over again that he was against violence. He wouldn't hurt a fly. What could he possibly have done that elicited this?

"But why would they do that to you? You've done nothing wrong." She tried to keep her voice steady. Panic was rising in her throat.

"Not in my eyes. But in theirs, I'm a suspect. Anyone who speaks up against them is a terrorist. You know that, Pix."

Deborah shifted closer. "But what did they want to know?"

Chris shook his head firmly. "I can't say. It's better if I don't tell you anything. Jeez, Pix, why can you never understand this? I don't want to draw you in."

She pulled at a thread on her blanket. "But I need to know."

He jerked away and put his head on his knees. When he spoke again his voice was gentler. "Pix, the less you know the better for you. Believe me."

"I'm in this with you. I want to—"

Chris put his finger over her lips. "Trust me on this one. I'm trying to keep you safe."

Deborah turned her face to the wall. Her eyes stung. She felt very far from him then. She could understand the logic of what he was saying, but she couldn't accept it emotionally.

He reached out and stroked her face with his index finger. "You have no idea how terrifying it is. You think you'll say nothing, but when you're fighting for breath, you could say all sorts of things."

"Did you tell them?"

"No. No, I didn't tell them anything. But it was touch and go, believe me."

Questions tumbled over each other in her brain, but she couldn't ask them. Instead she murmured, "I'm scared."

Chris put his arms around her and buried his head in her neck. "They won't touch you, Pix."

She pulled away to look at him. "But if they did?"

"That's exactly why I don't want to talk about it. Don't you understand that I'm trying to protect you?" He punched the pillow.

She clasped her hands together and squeezed until the tips of her fingers turned white. "No, what I'm saying is, I would never betray you. You know I wouldn't. Nothing they did to me would make me say anything. Why don't you believe me?"

Her words seemed to touch a nerve and he covered her hands with his own. "I do. I know, but—" He gently separated her stiff fingers. Placing one of her hands on his knee, he stroked it with the flat of his hand as though he were smoothing out crumpled paper. He took a deep breath. "You see, I can take … I know I can stand up to their treatment if I need to, but I can't put you in that kind of danger."

"But I—"

"No, don't say any more. I know you're brave, but can't you see that I can't, I just can't do what I need to if I'm worried about you? I need to know you're safe. Will you do that for me? Will you stay safe for me?"

She sat quietly for a few minutes before she spoke again. "At work they're all talking about these pamphlet bombs. Apparently they're being dropped all over town. Gold, green and black flyers. Do you know anything?"

"Have you been listening to a word I've said?" His voice rose and she picked up the tray.

○ ○ ○

Chapter Nine

Deborah struggled with the sticky doorknob and pushed the swollen wooden door open with her knee. The rain didn't help matters, and she shook her umbrella before leaning it against the hat stand. Bob's tail swiped her legs and she patted him absently.

"Julia?"

"In here."

Julia was making chicken soup, and lemongrass wafted down the narrow passage. There was fresh baguette, still warm from the oven, and three neatly laid places on the counter.

"I presume Chris turned down the supper invite." Julia stirred her soup vigorously.

"He's got some work thing on." Deborah wanted to say more, but she decided against it. Why would Julia just assume? That wasn't fair. Chris was really busy with "Varsity stuff." He couldn't always make it. It was true that he was here less and less. In fact, she hadn't seen him since the interrogation night. She winced at the memory of that. But still. Julia was being mean about him. It would be so much easier if they got along. Julia just wasn't open to a friendship with him. Deborah wished she could change that.

"Boetie's coming." Julie glanced up from her pot as she spoke.

Deborah smiled at her softer, almost apologetic tone. "Good. I'm glad."

She chucked her bag on the chair, slipped out of her work shoes and leant against the counter. "Guess what?"

Her friend looked up expectantly.

"I've been invited to a function at the French Embassy on Wednesday evening."

"Wow."

"Charlie wants me to tag along. Says I need to see how the other side lives." Deborah swirled, causing her skirt to balloon around her legs. Then she stopped. "Oh shoot. I can't go. I forgot about dinner and movies with Chris."

She watched that evil look creep onto Julia's face. "This is going to be easier than I thought."

"What do you mean?"

"You're going to stand Chris up!"

Her head shook vehemently. There was no way she'd let Chris down.

"Yes. You are. This is the perfect opportunity."

Deborah waved it away. She would never do that to Chris.

"Come on, Debs. This is a legit reason. You have a work function. Did Chris take you to his thing last week? Did he?" Julia shook her head. "You have to stand up to him, girl. Tell him you can't make it on Wednesday. Square your shoulders and do it!"

Deborah looked miserably at her friend.

"Just once. Let him down once. It'll be good for you."

She hesitated a moment longer, then nodded reluctantly.

"Yes! She's developing a backbone."

Deborah felt herself swooped up in a massive hug and freed herself to breathe again.

"Wat gaan hier aan?" Boetie was striding down the passage, with Bob announcing his arrival. He put his bottle on the counter and pecked both girls on the cheek before rummaging for the wine opener. "This drawer needs a good tidy up."

Julia put her hands on her hips and turned to Deborah. "We'll need to go shopping then."

Boetie opened the wine and poured three glasses. "Fill me in, girls. I'm out in the cold here."

He clinked glasses and settled onto a barstool. Julia scooped chicken soup into each bowl and broke off some bread. Supper was always a precious time in the cottage. Deborah loved it that they sat down together and had a "family" meal. She lit the candle and rearranged the posy of garden flowers.

"So, what time will Charlie fetch you on Wednesday?"

Boetie perked up immediately and looked from one to the other. "Who's Charlie? What's going on?"

"Shush, Boetie. Just listen and you'll get the picture." Julie turned towards Deborah and dropped her voice a little. "I can whip up a dress, if you like."

Deborah watched Boetie out of the corner of her eye. She felt bad about cutting him out of the conversation and shrugged her shoulders in apology. He shook his head and helped himself to more soup.

"Something chic. Sophisticated. Not too many bows and frills. You should look womanly. Not too girlie."

Deborah wasn't sure if her friend was complimenting or insulting her, but she laughed anyway. Julia stopped talking for a few seconds, and then a new idea struck her.

"How much French do you know?"

Deborah frowned. She had done French at school, but didn't remember much. "Let's see. Merci beaucoup. S'il vous plait. Je t'aime."

"A do at the French Embassy," Julia finally whispered into Boetie's ear.

Boetie's laughter echoed around the room. "That'll get you a glass of champagne at least."

Julia winked at Boetie before asking, "Does Charlie have a little thing for you?"

Deborah shot her friend a withering glance. "Of course not. I'm the new kid on the block, the little intern. He's just trying to be nice."

Boetie and Julia exchanged a look.

"Aw c'mon, guys. Give me a break."

No one had heard Chris open the front door. He appeared suddenly and looked awkward, as if intruding on a private conversation. "My appointment ended earlier than I thought, so I decided to pop in. Hope I'm not disturbing anything."

Deborah offered him wine and he sipped it slowly, making an effort to join in the conversation. Deborah slipped her arm around his waist and felt relieved when he chatted to Boetie about his latest electrical job and asked Julia about her wedding plans. Boetie cleared the bowls, while Julia wiped the counter vigorously. Chris ran his hands through Deborah's hair and then propped his elbow on her shoulder.

"We still on for Wednesday night, Pix?"

Everyone seemed to freeze for a split second and then carry on with whatever they were doing. Deborah hesitated before she answered quietly. "I can't make Wednesday now."

Chris' cheek muscle tensed. He sat back on his barstool.

"I've got a work function."

She hoped he'd suggest another night, but he just kept looking at her. "I can hardly believe it. It's quite an exciting opportunity for me. I'll be shadowing Charlie at the French—" She was surprised when his eyebrows met. "Couldn't we go out on Thursday?"

Chris shook his head. "I've got something on. Let me think about it. I'll phone you."

His reaction was perplexing. Deborah took a sip of wine.

"Don't be like that, Chris. You cancelled on me last week, remember? In fact, you cancelled—"

"Oh, so now it's going to be my fault again."

Deborah put her glass down. This was really unfair. Chris must see that.

"I said I'll phone later in the week."

Boetie began packing the bowls away noisily. Julia strode down the passage to fetch Bob's lead, and his barking filled the air. "Cheers," she shouted from the front door.

Boetie closed the cupboard door, grabbed his jacket and held out his hand to Chris. "I'm going to be on my way, too."

Chris hesitated for a second and then said, "Wait for me. I'll walk out with you."

Deborah stepped towards him. "Stay for a few minutes, Chris. Please. Let's talk about this."

"I need to get back."

Halfway down the passage he turned to her. "I'll phone."

○○○

Charlie held the passenger door open and closed it carefully. Deborah propped her clutch bag on her lap and smoothed out the brand new dress Julia had made for her. She suddenly felt self-conscious and hoped he wouldn't think she'd gotten all togged up for him. She glanced at him as he pulled off the kerb.

"You look all grown up tonight, kid."

"Thanks, grandpa."

"Touché." A wry smile formed at the corner of his mouth.

He took all sorts of shortcuts through the streets, and wintergreen lawns whizzed by. After the day's rain, Cape Town looked clean and fresh. She pulled her shawl around her shoulders and admired her new black shoes. Charlie turned into Southern Cross Drive and wound his way to the hidden entrance of the French Embassy. The ornate black gates opened, and a guard indicated the parking area. Deborah stepped out onto the paving and waited for Charlie so that she could follow him into the party.

Trays of champagne drifted past and he nabbed two flutes. "Mingle," he whispered into Deborah's ear. But she stuck by his side and moved wherever he moved. Much as she revelled in the ambience, it was still a little intimidating. She needed some time to feel her own way.

He offered her a caviar-topped blini, which melted in her mouth. Platters of canapés appeared miraculously, and she made sure she tasted all of them.

Charlie introduced her as "our young fledgling" and seemed to be greatly amused by his witticism. Deborah didn't mind. In fact, she loved it. The Ambassador's wife admired her cocktail dress and told her she was "veree chic." French gentlemen with sexy accents kissed her on the hand and plied her with champagne.

Charlie drifted off and seemed to speak to everyone in the room, stopping back occasionally to check on her. After her third glass of champagne, he appeared at her side.

"Enjoying the bubbly?" he whispered. Edith Piaf's husky voice filled the room with "Non, je regrette rien …" and women drew in smoke through long silver filters and then puffed out thin wisps. Deborah thought about lighting a cigarette herself, but decided against it. She'd have one at home, over coffee.

She really needed the loo, after all that champagne. "Toilet?"

"Voila," a waiter waved her down the passage.

She stopped as she was about to push the door open. Women's voices filtered through the keyhole. "This country is a police state … terrible … getting worse." She took a few steps back and waited. "The Security Branch men … asking innocent people questions, questions, a catastrophe!" There was a longer pause and then the other voice said, "Yes, everybody is a suspect now. How you say, terrorists around every corner."

Deborah walked back outside. She wasn't desperate. She'd wait till she got home. When Charlie indicated "time to go," she didn't plead to stay a little longer.

"You seem a little pensive, Debs."

"No, no. Just had too much champers, I think." She didn't want to tell him what she'd overheard. It had been a fabulous evening. She'd just forget about that. People exaggerated, anyway.

As he opened the car door for her, she noticed his notepad on the backseat. She reached back for it and saw that he'd already managed to jot down a few pages of quotes.

"When did you do that?" she asked in amazement.

"It's my job, girl." He shot her a cheeky grin. "You'll be doing that one day soon."

She somehow doubted that. While she'd just been simply enjoying herself, Charlie's brain had been whirring, picking up snippets, story ideas, asking questions. She suddenly felt foolish and inadequate. He seemed to sense her discomfort and patted her knee.

"Come to think of it, jot down your impressions of the evening. What people wore, what we ate, snippets of conversation; that sort of thing. You're a great observer. *Panache* would snap it up. You're almost part of their team, anyway."

The words "police state" came to mind. She murmured a hesitant, "Okay."

The streetlights lit up the expansive homesteads. Rows of freshly pruned rosebushes lined the driveways, and a whiff of horse manure tickled her nostrils. It was easy to imagine herself in a world that wasn't really hers.

Huge gardens gave way to smaller, contained ones, and she imagined herself married to Chris and living in one of these suburbs. A toddler or two would be hanging onto her skirt and—

"Are you planning to spend the night?" Charlie had pulled up outside the cottage. He sniggered at her embarrassment.

"Would you like to come in for coffee?"

He hesitated and then nodded. Julia opened the door before Deborah could struggle with the knob.

"Come in, hobnobbers."

Julia gestured expansively and Bob led the way to the lounge. Deborah rummaged through the pantry for freshly ground coffee beans and Julia produced brownies. Charlie settled on the sofa and sunk his teeth into one. "Hmmm. Are you already accounted for?"

"She's engaged, Charlie. Tough luck."

"Cheeky, now that she's back in her own territory, I see."

Charlie reached for another brownie. The phone rang insistently, and Deborah heaved herself up to answer it.

"Chris?" She was puzzled at his call.

"I just wondered if you were home yet."

He sounded weird. Was he checking up on her? Was something wrong? She held the phone closer to her ear and whispered, "Chris, are you okay?"

He didn't answer at first, and then eventually it came. "What were you doing for all this time? And who is this Charlie guy, anyway?"

She reassured him hurriedly. "Are you crazy? You know how I feel—"

"I need to see you, Pix. There are some things I want to talk about."

Even though she wanted him to step through the door immediately, Deborah stopped herself from inviting him round. "Can we talk tomorrow?"

"Okay."

She knew he was disappointed. But Julia's glare, when she'd risen to answer the phone, had spurred her on. They had both known that no one else was likely to phone at this time of night. He could wait until morning.

She was just putting the phone down when Charlie's voice boomed down the passage, "Is that the mysterious man? Tell him not to be so scarce in future."

She tried to snap out of her sudden dip in mood. Julia stepped into the gap and entertained their guest, but every now and again Deborah caught him watching her. When she met his eyes, he gave her a kind wink and a grin. She wished Chris had waited till the morning to phone.

○○○

Annie held the lift and she squeezed in next to her friend.

"How was the French Embassy thing?"

"Amazing. Another world."

"Who did you meet? What did you wear?" Annie ran her hands through her spiky hair.

The lift pinged and Deborah headed for the coffee table. She poured coffee for both of them, lit a cigarette, and began to describe her evening.

Ginger stood up and indicated to Deborah that he needed to see her. She put out her cigarette quickly and made her way down the room. He looked serious and she braced herself for a dressing down.

"Did you enjoy the French do?"

She nodded a little nervously.

"Good." He hesitated a little and then seemed to dive in. "I've been meaning to talk to you about Charlie."

"Oh, he's been very kind. He—"

"Yes, well, as long as you're learning the ropes from him. That's good, then."

Deborah felt confused by the conversation. Was he just checking up on her? "Thank you." She shrugged and walked back to her desk.

Annie was waiting for her at her desk. "What was that about?"

"I'm not sure. I think he was just checking up on me."

Charlie's face appeared around the corner at that precise moment. "Who's checking up on you?" He rubbed his hands in glee.

"Nobody, you fool." Annie smacked his arm.

"I wouldn't do that, Annie."

His eyes lit up and the game was on. Well almost, except that Ginger hollered down the passage. "Charlie. I need to see you."

Charlie tipped his imaginary hat and strode down the passage. It was a good hour before he reappeared, looking serious. Must be a new story breaking.

"Drinks tomorrow night?" Annie raised an eyebrow at Deborah.

"Can't. I'm making a curry for old school friends. Next week?"

Annie gave her a thumbs down and then slowly inverted it as she turned towards her typewriter. Deborah wrote, "Drinks with

Annie" on her calendar before turning to her scribbled notes on the "stray cats threatening the squirrels in the Gardens" story. She struggled to find a new angle. This needed to be good, or she'd lose her chance of shadowing Charlie ever again. Her phone rang just as she typed the final word. Chris' voice was shaky, unsure.

"I'd like to take you to dinner on Saturday night, Pix." She bit her lip and waited for him to go on. "Somewhere really special. Just the two of us. There are things I need to say to you, before I go away."

"Where are you going?"

"Wear your prettiest dress."

ooo

Deborah stirred the spices into the onions, which were slowly turning golden. She spooned in garlic and ginger and added tomatoes, to give the curry more liquid. The halaal lamb was resting in the spicy mix, and she fried each piece quickly, to seal the juices, before adding the meat to the simmering curry base. Cinnamon sticks and star aniseed filled the kitchen with Malay aromas. She began dicing the potatoes while her curry simmered. She would keep it on a very low heat for a few hours, so that the meat just fell away from the bone. Basmati rice, bananas, coconut and chutney, tomato, onion and cucumber. She kept the poppadums aside to fry at the last minute. She prepared the bowls and mentally ticked off her list. She really wanted to surprise Ayesha and Shamilla with a good curry.

"This looks amazing!" Julia folded the serviettes and laid out plates and cutlery. "You should cook more often."

"My repertoire is rather limited, Jules. I'm sure you'd get sick of it pretty quickly."

Boetie put the three bottles of dry white wine on the counter. "I hope this'll be enough."

He lifted the lid to sniff the curry, but Julia smacked his hand away. He backed out of the kitchen and was just in time to pick up the ringing phone. He held it to his ear for a minute and then put it down.

"Somebody hung up on me." Boetie rubbed his chin for a minute. "That phone is tapped, man. There's a strange sort of ticking sound." He examined the phone and shook his head.

The doorbell tinkled as he was putting it back. Deborah answered it and did the introductions.

"Ayesha, Shamilla, her brother Noor, Boetie, Julia."

Boetie stepped into the role of barman and poured wine, Coke and orange juice. Glasses were clinked. Shamilla kicked off her shoes and settled onto the couch with Ayesha.

Spicy aromas from the kitchen added to the warmth, and Deborah joined in the conversation as she stirred her pot.

"Do you see any of the other boarders from school?"

Ayesha looked at Shamilla. "No, not really."

"One or two," Shamilla added.

"Ayesha was the first Muslim 'head girl' at the convent." Deborah clinked glasses with her, and Boetie shook his head in amazement.

"And the Catholic nuns allowed that?"

"Yup. They were pretty amazing, in some ways."

"So the convent isn't fazed by, I mean, anyone could go to your school?"

Ayesha held out her glass. "The nuns ignored the race laws, Boetie, if that's what you mean. They interviewed anyone who wanted to go to their convent and then accepted you if they chose to. Simple as that."

The conversation shifted into the ways in which they were not so amazing, but it was Ayesha who jumped to the nuns' defence.

"C'mon, girls. You must admit we were pretty terrible. I wouldn't be a teacher if you paid me a million rand."

Heads nodded reluctantly and Noor chuckled in agreement.

"Remember when you kept getting detention for not doing your homework, Debs?"

Deborah blushed to her roots as she replied, "Yes, and I could never go because I was always rehearsing for an eisteddfod."

Shamilla guffawed and Ayesha shook her head despairingly. "And the Prefect told you not to bother about coming to school as you were forever dancing, anyway."

"Well, look at you now. I wonder what the stupid girl would have to say now," Noor added loyally.

Boetie put on jazz, but kept the volume to a background level. The candle flickered on the coffee table, and Julia dimmed the lights a little more. Deborah was about to say supper was ready when the doorbell rang once more. Strange. Had she invited someone else and forgotten?

She hurried to the door and opened it to two policemen. She felt the breath catch in her throat. "Can I help you?"

"Miss Morley?"

She nodded and felt her forehead creasing.

"We have reason to believe you are entertaining coloured people in your home."

Deborah stepped outside and closed the door quietly. "I have some friends here for supper. Yes." She looked at the men in amazement.

"Your neighbour complained."

"My neighbour?" Now she felt blood rushing to her head. "My neighbour complained?"

The policemen didn't react at first. After a long pause, one of them stepped towards her and said, "We need to investigate all complaints, ma'am."

"Everything okay, Debs?" Julia's voice called down the passage.

"Be there in a sec. No problem." She found herself biting back tears. This was shameful. How dare her neighbour do this to her?

The policemen towered over her. "Will your guests be staying overnight?"

"They're here for dinner." Her voice was sounding hysterical, and she tried to take a deep breath.

The men hovered on the doorstep and seemed ready to push past her. She stepped towards them, instinctively barring the entrance with her body. They would have to physically move her out of the way to enter. She stood her ground. Eventually, one of them stepped back.

"Well. You don't seem to be making any noise. No one is being disturbed. We'll take our leave, ma'am."

He began to retreat, but the taller one hesitated for a moment, took a few steps back and then turned. "Your boyfriend's Christopher Jarvis, is that right?"

Deborah stared at him in disbelief.

"He here tonight, too?"

Deborah felt her throat tighten, but she didn't utter a word.

"Where is he then?"

"Why should I know that?"

She knew she was sounding defensive, but she couldn't control her tone. The policeman tipped his cap and then turned on his heel. Deborah's hand shook as she closed the door. She took a deep breath, walked back to the kitchen and forced a smile as she stirred her pot unnecessarily.

"What was that about?"

"Oh, wrong house. Someone looking for our neighbour."

As her guests helped themselves and complimented her on her curry, Deborah struggled to regain her composure. She thanked her lucky stars that they were all talkative, and only Julia suspected that she was not okay. When the evening faded and her guests hugged and kissed her cheeks in farewell, Deborah closed the door and then burst into tears.

"What's wrong?" Julia was at her side instantly.

"I hate this stupid government and their insane laws. I hate it!"

"Wat's fout?"

Boetie switched the tap off and pulled her onto the sofa. Both their concerned faces seemed to zoom in on her suddenly, and Deborah got up.

"Would you mind very much if I left the cleaning to you?"

"Sure."

"Anytime."

At the door she turned to face her friends, who were still watching her. "It was the police at the door. They said the neighbours complained."

Julia jumped up immediately. "About what?"

Deborah hadn't wanted to blurt this out, and now she struggled to contain her rage. "About our 'coloured guests.' He actually complained about our guests!"

Boetie took her arm and pulled her back into the lounge. "Kom, sit nou. I'll make some tea. Jissie man, this is horrible."

Julia pressed fists to her cheeks, as she ranted. "The cheek of it! Our down and out neighbour, who can hardly hold down a job and spends his days drinking beer and watching TV. I could happily slap him through the face so hard he'd be reeling. I hate him! I hate all these bloody lunatics. Just because their skins are white, they think they're better than everyone else. How absurd is that?"

Deborah buried her head in a cushion and Boetie put her tea within reach. As he squeezed onto the sofa, he put his arm around her and pulled her towards him.

"Did they say anything else, Debs?"

"Yes. No, not really."

She sipped her tea. Thank goodness for her friends. She couldn't imagine dealing with this on her own. Well, there was one bit she had to keep to herself.

She needed to be alone suddenly and mumbled an apology as she disappeared to her room.

Her bedroom ceiling seemed to press down on her. How did the policemen know about Chris? Maybe Boetie was right about the phone. She should phone Chris. But no. What if the phone was tapped?

Terror tingled in her fingers. She needed to see him. She knew he was involved in underground politics, but what part did he actually play? Had her neighbour phoned, or was this just the police's way of intimidating her? She felt angry and hurt and physically sick. She was ashamed. She was ashamed of being associated, in any way, with the policemen, the government; in fact, right at this moment she was bitterly ashamed of being white. She hid her head under the pillow.

Chris was right. It was going to take a lot more than marches and placards to change the country. The years of entrenched racism were not going to just disappear without a fight. Her beloved country was so entangled in this hatred and malice; it would take a miracle to find a peaceful solution. Was it even remotely possible?

She laid there for a little longer and then got up and eased her door open. The phone was just a step away. She pulled her tracksuit on and grabbed her takkies. If she eased the front door open very slowly, no one would hear her leave. There was a tickey box at the end of the road. She would phone from there.

Bob seemed to understand the need for silence, and he slunk after her as she closed the door soundlessly, pushed her bicycle off the front stoep carefully, and then swung a leg over it.

Chris picked up on the first ring, and she whispered into the receiver, "I need to see you urgently."

○○○

He was waiting outside when she arrived. She leant her bicycle against the railing and patted Bob. He'd been confused by her late night ride, but seemed to understand that his protection was needed. She allowed Chris to pull her inside, and she gulped the beer shandy he'd ordered for her. He rubbed her back and wrapped his jacket around her to stop her shivering. She came out with the story and he listened in silence until she faltered. Then he raised two fingers at the barman and slid the empty glasses to the edge of the table. She watched his cheek twitch as he concentrated on her words. The clock behind the bar ticked loudly in the silence.

Eventually he spoke. "I'm still a pacifist, Pix. You know that, don't you?"

She nodded. "I know."

"I'll always reject violence. I want you to understand that. But people are growing impatient with just talks. I totally get that, too."

Her eyes remained glued to his. "You're not becoming involved with the armed?"

"I've already said that. No. But we need to understand the frustration on the ground. That's all I'm going to say. If something happens to me, you mustn't—"

"Nothing's going to happen," she said unconvincingly.

"I'm still a part of the group involved in secret talks. It's vital that we talk to certain organizations."

Deborah held onto his hand and squeezed it tightly. "I understand."

"I'm not sure that you really do. This government is leading us into a civil war. We're heading for a bloodbath, I'm telling you. You have no idea what's going on. I wish I could—"

He banged the table with his hand and seemed to reconsider what he was about to say.

"I shouldn't be telling you any of this. It's dangerous for both of us. I don't want to—"

She felt the hairs on the back of her neck tingle. What if The Pig was bugged? Perhaps they were being listened to, right now. Any moment, the door could burst open. They could be taken in for questioning any second. Their lives could change in a flash.

She brought his hand to her lips and kissed it. "I think my phone is tapped."

His brow creased as he shook his head sadly. "I'm sorry, Pix. I didn't want you involved in all this."

She shuddered involuntarily, but reassured him quickly. "No, no. It's okay, Chris. Really. I'm right behind you."

Mandela's speech from the dock was still pinned to his satchel. Her eyes scanned the words again, as Chris excused himself and walked towards the toilets.

"… dedicated my life to this struggle of the African people … fought against white domination and fought against black domination … cherished the ideal of a democratic and free society … it is an ideal for which I am prepared to die."

A shiver rippled down her spine.

He buttoned the jacket and pulled the belt tightly around her waist. "I'll drive you back."

Deborah trembled as he flung the bicycle into the back of the bakkie and heaved Bob up beside it, before he held the door open for her.

"I hate this stupid government. They're bringing us nothing but pain. More than anything, I want them to release Nelson Mandela and un-ban the ANC. I want to see this government toppled, Chris."

He turned to look at her, as she hesitated.

"… But I don't want to lose you to the struggle."

He glued his eye to the road.

"You're more important to me than anything else in the world, and I'm scared, Chris; for you, I'm scared for you."

She watched his face tense up for a moment before he squeezed her leg in acknowledgement.

"But don't you understand? We're part of the struggle. It can't be a separate thing. We're making history here, every day of our lives. We can't opt out. At least I can't."

Deborah struggled to keep her tears at bay. "I care very much. About everything. I try to make a difference in peoples' lives. I teach dancing to kids who can't afford lessons. I help wherever I can, with the skills I have, but I don't want you to be arrested. I'd die if that happened. I just want us to be a boy and girl, in love, in an ordinary city."

She could see Chris tensing his shoulders and she stopped. His voice went up an octave when he next spoke.

"But we were born into extraordinary times. Can't you get that? We need to be the change, Pix. It's not just going to happen. And you, you have all the knowledge at your fingertips. You should get involved in the struggle. You could be making a valuable contribution. And yet, you hide behind your shyness; bury yourself in your job at *Panache,* writing frivolous stories about unimportant events. Sometimes I feel as if I no longer understand."

Her shoulders shook, and try as she might, she could not gulp back the stream of tears.

"I'm sorry, Pix." Chris' hand reached for hers. "Forgive me. Please forgive me. I had no right to—"

He stroked her cheek and smoothed back her hair. "I do still love you. It's just that—"

She shook her head and dropped her face into her hands.

"On Saturday night, I'm going to whisk you away on a magic carpet. Your feet won't touch the ground for a second. It's going to be your night. I promise."

○○○

Deborah pulled out several outfits and threw them on the bed. She held up the black strapless number and decided it looked good. But no. Chris hated her in black. She slipped on the cheesecloth dress. Not special enough. Made her look a bit insipid. Lime green cocktail dress? A possibility, but not Chris' scene. She just didn't have the extra cash for a new dress, and she could hardly expect Julia to whip up another one. One of these would have to do.

"Jules," she hollered down the passage.

Julia slid into her room and pulled her legs up under her on the edge of her bed. "Put some on and model for me. I'll tell you which one is going to knock him out."

Deborah tried on one after the other, and Julia picked them up off the floor as she discarded them. "Aaargh!" Nothing seemed to look right. She tugged her hair and threw a pillow at Julia.

"Wait. Let me have a look." She allowed her friend to push her onto the bed and take over the wardrobe.

Julia eyed each dress critically and finally pulled out a silky pastel mix. "This one, Debs. It's smart, but sort of gypsy-ish. Blues and greens. You look good in a halter neck. Just up Chris' street, I think."

Deborah pulled it over her head and swirled. "Yes!"

She stood in front of the mirror and tried on jewellery until she settled on a plain silver chain and her usual silver bangles. Chris had always loved those. He said the sound of them made him think she was about to read his fortune.

"Try the plain black kitten heels. I think they'll do the trick. And do something special with your hair." She scrunched it up in a loose bun. "I've got a pretty black hair clip, which will look great in that mop of yours."

Deborah slid out of the dress and hung it up as Julia disappeared down the passage.

"Come and fry the bacon," she called over her shoulder. Deborah grabbed her jeans off the chair and rummaged for a clean t-shirt. She should tell Jules everything that happened the other night. She felt disloyal keeping such a big secret. It was often the unsaid things which hung in the air and unravelled friendships slowly. Well, not only friendships. The secrecy around Chris was chipping away at their relationship. If only she was brave enough to confront him—about everything. She slipped on some takkies and made her way to the kitchen.

"Jules, I've been meaning to tell you more about the other night."

ooo

Chapter Eleven

The doorbell chimed at exactly seven o'clock. Chris was always punctual. Deborah, naturally, was still under the shower. She could hear his infectious laughter. She dried and dressed as quickly as she could. A smudge of lip gloss and a little mascara would do. Julia appeared at her door and mouthed, "Hurry up." Deborah scooped her hair up, sprayed a little Chanel No. 5 onto her wrists before she clip-clopped into the passage.

Chris was already up to greet her. "Wow!"

She smiled up at him. "You look handsome, too."

She reached to straighten his red satin bow tie and couldn't help noticing how the dinner jacket stretched across his shoulders. His hair waved up slightly as it tipped the collar of the starched white shirt.

"Shall we go?" He winked at Julia, walked round to the passenger side of the Volvo, held the door open, and handed Deborah a little parcel as she sat down. She waited for him to start the car before she fingered the silver tissue paper.

"Shall I open it now?"

The paper held something fragile and she moved it aside gently. Her eyes welled up as she picked up the necklace. It was meticulously strung with tiny shells of different hues. Mother-of-pearl shone delicately next to smooth cream. A soft pink, nestled next to sand-washed white. It was painstakingly put together and filled with pure love.

"You made it?"

A smile lingered in the corners of his mouth.

"Where are we going?"

"A surprise."

The trees flashed past as the road wound its way upwards. Lush undergrowth gave way to ferns. Pine cones rolled towards the road and settled in the fynbos, waiting for someone like Deborah to pick them up for winter fires in fireplaces. She opened her window and breathed in the smell of pine and moss and clean moist air. As the Volvo turned the last corner, the Constantia Nek restaurant came into view. Deborah reached over to kiss Chris' cheek.

"I thought you'd like to dance, after dinner."

She slipped her hand into his. He held it so tightly it almost hurt, and she felt her stomach lurch. The thatched building seemed to peep through the evening mist, and a roaring log fire welcomed them to the room. A single deep red rose rested on the linen tablecloth. As the waiter pulled her chair out, she picked it up and smelt the heady aroma.

When the menus came, Chris suggested choices. Mussels in a white wine sauce, followed by lemon buttered sole and vegetables of the day. Crème brûlée was to end the dinner, and a KWV wooded Chardonnay was already in the ice bucket. When the waiter poured the wine, Chris stood up.

"I'd like to make a toast to my one and only Pixie." Deborah looked around to see other dinner guests smiling knowingly. "I know I haven't been the best boyfriend to you for a long time now, but—"

She tried to interrupt him, but he hushed her as he sat down again. "Let me speak."

She leant back in her chair and focussed on his words. "That's all going to change. When I get back from this trip, I want things to be different. I love you, Pix. Give me a chance to make everything up to you.".

"But ..."

"You won't understand yet, but I promise, things are going to get better, much better between us. We do have a future together. I'm going to make sure it happens. Perhaps I can't wave a magic wand and change the country, but I can change things between us."

Deborah wanted to ask a thousand questions. She knew he meant every word, but there were puzzling things she wanted answers to. Who was the girl riding Hercules, for a start.

She swallowed her last bite of creamy mussel and then put her knife and fork down. "Chris."

He got up and led her to the dance floor. Gloria Gaynor was belting out "Back from outer space," and he eased her to the middle of the floor. He moved well and she followed his lead. The rhythm coursed through her body, and she allowed herself to relax into it. The floor filled up and she was in her element.

Chris stepped back to watch her for a minute. He shook his head and stepped forward to take her into his arms again. "You dance as if you were born to it," he whispered.

They got back to their table as the main course arrived. Chris topped off the wine glasses, and Deborah savoured every mouthful of the lemony sole. "To us," she said as she raised her glass to Chris.

A silver-haired, distinguished gentleman stood up and walked towards their table. He bowed slightly and addressed Chris. "May I dance with your beautiful lady?"

Chris looked questioningly at Deborah, and she got up and took the man's arm. The strains of "Por una Cabeza" enticed them into a tango, and as she laid her hand into his firm grip, he manoeuvred her feet backwards in long strides.

"Close your eyes and trust me," he said.

She allowed his feet to guide hers. He pulled her waist in closer and she leant into his frame. The music coursed through them as they moved across the floor, and when Deborah was dipped into the finale, she heard the crowd clapping. Chris was staring at her as if he'd only just noticed her.

"I didn't know you could do the tango. You are a pro." She smiled and took his hand. "Teach me that. You're going to dance like that with me."

He pulled her chair out for her and moved his closer before he sat again. His eyes studied every feature of her face, and he buried his mouth in the palm of her hand. "I wanted to grab you away from your partner in the middle of the dance and pull you into my arms."

Deborah laughed happily. "You were jealous?"

"Of course I was. Here was my Pixie dancing like an angel, and everyone in the room was watching her."

This time, she pulled him up and led him to the dance floor. She wrapped her arms around his neck and moved him into a slow shuffle.

"You should have carried on dancing, not studied politics," he whispered in her ear.

By the time the dessert arrived, she was a little tipsy and deliriously happy. "I don't want tonight to end."

A flash of anxiety swept over Chris' face, but it was gone almost as soon as she noticed its arrival. When it was time to leave, Chris wrapped her in his jacket and kept his arm tightly around her until they got to the car. The drive home was meandering, and a full moon lit their way between the trees.

They reached the cottage and Chris took her to the front door. "Please stay," she whispered.

He shook his head. "I can't, my darling. We leave in a few hours."

"Tell me where you're going this time."

He put his finger on her lips. "I'll be back before you know it. Promise."

"But Chris, I—"

"You know it's for your own protection, Pix. I've already drawn you in too much. Please don't ask."

She reached up to kiss him. She didn't want an argument. Not now. Not after a heavenly evening.

"Remember what I said tonight. I meant it. Every word."

Chris walked to the gate, but before he pushed it open, he turned. "I almost forgot." He fumbled in this pocket for a slip of paper and held it out to her. "Memorize the number and then burn it."

Deborah closed her palm over it. "What is it?"

He put his finger to his lips. "If there is a real emergency, you can get hold of me there." He blew her one last kiss, before the gate slammed behind him.

The Volvo pulled away slowly. She stood watching him until he was a speck in the dark. Then she closed the door and slipped into her room. The moon streamed silver light, and stars still lit up the sky. It was a magical night. Everything she could have wished for. And yet a tight knot was developing in her stomach and she couldn't wish it away.

○○○

"There's a protest going on in Adderley Street, guys." Annie was leaning over the balcony, trying for a better view.

"Go, Annie. Take a photographer with you, and take Deborah." Ginger gestured towards the entrance.

Deborah seized her jacket and Annie raced her to the lift. In minutes, they were in the middle of the placard-holding crowd marching towards the fountain, where a phalanx of blue uniforms awaited them. Their shouts bounced between the buildings.

Deborah found herself struggling to keep up with the crowd. The Indian girl next to her looked much too young to be there by herself. A copy of *Macbeth* protruded from her blazer pocket, and Deborah wanted to push it back more securely. An elderly man beat her to it, and they exchanged a look. He looked like an academic type, with his faded denim jeans and leather patches on his jacket elbows.

She was propelled forward by the crowd and noted youngsters, intermingled with middle-aged people, all dressed in casual clothing, all united in a common cause. The air was electric.

"Free Mandela!"

"Amandla!"

"Awethu!"

Deborah absorbed the energy. It was tinged with fear, but the big crowd drew together and seemed to take comfort in their closeness. Apprehension was overridden by a wave of idealism. She looked around to say something to Annie, but she was no longer by her side.

"Ready for this?" A young bearded man pushed through the crowd to get to the front. Deborah nodded uncertainly.

"You're Chris Jarvis' girlfriend, right?"

Her stomach spasmed. She needed Chris there. The young man hesitated for a second.

"I'm Tom Smith, by the way, in case you need my name," he said over his shoulder.

The *Macbeth* girl stumbled and fell. The crowd surged forward, and a tall, elderly man pulled her up quickly before she was trampled. He put his arm around her shoulder and kept it there as they moved forward.

Tom was addressing the crowd through a loudspeaker. Deborah looked around to see where his voice was coming from, but she couldn't spot him in the dense crowd.

"Mandela must be released. We must never, never give up!" People raised their fists and shouted.

"Power to the people."

"Amandla."

She unclenched her fist as she remembered her role here.

"There is no room for complacency. We all need to get involved. Make this country ungovernable!"

Words swam around in her head, and people pushed in front of her. She saw the speaker up ahead. Strong arms had lifted him so he could be seen. People were cheering and clapping. A piece of cardboard with "real education for all," scrawled in black khoki pen, flapped in front of Deborah's eyes, and she stepped out of its way. Bits of cardboard bearing angry slogans waved all around her, and she tried to read as many as she could.

"Nigel, can you get a shot of that placard? The 'real education' one?" He was weaving in between people, angling for the best shot.

"We must force the apartheid government to step down. Time for negotiation is over. No longer accept the murder of our children. The power must be in the hands of the people. Dream of a new South Africa!"

"Can you see Tom Smith? He's the one with the loud hailer."

Nigel shook his head. "No, I'll push closer. See if I can get a shot."

Nigel was snapping pictures rapidly, and the crowd heaved towards the human barrier. Deborah tried to steady herself as they reached the policemen. Her press card was not going to be much protection. Her mouth felt dry. Two policemen grappled with Nigel, wrenching the camera out of his hand.

"I'm a press photographer."

He was shoved to the ground. Deborah elbowed through to help him. Her hand stretched out, but she was flung back by the crowd. Her head throbbed. She pushed desperately to reach Nigel. She had to find him.

Police coursed forward. Their batons held high, ready for action and daring the crowd to cross the line. She looked into a pair of steely grey eyes, and a shiver ran down her spine. He began thumping his weapon into the palm of his hand as he made eye contact with her.

Batons swung and people scattered in all directions. One minute a loud hailer was warning the crowd to disperse, and the next, tear gas canisters were hissing as they hit the ground. One landed next to her, and immediately her eyes clouded and stung like crazy. Tears welled up. She tried to brush them away to see where she was going, but it was no use. She felt the panic rising in her throat. A hazy mob swam in front of her.

"I can't see." She could feel bodies bumping her, but couldn't make out any faces. "Help me. I can't see anything." Her voice sounded far away, and she covered her eyes with her hands.

"It's okay. Come with us. Grab my arm."

A voice and strong hands on her shoulders allowed her to breathe out, and she felt herself moved forward.

"I'll steer you. Stick with us."

Her knees buckled as she felt a body running into her, and the stranger stopped her from falling. Somewhere in the crowd a woman was screaming. She froze as her eyes cleared a little. Two policemen right next to her wielded batons at a group of students. She could make out the bulk of a policeman swinging at a figure in a blue sweatshirt, curled in a foetal ball. A muddied book lay in the dirt beside the body.

Deborah took a step forward. "Stop it!" She felt herself heaving, sobs rising in her chest. "Stop it. Just stop it."

The policeman turned, baton still raised. She couldn't see his face through the sting of tears, but he stepped towards her. She wanted to run but her legs wouldn't move. She heard Annie's voice and turned to see a figure pushing through the crowd towards her. Deborah couldn't make out what she was saying until Annie roughly grabbed her sleeve.

"Run!" Annie growled at her. "Run, run!"

She felt the life return to her legs, and she turned and fled with the others. The sound of Annie's pounding steps just behind her gave her the courage to run faster, harder. When her legs gave up, she turned back towards her friend. Annie was gone. Shit! She looked around wildly.

"Annie!"

"Nigel!"

Her screams echoed around her. She'd lost them. She ran towards a young man huddled against the pavement.

"Nigel?" No. It wasn't him.

Her eyes still stung, but she was beginning to see again. She followed the now smaller crowd to St George's Cathedral. Her eyes scoured the pews quickly as she squeezed into the shadowed interior, past the crowd at the massive doors. No sign of Annie or Nigel.

Her heart pounded, and she turned away and walked back to the newsroom. The sound of sirens echoed down Adderley Street. People ran in the other direction, to the sanctuary of the cathedral. She dodged a police patrol car as she wound her way between people and resisted the urge to throw up. What if Nigel was badly hurt? And where was Annie? She shouldn't have left Nigel's side. She should have made sure Annie was behind her. She'd let them both down so badly. She'd never forgive herself if either one of them was hurt. She forced herself into a jog now. The comfort of the newsroom propelled her forward. With immense relief she found herself back in the newspaper building at last. As the lift door opened, she stumbled out into the familiar, comforting territory of the newsroom.

Nigel steadied her as Annie reached for her hand.

"Chill, girl. Just chill."

Deborah inhaled the air-conditioned oxygen.

"A cigarette. Please."

ooo

"You okay, my friend?" Deborah took Julia's outstretched hand. "We read the news. Were you slap-bang in the middle of all that?"

"I was right in the middle."

Julia shook her head. "I was so worried. Thank goodness you're okay."

Deborah rid herself of extra layers. The smell of tear gas and sweat was overwhelming.

"Boetie thinks we should all go out tonight. Take your mind off of this. Have some good clean fun. You up for it?"

Deborah made her way to the shower wordlessly.

"Okay, think about it—after your shower," Julia called after her.

She needed to wash away the tear gas, the fear, the hurt. She scrubbed her body roughly and flinched as the brush moved over a yellowish-green bruise on her thigh. Her thumb throbbed and seemed to swell up as she turned the water on full blast. She stood on the edge of her left foot so as not to pop the blister which had formed under her heel. Her eyes closed, and she allowed the stream to pound against her lids. Only when she felt purged did she turn the water off and wrap herself in her towel. Her mind felt numb, and she brushed her teeth vigorously to rid herself of the bitter taste of tear gas and terror.

Boetie was already hooting by the time she'd pulled on fresh jeans and a t-shirt. She patted a plaster over her blister and slid into her ankle boots as she picked up her jacket.

The Pig was rocking and Boetie led them to the bar, where his buddy Joubert was already well into a castle.

"Beers?"

"Bye, Bye, Miss American Pie" was blasting across the room, and the crowd grew steadily. This was what she needed, no thinking, analysing, trying to make sense of what had happened, just mindless fun and a tall glass of alcohol to blot out the chaos. She envied Boetie, relaxing into his pub night, and wished she could just flip a switch. Joubert was building the Jenga blocks into a tower.

"Jack on the rocks. Make it a double."

Boetie shot him a quizzical look.

"Are you going to keep up or what, Boet?"

Deborah shook her head at Boetie. He ignored her, nodded at the barman and adjusted his stool so that he was facing his friend.

Julia clinked glasses with her and pulled her stool closer. "Are you enjoying yourself?"

Deborah accepted a cigarette and bent her head to light it from Julia's match. Her hand shook a little as she cupped the match. Flashes of the morning's protest kept popping up in her mind, and, as much as she wanted to, she just couldn't block them out. One minute it was peaceful, and the next it was a war zone. The thing was, only one side was armed. She shuddered at the thought of what could have happened. Annie could have been seriously hurt. Nigel was lucky to have escaped at all.

She gulped the beer and took a deep drag of her cigarette. Boetie and his friend were on another planet already. She half-wished she could join them. A mixture of jealousy and annoyance at their ignorance overwhelmed her. The whole country was collapsing around their ears, and these two were fooling around as if there was nothing wrong. Hadn't they heard about the protest in town? Hadn't they seen the newspaper headlines? Did they just not care?

"Earth to Deborah." Julia was frowning at her now. "C'mon. We're supposed to be having fun."

Deborah forced a smile. She must try to chill. It was no use spoiling everyone's evening.

"Stop thinking about what happened. We're here now."

Julia was right. For her friends' sake, she should just block it all out, for tonight, anyway.

Boetie was trying his best to communicate with his drunken friend. "Wat's met jou, man?"

Joubert toppled the tower of blocks with one swipe. Then he started balancing them again, one by one. He slipped a Camel from Boetie's pack and swiped at the lighter viciously, until it finally lit up. The blocks toppled. Joubert downed the last of his Jack Daniels and banged the glass on the counter. The barman looked up, and Joubert lifted two fingers. Joubert looked down again, sucking deeply on his Camel. Boetie caught the barman's eye and gestured to the water jug.

"Add water," he mouthed. The barman nodded, giving Boetie a quick smile.

Joubert kept his eyes on the scattered blocks.

Boetie leant forward and grabbed his friend's arm. "Cheer up, man. It can't be that bad." Joubert shook him off roughly, and Boetie clutched the edge of the bar to steady himself.

"Hey! Praat met my, man. I'm your mate, remember? Same side."

Deborah looked away. A woman wearing a tight pencil skirt and stilettos was making her way to a stool close by. Her skirt flapped open at the slit as she swung her pert butt onto a stool. Stilettos balanced precariously on the rim, she leant forward and gave a little wave to the barman.

"Gin and tonic," she said peremptorily.

Joubert caught the barman's eye and slipped a folded R50 note under his hand. The barman nodded.

"Paid for, miss," he told the woman, who was still rummaging through her bag. Joubert seemed to keep his head forward so that she couldn't thank him easily. Deborah noted the tell-tale cheek muscle flinch as the woman's stool shifted closer, and her violet eyes summed up Joubert. He was running his fingers through his mop of black curls.

"The next one's on me then."

He didn't turn, but he nodded and the slight upturn of his mouth was enough to encourage more conversation.

"Are you guys from around here?" The woman was as smooth as a silk scarf.

Boetie had shifted in and was giving Joubert a "don't go there'" look. He turned towards the woman. "Ja we are. You? I think I've seen you in the Standard. You're one of the tellers there?"

Before the woman could answer, Joubert spat out, "Boet, she's the bank manager."

Boetie clinked the ice around his empty glass. He seemed to shrink back onto his stool. "Oh. Sorry, man. I didn't recognise you."

The bank manager smiled generously and indicated drinks all round to the barman, who was pretending to polish glasses.

"No thanks. We've had more than enough. Joubert's meisie will be waiting."

"Boetie is jy nou mal. I don't have a meisie, man. Come to think of it, neither does he."

He grabbed Boetie around the neck and planted a kiss on his cheek. Despite herself, Deborah felt hysterical laughter bubbling up inside her. Julia joined her, and as Boetie wiped his cheek in disgust, the bank manager started to laugh.

"Our charming Boetie here doesn't have a girlfriend, yet. But we're interviewing. Any takers?" Julia looked around cheekily. Boetie's expression brought on more wild laughter. Deborah hadn't laughed so hard in ages. It was laughter of release, of panic relinquished. She caught the bank manager's eye. The laughter started up again. Her stomach ached and she put her hands up. "No more. I can't laugh any more, guys."

She moved her stool in closer, to complete the circle. "Anyone else want a hamburger? I'm ravenous."

Julia looked around for a waiter. By the time they were all ready to leave, Julia had got everyone to swop telephone numbers and was arranging a braai at the cottage. The bank manager was becoming quite chatty, especially to Boetie. Deborah tried her best to hold onto the laughter. Her mind kept trying to replay scenes of tear gas and batons. She couldn't believe she'd lost Nigel, and then Annie. The woman's screams reverberated in her head.

No. She mustn't think. She needed to push it all away. Just enjoy this evening with her friends. She grabbed her bag off the back of her stool and followed them to the door. Out of the corner of her eye, she took in the two men approaching the bar, and a sixth sense made her neck prickle.

Had they been there all the time? She couldn't help feeling that she'd been watched. She turned to look at them and they stared straight back. The safari-suited one clearly recognised her. She felt her stomach churn.

But this night was supposed to be about fun. She tried to push the creeping terror to the back of her mind. Chris was right. They had been born into extraordinary times. And the backdrop to their lives was South Africa's crazy politics. They had to be a part of it all, but she needed time out, even if it was just for a night.

As she drifted off to sleep, she heard the hiss of tear gas canisters, looked around frantically for Chris, felt the stinging in her sightless eyes and saw the silhouettes of the strange men in the bar. She woke up screaming, as if she'd never stop.

ooo

The early train drew to a sudden halt. It couldn't be Cape Town Station already.

"Why've we stopped?" A young mum lifted her baby out of his pram to soothe him. A conductor dashed into the compartment. He was shouting something in Afrikaans.

"What's happening?" The young mum tapped the conductor's shoulder. "Why are we stopping here?"

People were standing up, peering out of the windows. "We're not moving." Deborah glanced out. The Salt River Station was still visible behind her. "Why?" someone shouted. "What's going on?"

The sting of tear gas wafted through the windows into Deborah's nostrils and eyes as soon as the train moved forward. She stood and made her way to the door. Then she changed her mind and slid back onto her seat. She'd just wait. The words "pamphlet bomb" were being bandied about all around her. She'd heard about them but never actually seen one in action.

She reached for her book, read the same paragraph a few times and then gave up. People were sitting down again, but restlessness hung about the whole compartment. The idea of a pamphlet bomb sent a ripple of anxiety through her body. She wanted to talk to Chris. Maybe he'd heard more.

The train edged forward. There was a sudden commotion on the platform. A conductor was blowing his whistle frantically. Police appeared from nowhere and began searching bags, grabbing people, redirecting the crowd.

"Pamphlet bomb," someone else shouted from the back of her compartment. A handful of gold, green and black pamphlets flew through the window.

The young mum had grabbed her baby and covered his head with her hands. The compartment erupted into a frantic buzz of people, trying to squeeze through the doors.

Deborah felt queasy. She'd landed herself in the middle of something big. She stepped onto the platform, picked up a pamphlet with a heel print on it and scanned it quickly. *Time for talking is over. The ANC is the future. The people must rule.* She folded it, reached for her bag, changed her mind and dropped it on the nearest seat.

The platform was teeming with people, screaming and running in every direction. Policemen with huge rifles were grabbing handfuls of pamphlets, searching bags, shoving people on. Shouts rang out, and a few students in UCT hoodies ran along the side of the train, waving pamphlets in the air and dodging the policemen who chased after them. It felt like something out of a movie.

Despite the chaos around her, Deborah felt a growing fascination with the whole scene. It was a brave thing to do. Whoever had masterminded this was putting themselves in real danger. They'd be detained for sure. Yet they'd done this, brazenly.

There was an excitement in the air that she couldn't quite put her finger on. People seemed to be caught up in a spirit of adventure. She looked at the hopeful faces around her. A grey-haired woman was shaking her head, but the hint of a smile played at her lips. "Stoute studente," the cleaner mumbled, as he chased pigeons away from the morning's sandwich crumbs and swept up more of the pamphlets. "Pamphlet bomb," was whispered all around her. She would never have orchestrated something like this, but she couldn't help admiring the people who had. Their mission had been accomplished, that was for sure. The audacity of it made her curious.

A camera jammed into her hip as someone elbowed her out of his way. She glanced at the retreating sports jacket. He met her eyes for a second, but not in apology. She checked the station clock and lengthened her stride as she made her way to Adderley Street.

ooo

Chapter Twelve

Deborah kicked off her duvet and pulled up the sheet. She was born to wake up only in the light. Weekday mornings, when she had to walk to the train station in the pitch dark, were enough to make her wish she could work from home.

"Hey, sleepy head."

Julia was already bouncing off the walls. She was like an energetic bunny, and Deborah pulled the sheet over her head to avoid her.

"How about a beach walk?"

Deborah smelt the aroma before Julia waved the mug of Earl Grey under her nose.

"Come on, girl. We need to keep fit and trim. Only a few months to the wedding now."

Julia waited until she'd swung her legs off the bed before she turned to leave. Deborah hauled herself to the bathroom for a quick wash and then slipped into her bikini. She pulled on her jeans and a t-shirt and grabbed her straw hat off the coat rack.

"I'm ready."

Julia was rummaging for her keys. "Kommetjie?"

Deborah rubbed her chin. "Yes. Actually, no. Clovelly, rather. I want warmer water." She lit two cigarettes and handed one to Julia. Then she wound down the window. Julia zipped through the avenues and headed towards Tokai. Pollsmoor Prison loomed ahead. It always made her uneasy to see it. She thought of the young activist, Tom, who had addressed the crowd in Adderley Street and the girl she was sure she'd seen curled up on the ground. She hoped neither of them had been arrested and taken there. She hoped she'd never have to see the inside of the place. As Julia turned towards Muizenberg, Deborah let the sea air tickle her face.

"Penny for your thoughts." Julia turned her head, so that she could see her friend.

"None really."

Julia shook her head.

"Actually, I'm worried about Chris. I haven't heard from him yet, and it's been a week already."

Julia nodded sagely, but didn't offer any words of comfort.

"He said he'd write."

Deborah took a deep drag of her cigarette. Julia still didn't respond. Her hands seemed to grip the steering wheel. Deborah kept her gaze on her friend for a moment, but Julia concentrated on the road. "I've been meaning to tell you about the train thing yesterday." Deborah waited for a response. When there was none, she carried on with her story. "Our train was held back and we didn't enter the station for a while. Some people had dropped a pamphlet bomb. Can you imagine? There was complete chaos on the platform. Pamphlets all over the place, police chasing students, hundreds of confused passengers, tear gas, the works. I thought I'd landed in a movie set." She leant forward to catch Julia's eye.

After a long silence, Julia said, "I heard a little about it."

That was it? After her whole story, Julia gave her a one-liner? She drifted back into silence, and soon Julia was turning towards Clovelly Beach. When the car stopped, Deborah ducked as Bob jumped over and bounded off across the beach. Julia sought out a good spot, spread her towel, and Deborah slipped her clothes off.

"Shall we walk?"

Julia kicked off her slip-slops and put them on top of the pile, in case the wind came up. Deborah's feet sank into the soft sand. The sun warmed her shoulders, and she moved towards the foamy edge of the water to gather freshly washed-up sea shells. Spirally snail cones lay next to lustrous mother-of-pearl pieces. She picked up as many as she could fit into her hat and then sorted through them to keep the perfect ones. She waded in farther and held her hat above her head. Sea water prickled against her skin, making her shiver. She turned back to watch Julia, who was also collecting shells, throwing back the flawed ones fiercely. She could see the muscle in Julia's jaw flinching.

Something was clearly wrong. Deborah waded through the waves foaming at her calves and put her hat down.

"Want to come for a swim?"

Julia shook her head and focussed on the sand running through her fingers. Deborah sprinted to dive under the next wave. Cold sea water hit her face as it broke into her and she resurfaced. She turned on her back and soaked up the sun and salty water. She kicked, causing salty spray to glisten in the sunlight. A single dark cloud floated in the sky above her, and the faint outline of the moon appeared. A seagull shrieked and circled for a catch. "One last wave," she called.

Deborah rode the wave into the shore and only stood up when it turned into foam on the sand. Her toes sank into the bubbles, and seaweed wrapped itself around her ankles as the water retreated. She bent to brush it off, and as she stretched up, she saw Julia walking to meet her. She seemed about to say something, but stopped herself. The tension in the air was palpable now. Deborah couldn't take another second of this, and she felt the blood rush to her cheeks.

"I'm not sure why you're so tense, but I suspect it has to do with the pamphlet bomb." It has to be. Why would she be angry about it? Surely she can see that it was a brave thing to do? People needed to be aware of what is happening in their country.

Julia picked up a pebble and threw it into the sea. "Was Chris involved in that?"

"So that's why you're being weird? You think Chris is involved. I don't think that at all. But even if he is, why is that so bad? It's not as if he's committed a terrible crime, you know."

"I'm not upset about that. It's something else, Debs."

She watched Julia shifting the wet sand with her toes and waited for her to spit it out. "Those books you put into your shelf the other day. Are they yours?"

Deborah stopped and gawked at her friend. "How did you know I'd put some books there?"

Julia didn't answer and shifted from leg to leg.

"Have you been snooping around in my room?"

Julia seemed awkward. She opened her mouth to reply and then didn't. They walked along in silence for a few moments before Julia spoke.

"*Are* they your books, Debs?"

Deborah faced Julia. "Why do you ask?"

"Because if they're Chris', I don't want them in the cottage."

Deborah's stomach churned. Julia looked down at the sand. Eventually Deborah said, "I offered to keep them while Chris is away. That's not such a big deal, is it?"

"They're banned books. Of course it's a big deal. Karl Marx, the Rivonia trials, even I know that."

Disappointment rose in her throat. This was her best friend talking, and it seemed as if she came from a different planet.

"I can't have them in the cottage. The wedding is in a few weeks now. Guests will be arriving from France; people will be in and out. What if the police decide to raid us then? They've already been at our door. I don't want any trouble. I don't give two hoots about what Chris has in his place. I really don't. But when he starts bringing stuff into our cottage, that's a different story. And anyway, he's got a damn cheek asking you to keep his books for him. That's putting you at risk for a—"

Deborah stopped her before she said any more. "That's enough. And he didn't ask me. I offered."

She turned away from Julia and took off down the beach running, as fast as she could. She heard Julia calling after her, but she didn't turn around. She ran until she couldn't anymore and then slumped down onto the sand. Waves rose and crashed and seagulls called, before swooping down onto the sea. The weather was changing and dark clouds were building quickly.

Julia puffed down next to her. "I'm sorry." She tried to take her hand, but Deborah pulled away. "It's just that Pierre wouldn't like it. He's very protective, and I can't say I blame him."

Deborah couldn't listen to more of this.

"This is my stuff, my room, and those books belong to the man I love."

"But you don't believe in what he does, Debs. He's drawing you into dangerous stuff."

Deborah felt her cheeks heat up. "I do. I do believe in what he does. He's fighting for justice. Of course, I do. Who wouldn't? So should you. How can you even be so selfish as to think only of something as bourgeois as a wedding when people are risking their lives for their ideals?"

She watched the hurt appear in Julia's eyes.

"Listen to yourself. This isn't you talking. You love weddings. You've never considered them bourgeois before. Who's talking about selfish? You're putting other people at risk."

Deborah stepped forward towards Julia. "I'm not just getting this from Chris. Do you think I don't have a mind of my own? Especially after what I got involved in on Friday, how can you even ask that?"

Julia's eyes misted up and she changed tack.

"I love you, Debs. You're more important to me than you could possibly realise. I want the best for you. I want you to meet someone who makes you deliriously happy, who treats you the way you deserve to be treated. I—"

Raindrops came sporadically and Deborah stood up. "We'd better start walking back."

She was aware of Julia's hand reaching out to her, but her friend seemed to think better of it and dropped it to her side. The raindrops came steadily and Julia huddled closer. When the heavens opened, they ran to collect their things and dash for the car. They cursed the broken heater. Bob shook the water off vigorously and looked disappointed when he got shoved to the backseat. Once the engine burst into life, Julia pulled off quickly and wound her way back to the cottage and the promise of hot chocolate and marshmallows at the fire.

ooo

Logs crackled and Deborah watched the yellow-red flames being drawn up quickly into the narrow chimney. The smell of burning pine cones sweetened the air, and she savoured her steaming chocolate. Julia arranged the blanket over both their legs and rubbed Bob with her foot.

"I'll remove the books." Deborah turned her marshmallow until it was crispy brown on the outside and a gooey mess in the middle.

"Ag, Debs, if it matters that much to you, then I can't ask."

"No, you're right." Deborah eased the marshmallow off the stick with her teeth and let it melt onto her tongue. "It's not your issue and it's half your cottage. I can't endanger you."

Julia added another log to the fire.

Deborah sat up abruptly and snapped her fingers.

"Hercules."

"What?"

"Just you and I. We'll go out there tomorrow and hide the books in Hercules' stable."

○○○

Deborah pushed the gate and held it open for Julia. She waved at Prins, who was cleaning stables at the other end of the farm. The rain had softened the earth, and her boots sank into the mud with each step she took. She took in the smell of horses and fresh manure.

"Don't look guilty, Debs. Just act normal."

Deborah smiled at Prins and strode alongside Julia. When they reached Hercules' stable, she held out the huge carrot and he chomped it. He let her stroke his velvety nose, and she opened her palm so he could take the last bits.

Prins came strolling over and offered her a brush. "More nooi."

"Hello, Prins."

"You've come to visit my favourite boy again, ne?"

She tried not to remember the last painful conversation they'd had. She took the brush he held out.

"This is my friend Julia, Prins."

Prins held out a muddy hand and Julia hesitated for a second before she shook it firmly. Deborah needed him to go back to whatever he was doing.

"I'll brush him nicely, Prins. You don't have to worry about us."

Prins dipped his head, but still hung around.

Deborah examined the brush, patted Hercules for a bit and then tried again. "Prins, is it all right if I call you when I need your help?"

He took the hint now and backed off reluctantly. "Okay nooi. Just shout for me, if you want me to come."

"Thanks."

She watched him saunter back to the stables on the other side. When he was far enough away, she turned to Julia for the go ahead.

"Start brushing. I'll do the digging. Keep your eye on Prins, okay?"

Deborah slipped the brush over her hand. She stroked Hercules and nuzzled his neck for a moment.

"I miss him too, boy. He'll be back soon." She began massaging him in small circles. He neighed and stamped his hoof. Then he settled into a contented trance as she increased her pressure a little.

She could hear Julia shifting sawdust aside and digging. She'd brought their garden trowel and was gradually making a hole deep enough to bury the books, which they had wrapped carefully in several layers of plastic. Deborah sneaked a backward glance.

"Deeper, Jules. We don't want Hercules to dig it up accidentally."

Her friend barked back immediately. "Keep your eye on Prins. I'll need enough warning if he starts walking back."

Deborah concentrated on Hercules' back now. His head was in his food trough and he was munching away contentedly. She worked her way over all his muscles and admired his now-shiny coat. He allowed her to untangle his mane and even brush his ears.

She was brushing his tail when she saw Prins making his way towards the stable. "He's coming."

By the time Prins reached them, Julia had packed away her trowel, and Deborah held out a wrapped food parcel for Prins.

"This is for you and your family, Prins."

His face lit up and he put out both hands. "Haai nooi. Baie dankie, baie dankie." He bowed in thanks and she grinned at him.

"Enjoy it. I made it especially for you."

He sniffed the fresh bread and shook his head in amazement.

"You are kind nooi. Very kind."

Deborah handed him the brush and gave Hercules one last caress. "We're going home now."

She looked back at Julia, who was quietly shifting sawdust with her feet.

"Right. Let's be on our way then."

Prins walked ahead so that he could open the gate, and as they climbed into the car and pulled away, he waved them off.

"Don't look back," said Julia. "Just keep looking ahead."

As the car took the first turn towards home, Deborah slapped her friend on the shoulder.

"Well done."

Julia inhaled deeply and blew out quickly. "Mission accomplished!"

Deborah handed her a lit cigarette and then took a deep drag on her own. Then she opened her window and blew out the smoke.

ooo

Deborah leant back into the hard leather and tried to move her head into a comfortable position. *Panache* had requested her again, and she'd been asked to write about a cocktail party for Fashion Week. The lifestyle editor seemed pleased with her, and Ginger was surprisingly encouraging. He'd said she should work on as many different types of stories as possible. That was the only way she'd find her niche.

Her internship was coming to an end soon, and she was holding thumbs that *Panache* would offer her a permanent job. She was better there than in news. She tried not to think about Chris' reaction. He'd think she was selling out. But she was better suited to lifestyle and design. She just didn't have it in her to be a political reporter, no matter how interested she was.

Now, she could do with being home, in the lounge with Julia. Hopefully Boetie would pop in, too. That would be really nice. It was Julia's turn to cook, and she wondered what was for supper. Five-thirty and the train was a little late today. Still, she'd be home in about twenty-five minutes.

She took out the postcard from Chris and read it for the umpteenth time. He'd be home soon. He couldn't say much; just that he missed her and would see her any day now. She pressed the card to her lips and then slipped it into *Cry the Beloved Country*. It was a fitting bookmark for one of her favourite books. The train's rhythm would soon sooth her jangled nerves, and she relaxed her neck. Rain pelted down. Sheets of it swished against the window. Deborah stifled a yawn as the doors opened again and a burly young man made his way towards the empty seat next to her. He shook his head and a few droplets fell onto her book. She jerked it away.

"Oops. Sorry!"

Deborah found herself gushing an "It's okay," and arranged her paraphernalia neatly, to make room. She could feel her pink cheeks under his gaze and turned to the window as he stretched his legs across the linoleum.

Would it seem rude to just carry on reading? She wasn't all that hot at small talk, and, anyway, she'd had a day full of news stories. He glanced at her, and she turned the page firmly before bringing it a bit closer to her face. The light began to fade slowly and the train hadn't moved. People were still getting on and jostling for seats now. When the train eased away from the platform, people reached for the roof straps. Deborah sat stiffly and tried not to let her knee touch his. He seemed to have spread himself comfortably and taken ownership of the space. She could smell Brut and pipe tobacco. Funny how attractive men seemed to impose their presence, as if it were their right.

Legs slightly ajar, shoulders back against the seat, muscled arms straying over the invisible line. She smiled a little. There was something charming about this manly confidence. Owning the world must be awesome.

Salt River drifted by. Woodstock would be next. Deborah always counted all the stops before Rondebosch. People crowded the doors and elbowed their way to the few available seats. Her neighbour got up to offer his to a silver-haired lady. Deborah loved the old fashioned chivalry.

"Wish there was more of that around," she mumbled to herself.

Closing the book, she leant forward to slip it into her bag. The train eased into Woodstock Station. People spewed out and more streamed in. The silver-haired lady had dismounted now, and Deborah moved her knee to make way for Mr Chivalry's legs.

Observatory came into view, and the compartment emptied a bit more. Deborah kneaded the tension in her neck and looked out of the window to see Mowbray slowly appearing before her. She loved this part of the journey. It got prettier and prettier, as Rosebank came closer. The rain hadn't eased up, and she hoped her fold-up umbrella was still in her bag somewhere. She picked it up, rummaged for the umbrella and put her ticket back into her purse. There were more people than usual on the platform. Usually it was pretty empty by this time of the afternoon.

"Your stop coming up?"

"Yup," she smiled at her neighbour, who had gradually taken over more of the space again.

ooo

Something whizzed past the back of Deborah's head. Broken glass tinkled onto her lap. A half-brick dropped onto the floor behind her, as a burly dad grabbed his toddler and pulled him into a tight embrace. The compartment erupted into a frenetic buzz of people. Deborah felt glued to her seat. Her heart beat above the cacophony around her, and she shut her eyes to block out rising panic.

The train moved into a steady click-clack, click-clack once more. It seemed out of sync with what had just happened. Was that brick aimed at her? It had come straight towards her seat. She felt her neighbour's eyes.

"You okay?" He stared at her for a moment.

"I'm okay."

She pretended to read her book. The same words swam in front of her eyes until she closed it again. She couldn't shake the idea that she was being watched.

"Don't be ridiculous," she muttered to herself. She was just being paranoid. Why on earth would anyone watch her? She was someone who was about to spend a week at a Design Indaba. She was hardly a threat to the country's security. But she was connected to Chris.

"What the hell happened here?" The conductor was stepping over shards of glass and shaking his head as he demanded tickets.

"A brick came through the window." Her neighbour indicated its position behind their seat.

"Donner se skollies," the conductor mumbled as he pushed pamphlets and shards of glass away with his boots. "Ek gaan hulle slat."

Deborah clutched her bag in her lap and tried to stop her knees from shaking.

ooo

Bob was barking wildly when Deborah pushed the gate open. Julia was waving something in the air. "Another postcard for you. I think it's from Chris! " She walked past her friend wordlessly, flopped onto the sofa and glanced at the postcard.

Back any day now. Remember what I said. I meant it. All my love, C.

"Oh thank goodness. He's nearly home."

Without asking, Julia poured two glasses of chilled wine and sat down beside her. Deborah took a gulp and clinked glasses.

"You okay?"

"I'll be fine. Just give me a minute." She tried to slow her breathing down, while Julia rummaged in her bag for some cigarettes. Then she blurted out the story in one breath. Julia seemed to grow pensive as the story went on, and when she'd finished the two sat in silence.

"Say something, Jules."

Julia hesitated for a moment. "Maybe some delinquent kid just threw a brick at the train. It could have just been a random act. Perhaps it wasn't meant for you at all."

Deborah shifted the cushion into the small of her back. "But the pamphlets?"

Julia topped up the glasses.

"Just coincidence. Think about it, Debs. It could really have been bad luck that it came your way."

Deborah took a sip of her wine and looked at Julia closely.

"Seriously. I would take it as a freak thing. It could have been anyone sitting on that seat. If the train was fuller, you'd have been standing, anyway. Not so?"

Deborah rubbed her eyes. Julia punched her arm.

"You were just in the wrong place, at the wrong time. Really."

Deborah sipped her wine again. "Maybe you're right."

"Course I'm right. Aren't I always right?"

She raised her glass and proposed a toast. "To freaky things and lucky escapes."

She picked a few pieces of glass out of Deborah's hair. "Want to get yourself cleaned up, while I start the soup?"

ooo

The next morning, the men seized Deborah, as soon as she stepped through the gate. She was bundled into the back of a car and it sped off instantly. Once they had turned the corner, the moustached one took the hood off her head.

"It's okay, Deborah. We aren't going to hurt you. We just need to ask you a few simple questions."

The car turned down a side street, and Deborah was led into the police station. The taller man unlocked the door of a tiny room and indicated that she should enter it. "We'll be back soon." The door clanged behind them and Deborah was alone. The key turned and footsteps drifted away.

She stared at the table and two chairs. In the corner was a tin filing cabinet. She paced the room and checked her watch every few minutes. There was still time to get to work. No need to panic yet. She could get the next train, in fifteen minutes. Surely they'd come back any minute.

She sat down. What did they want from her? Was this about the books? They couldn't possibly know about them. No, she mustn't be silly. There was no way they could have. She mustn't start imagining things. She could hear birdsong coming in through the small window in the corner. She drummed her fingers on the table. Five minutes left. If she ran she'd just make that train.

Where were they? She really needed to get to work. She watched the big hand go round twice. Blast! She couldn't be late this morning. She still had a lot of work to do on the Design Indaba story. Her watch was the only sound in the room and she tried not to look at it anymore.

The white walls began to close in on her. There was nothing to break the glare. No curtains softened the meshed window. There were no pictures, ornaments, green plants, nothing, except the table, chairs and the ugly cabinet.

She checked her watch again. Damn! She'd missed the next two trains. Gloria would be worried by now. She'd probably asked Annie if she knew anything. There was no way to get a message to them, either. Beads of perspiration broke out on her forehead. She got up again and paced.

What did they want from her? Why hadn't they come back? Her breath was coming in shallow gulps now, and she tried to calm herself down. If they didn't come soon, she would not be able to stop from weeing in her pants. She was desperate. She walked briskly around the room again. She checked her watch. Two hours! She'd been in this room for two whole hours. Maybe they'd forgotten she was there. She tried the door. Locked. If she banged her body weight against it, she could force it. It didn't give at all.

"Hello. Anybody out there?" Her voice ricocheted across the room.

There wasn't a soul around. They had forgotten her. She glanced up at the window. Perhaps she could just squeeze; she stood on the chair and went up on her tiptoes. No. There was no way she could get to it. She tried jumping up, but it was no use. Just too high.

When the door finally opened, she rushed at the men. "Please, I'm desperate for the toilet."

"All in good time." The tall man gestured for her to sit.

"But I—"

His cold eyes stopped her. She crossed her legs tightly.

"Deborah, if you co-operate with us, then you can get to work and go on with your day. However, if you do not, I cannot guarantee that things will go well for you and your friends. So think very carefully about the questions we're going to ask you."

He got up and left the room without a backward glance, as his companion stepped forward and sat down.

"Please. I really need the—"

The moustached man took her by the arm, ushered her to a toilet opposite the room and turned his back. "The door stays open," he said by way of explanation. When they were back at the table, he smiled at her.

"Feel better now?" He folded his arms and looked closely at her. "I can't imagine that you've done anything wrong, Deborah."

Deborah stumbled over her words.

"No. No, I haven't. I don't understand why you want to ask me questions. I really …"

A wry smile swept over his face and he got up abruptly. "I'll be back."

What was happening now? Deborah put her head in her hands. Why were they doing this to her? She got up and paced again. She checked her watch once more. Shit. She was now hopelessly late. If only she could contact someone, anyone. She glanced up. The wind had gained momentum, and it was battering the broken glass in the window. She slid down the wall and curled up into herself.

Her head hurt and she could barely swallow. She needed some water. She got up again and walked to the door. Then she banged on it with her fists. "I need water," she croaked. The metal taste in her mouth made her feel nauseous. Her watch ticked and the sound of footsteps grew closer. Then they faded away again. Deborah slumped into the chair. Her forehead fell onto the table and she covered her head with her hands.

A sudden thought made her bolt up again. What if they had taken Chris at the same time? They could pretend that she'd said things about him. She never would, but what if he believed them? She'd rather die than have Chris believe she'd betrayed him. She didn't know anything. But they could pretend she'd given information. She wished she knew where he was. She wished he'd contact her. She really needed to speak to him.

It was dark by the time the door opened again, and she was relieved when a light went on. This time, the men brought a glass of water, pen and paper. "You ready to answer the questions now?" the tall one barked. He nodded at his partner who picked up the pen.

"Where did you go to university?"

Deborah answered immediately. "Grahamstown. I went to Rhodes."

She watched the moustached one labouriously write down the answer.

"Why politics?"

She hesitated. Why was he asking that? Both men folded their arms and stared at her.

"I'm interested in politics." Was that the wrong thing to say? What were they getting at?

"Did you know Professor Nancy?"

"Of course. She was acting Head of Department."

The men nodded knowingly.

"I mean she lectured me. I didn't really—"

"What were the names of the other lecturers?"

Why would they ask all this? "I can't remember everyone's name. I—"

"But you knew them socially. You spent a lot of time with them."

She didn't. Yes, she went to the department functions. But not ...

"I went to the department's functions. Not to anything else." They were confusing her. She knew what she meant. But it wasn't coming out right. She rubbed her palms over her face.

"So you love this Chris guy, Deborah?"

What? Now they were jumping to Chris. She felt panic rising in her gut.

"Yes."

"You'd do anything for him, I guess?"

"Yes. No. I mean ... I don't know what you're asking me." She was in over her head. Whatever she said, they'd twist it. Already she'd said more than she wanted to. She bit her lip.

"I'm not going to say any more. I have nothing to tell you. I know nothing. You've no right. I'm just not saying another word."

"Have it your way then." The tall man rose and gestured to his companion. They slammed the door behind them.

"Wait!" They couldn't leave her alone again. She had to get out. She checked her watch as she paced the room once more. Her stomach ached. She hadn't eaten since breakfast. Bile shot up into her throat and she retched miserably. She leant against the wall. Then she slid down it and curled up. The room was darkening, and she could see grey clouds drifting past the small window.

The door creaked open and they sauntered in. This time Deborah didn't get up. She stayed on the floor until the moustached man pulled her by her hair and dragged her to the table. "Sit," he ordered and he spread photographs across the surface. "What do you know about the pamphlet bombs?"

Oh, thank God. They didn't know about the books. They wouldn't know—

"What pamphlet bombs?"

"Do you recognise yourself?"

Deborah put her hand to her mouth. It was a photograph of her on the platform. Green and black pamphlets were scattered all around her feet.

"That it is you, right?"

She mumbled a "Yes."

"What are you holding in your hand here?"

She stared at the photograph. There was a pamphlet in her hand—the one she'd picked up to take a closer look.

"I'm waiting, Deborah." The moustache man was in her face.

"I don't know. I—"

"I didn't hear you. Speak up, Deborah. What was that?"

She looked down at her lap. His hand pulled back and she reeled as it came across her cheek. The chair tipped and she just managed to balance it. Tears pricked behind her eyes, and she put the palm of her hand against her burning cheek.

"Meisiekind, you need to stop lying, otherwise things will get a lot worse for you."

"I'm not lying. I don't know anything about—" Her hairline prickled and she pushed her hair away from her face. "I caught the train to work. There was a pamphlet bomb at Cape Town Station. Pamphlets were scattered all over the platform. I didn't … I mean, that's all I can tell you."

The tall one thrust another photograph at her. "Who is the man in the middle here?" Deborah didn't answer. "Okay then, I'll tell you. Christopher Jarvis." She stared at the wall. "And what do you notice about the photo?" He was working himself up again. She tried not to make any eye contact. "He's the only white man. Don't you find that strange?" She shook her head. "Ah-ha. Now we're getting somewhere."

She shouldn't have shaken her head. What did he mean by— She'd already said too much. Chris was right. She could get someone into trouble without even meaning to. She wouldn't even be aware of it. She was way out of her depth. Her head spun and she put her hands up to her cheeks.

The moustache gathered up the photographs quickly and opened the door. "Gaan." She hesitated at the door. "Go! You can go!" She stumbled towards the entrance, but before she'd reached the front door, the tall one pulled her back and whispered, "The pamphlet in your hand. That's quite a coincidence, Deborah. Ne?"

ooo

Deborah crossed the stretch of lawn and looked down the road. The area seemed unfamiliar to her, but she couldn't be that far from home. It hadn't taken them that long from the Rondebosch Station. She looked up at the mountain to get her bearings. Okay, so if she zigzagged her way towards it, she'd reach Main Road. Then she'd know where to go from there.

The sky was darkening by the minute. Cars whizzed past her. A cyclist rang his bell as he overtook her on the right. Other pedestrians eyed her curiously. She was exhausted. Her hair was blowing all over her face, and she tried in vain to keep her skirt from flapping up. Her legs felt shaky, and she had to force herself to keep going. She tried to focus on one step at a time. Finally she could see Main Road up ahead of her. From there, it was just another block and she'd be home. The thought spurred her on and she lengthened her stride.

The sun had set by the time Deborah struggled with the door key. She patted Bob absent-mindedly and made her way to the kitchen. She poured herself a glass of wine and slid into the sofa. It suited her that the room was dark. She curled up and took a big gulp. A cigarette would be good, too. She shook one of Julia's Pall Malls out of the packet and lit it shakily.

Had this really happened? It didn't seem possible. She tried not to think about it. Best to just push the whole thing away. She pulled the mohair blanket up to her shoulders. Her body shook from head to toe, and she couldn't get it to stop. It was as if she was in shock. Her yoga breathing wasn't cutting it, either. She lit another cigarette and inhaled hungrily.

"It's okay now," she told herself. She hadn't told them anything. They wouldn't have let her go, if they really had something on her. She wasn't a criminal or a terrorist. She hadn't done anything wrong. And yet she felt guilty in some way. Violated, dirty, singled out; a mixture of awful feelings which left her confused. Had she let Chris down somehow? Was he involved in the pamphlet bomb incident? She could ask him, but he wouldn't tell her. She didn't believe he had anything to do with it, but what if he did? If the SB had merely wanted to rattle her cage, they had succeeded fully.

Bob's barking alerted her to Julia's arrival before the door creaked open and she heard boots tramping down the passage.

"Debs?" Julia flicked the light switch and sat down on the edge of the sofa. "You okay? Why are you sitting in the dark?"

Deborah took her last sip and stretched for the cigarette box once more.

"What's happened? Tell me. You look like death."

Julia struck a match and cupped the flame with one hand. After a long drag, Deborah turned to face her.

"The security police took me in."

"What? You serious, Debs?"

"But I'm fine now." Should she even be telling her this?

"What did they want? Did they hurt you?" Julia looked at her suspiciously.

"No, no." She put her hand up to her cheek. "But it was horrible. A nightmare."

Julia shook cheese and onion chips into a bowl.

"I can't believe it. Why would they want to question you? What have you done that's so bad?"

"I don't want to talk about it, Jules. I'm just so grateful to be home. It's over. I'm really okay now."

She watched Julia mulling over this and wasn't surprised when she asked, "Is this because of Chris? It must be because of—"

"No. It's not. It's not always about …" This was the last thing she needed now. She inhaled deeply.

"How did you get away?"

"They just let me go." She laughed a little hysterically.

"It's not funny."

"Well, it is in a way. The only insurrectionist thing I've done lately is argue about my bridesmaid dress."

Julia's laughter set her off again and they just couldn't stop.

○○○

Annie was already at her desk when Deborah arrived. She waved and began weaving her way towards the stairs when Annie jumped up and directed her onto the balcony. She accepted the cigarette and laughed at Annie's smoke rings. "I've been trying to get you all evening. You're pretty scarce at the moment, Debs. What's up?" She tried to copy the smoke rings, but failed dismally. "Useless," she declared.

It would be great to be able to tell Annie what had happened. Annie would know exactly what to do. "I've been meaning to—" No, she shouldn't. It would be dangerous. She imagined Chris frowning at her as she blurted out everything that had happened in the last few days. "Just been busy, busy. Wedding stuff and all that."

Annie studied her suspiciously. She wasn't fooled. But it would be stupid to confide in her. "I presume that's not yours you're talking about."

Deborah let out a giggle. "No, no. I wish!"

Annie was waiting for her to say more. Deborah stubbed her cigarette out in the dead potted plant and picked up her bag. "We'd better get in there."

She made her way down to the *Panache* section and checked the board for her work. Gloria lifted an eyebrow as Deborah fumbled with the three sheets and fed them into the typewriter. A wrap-up of the Design Indaba. Right. She flipped through her notes and highlighted the main points. She typed *Design Indaba* at the top of her page and then began her introduction. When she'd finished it, she re-read it carefully, ripped out the pages and began preparing a new set of three sheets. She needed to focus. This wrap-up was due by the end of the morning. "C'mon, Deborah," she growled at herself.

Gloria was watching her from a distance. Now she walked across. "Is there a problem? Something you want to discuss?"

Deborah cringed. "No, no. Just made a silly mistake. I'm starting it again." Gloria hesitated and then walked back to her desk.

Aaargh! Everyone seemed to be honing in on her. Did she have a sign on her forehead or something? It would be so much easier if she could talk about it. She wasn't good at bottling things up like this. But what option did she have? She had to keep her mouth shut. She tried to concentrate on the Indaba story. It seemed absurd to be writing about this now, when so much else was going down around her. Maybe Chris was right. She was burying her head in the sand, instead of getting involved. No wonder he pooh-poohed her job.

She typed the introduction again. It still sounded lame. She looked around to check where Gloria was, before she pulled the sheets out and began preparing a third lot to feed in. If only she could get hold of Chris. She rummaged in her bag for the emergency phone number he'd given her. She wasn't supposed to contact him at all while he was away, unless it was an emergency. This was one. He probably already knew she'd been taken in by the SB. Maybe he believed she'd said something. Betrayed him in some way. But she hadn't. She needed to reassure him of that.

She dialled the number and was relieved to hear the phone ringing. It rang and rang. "Pick up!" she whispered at it. Nothing. When Gloria made the rounds again, Deborah slid the receiver back and busied herself on the typewriter. She'd try again later. He had to pick up some time. She concentrated on her introduction and typed the last few words. Then she scanned it for mistakes. At last. This one would do.

By lunchtime, she was frantic. She'd dialled the number three times and no one had picked up. Her story was complete—at least that had gone well in the end. She had to speak to Chris now. Her stomach was in a knot, and she couldn't concentrate for a minute longer. "Please, please, pick up," she prayed as she dialled the number again.

"Hello."

"Chris, thank God you—"

The phone clicked and he was gone. Her hand shook as she replaced the receiver. Now what? Should she dial again? As she stretched to pick it up it rang. She had it at her ear in a flash and breathed out when she heard the words. "Pixie. What's up?" He paused. "I'll be back on the fourth. Then we can talk, okay?"

Deborah nodded into the phone.

"Pix, you still there?"

"Yes. I'm here."

She packed her pens into the desk organiser. It would be so much better if she could see him, look into his eyes, trust what he was saying.

"I'm so angry that you were taken in. Damn these people. What could they possibly want with you?"

"It's okay. I'm okay."

Gloria was watching her. It was as if she knew who was on the other end of the phone. Deborah turned slightly so that she was facing the window.

"No, it's not okay. I could strangle someone with my bare hands for this."

"I didn't tell them—" But what if she had. She could have said something without realising it. Was there anything she'd said that could be—

"I know, Pix. You did really well. You didn't tell them anything they didn't already know."

"But I—"

Chris was trying to control his irritation now. She could hear it in the way his voice rose. "Stop it. You were fine. Really. I'm proud of you."

She knew she should let it go. But she couldn't. "I could have let you down, without realising it. I'd die if that's the case."

Now he was shouting at her. She clutched the edge of her desk.

"That's enough! You handled yourself well. I don't want you to go over this again. Really, Pix."

Deborah held the phone at arm's length. She hadn't wanted to make him angry. But she needed the reassurance from him. She had to make him understand how she felt. She would give her life for him, if she had to. His voice was softer now. He was trying to calm down.

"I'm sorry, really sorry that you had to go through this."

"Okay."

She could hear his breathing and his voice trembled a little. "No, truly. I feel terrible."

"I'm fine now. I am."

She hadn't meant to upset him. If only she could see him, put her arms around him. She'd make him understand her.

"Do you understand now, why I wanted to keep you in the dark? It's frighteningly easy to be turned around. Even answering the simplest questions can lead you into trouble. Better to just keep absolutely quiet, see?"

He was trying to appease her. She could feel his concern. But she couldn't stop herself from saying, "I feel stupid now. I feel as if you don't trust me." She braced herself for his reaction. It came immediately.

"Pix, I do! How many more times must I say this?"

"But I let you down. Maybe you shouldn't trust me."

He was wound up now. She'd made it worse again. When was she going to learn to just shut up?

"You didn't tell them anything, you didn't let me down. I do trust you completely. Can you let this thing go now?"

Deborah bit her lip hard. She mustn't cry now. She needed to be strong. She could be, for his sake.

"Yes. I can."

"Thank you. I need you to keep it together, Pix. Okay?"

He was closing the conversation. She needed to know one more thing. This was her last chance until he came back.

"Chris, were you involved in the pamphlet bomb thing?"

There was a moment's hesitation before the answer came. "I knew about it, but no. No, no, I wasn't."

She wanted to believe him. He'd never lied to her. If she could look him in the eye, she knew she would.

"Pix, you still there?"

"Yes. I'm here."

"Good girl. I'll see you on the fourth, okay? Remember everything I said, before I left. I meant every word. I'll prove it to you as soon as I get back."

"Chris, I—"

"Love you."

The phone clicked and he was gone. She hadn't managed to say she loved him. An irrational, crazy thought flashed across her fevered brain. What if she never, ever got the chance to say it again?

○○○

It was Saturday evening, and Deborah couldn't think of anything she wanted more than a night in. She needed to put the whole interrogation thing behind her. She touched her cheek. The sting was long gone, but she couldn't believe the man had actually slapped her. No one had ever done that. A good talking to was about the worst thing she'd experienced, up to now. Thank goodness Julia had been there, when she finally made it home. They'd laughed about it, even if it was a bit hysterically. "It's over. Forget it!" She repeated this to herself every time the memory floated in. She had to find a way of blocking it out.

She was playing the phone call with Chris over and over in her mind. He kept saying she'd done well. She hadn't betrayed him. She tried to hold on to that. She closed her eyes and heard his voice again. She just couldn't wait for him to get home. Just a few more days now. It seemed like a silly thing to mull over, but she really wished she'd had the chance to tell him she loved him.

The smell of homemade chicken soup and fresh rolls made her hungry. She could haul out her wool and start knitting that jersey for Chris. Or perhaps just watch the Saturday night movie.

When the doorbell rang, Julia jumped up to answer it and came back into the lounge with Charlie and Annie following close behind her.

"All work and no play make Jack a ...?" Charlie fluttered some tickets under Deborah's chin.

"We've got two extra tickets for some boxing tonight. Have you girls ever been to a match?"

"Boxing? You've got to be joking."

Julia pulled her nose up at him and shook her head. Deborah was about to decline, too, when he pulled her up off the sofa, grabbed Julia by the arm and looked around the room.

"Do I look like someone who takes 'no' for an answer?"

Annie was egging him on from the side. "C'mon, Debs. It'll be a hoot."

"I don't like—"

Charlie swiftly cut her off. "Don't knock something you've never experienced."

"Try everything once. That's my motto," echoed Annie.

Charlie spotted the hat rack down the passage and took their jackets off it.

"You've got sixty seconds to change."

Julia pointed feebly at the pot of soup simmering on the stove, and Annie slipped around the counter to switch it off. Charlie gave her a wink before he chivvied everyone down the passage.

"We'll pick up some burgers on the way."

Deborah held Julia back for a second and whispered, "I never got the chance to say 'I love you,' on the phone."

"What are you talking about, Debs?"

"To Chris. I never said it to Chris."

Charlie flicked her arm with his rolled-up jacket.

"Shake a leg, girls. We need to be on our way."

○○○

"I love him, that's all."

Katie's words echoed in her head. It wasn't possible. Chris loved her, Deborah. He'd said so the night before he left. She handed her ticket to the air hostess and stopped at 24-C.

"I think you're in the wrong seat."

The elderly woman glared at her before shifting herself into the middle. Deborah didn't make eye contact, but felt the woman's eyes on her. Scrabbling for her seat belt, she glanced sideways. The woman was frowning slightly.

"Are you okay?"

She looked away. As soon as she could, she closed her eyes and allowed her mind to race. The plane took off easily, and she felt herself pushed back into her seat. When the plane levelled off and the seat belt lights went out, she unclicked her belt and released her chair a little.

A rush of angry questions flooded her thoughts. What the hell had Chris been up to? Was he really involved with Katie? How involved? How long had this been going on? She wanted to be by his side. Pound her fists on his chest. Scream her rage at him, be reassured and encircled in his arms. How could he do this to her? He was her only love, her life. And now he was in a coma. There was no way of finding out. She tortured herself with possible answers.

If he only recovered, it would surely be okay between them. Katie was an aberration. She had pushed herself at him. Anyone could see that. She shouldn't be thinking about Katie now. She didn't want to hear the gory details from her. In fact, if she never saw her again, it would be too soon. Whatever happened between them, she'd be happy if he just recovered. She loved him. That was more important than anything. She blinked hard and tried some yoga breaths to calm herself. A cabin attendant was touching her arm and smiling at her.

"Chicken à la king or beef fillet?"

She mouthed "chicken" and the hostess leant towards her to murmur, "Are you all right?"

Her voice quivered and she mumbled the words, "Yes. No. I'm just. I'm not prepared. I'm not ready."

The air hostess crouched beside her and offered her a glass of water. She raised a hand to indicate that she was okay. A few more deep breaths helped steady her breathing, and she closed her eyes. It was a long time since she had prayed. She bit her lip and concentrated on staying calm, until she felt the plane dipping towards Jan Smuts Airport. Perspiration gathered on her forehead, and she suddenly felt really weak.

After they'd taxied to a halt, she held onto each seat as she made her way down the narrow aisle. At the top of the gangway, she felt herself sway. She looked down, took a deep breath and willed herself to make it to the bottom. As she took the last step onto the tarmac, she put her hand onto a nearby shoulder.

"Excuse me."

The startled woman backed away, and Deborah fought against the blackness threatening to engulf her.

ooo

"You're going to have to be strong now, Cookie."

"I know. I will be."

Her mother's glance was anxious, and Deborah gave her the best attempt at a smile she could muster.

"If there's anything you need me to do, just—"

Deborah turned her face to the window and her mum gave up on conversation and concentrated on the road. The jacarandas drifted by, and she remembered the way the blossoms popped when you stood on them. Steam rose from the tar in the wake of a sudden thunderstorm. The air smelt fresh.

At every red light, she reached for her mum's hand. The hospital seemed incredibly far. The Coca-Cola which she had poured down her throat had helped to revive her, and she felt a little stronger. Debilitating terror was gradually making way for courage, and now she was anxious to be at Chris' side.

Her pointless anger had dissipated, and her thoughts were only about him and how she could make him better. A surprising wave of strength was building inside her, and she wondered about her short appeal to God. She breathed deeply. No space for thoughts about Katie. No space for panic. Chris needed her to be strong.

In the span of a few hours, she felt older. This was adult territory and she needed to be one.

"I'll wait in the car, Cookie."

Deborah stared uncomprehendingly. "Don't you want to come in, just for a moment?"

Her mum fiddled with the steering wheel and shook her head. "I'm not good at this sort of thing, you go. Take your time. I'll wait."

ooo

The hospital lift opened and she stepped into the cold passage. The silence was broken only by the sound of her heels on tiles. Glancing left and right, she spotted the porcelain hands held in prayer guarding the entrance to the ICU. Rows of white sheets covered bodies hooked up to machines.

A burly nurse barred her from entering, but she frantically scanned the beds for Chris before answering her questions. She glimpsed tanned flesh, incongruous in a room full of sickly pale people. She smiled involuntarily and ignored the raised eyebrow as she answered, "Chris Jarvis' girlfriend."

"Jammer. Net familie in ICU."

This wasn't possible. She had to see him. The woman seemed to spread herself out, blocking the entrance entirely.

"Please. Just for a few minutes? I've flown all the way from Cape Town."

The nurse shook her head firmly.

Deborah stood there and peered past her into the room. "But there's nobody with him. Couldn't I just—"

The woman shook her head and muttered under her breath. "Not even the Security Branch are allowed in to see him."

Deborah stiffened. "The Security Branch?"

"They wanted to ask him a few questions. But the doctor told them it would be many months before his patient would be able to answer anything."

Deborah stared at her in horror.

"Don't call me, I'll call you. That's what he said." She chuckled and seemed to soften a little. "Listen, we look after our patients. No one, not even the Prime Minister, is allowed to just pitch up."

Deborah didn't move. "I've come from Cape Town. Please."

After a few more seconds, the nurse shrugged. "Okay. Gaan maar. But if a family member comes, then you'll have to leave."

"Thank you, thank you. I—"

The nurse clucked in impatience. "Gaan in."

She felt the matron's eyes on her as she walked the length of the ward to Chris' bed. It all felt surreal, as if she were watching herself from above. No one was awake. Rhythmic breathing punctuated the silence. She reached his bed and was momentarily at a loss. Then she took his limp hand and pressed her lips against his cheek.

"It's me, Pixie. I'm here."

His chest rose and fell in time with the machine behind him.

She rested her head lightly on his chest and spoke to him quietly. "I've missed you so much. I couldn't wait to see you. There's so much to tell you."

She pulled up a chair and sat as close to him as she could. Her hand moved gently over his chest. Perhaps if he could feel her, know she was there; she started talking again.

"I groomed Hercules. He's missing you, too. You need to ride him soon. Maybe we can have another Noordhoek ride? I'd love that. I'm wearing the shell necklace you made me. Can you feel it tickling your chest? We could go to the Constantia Nek restaurant again, when you come back. I still need to teach you the tango."

A lump in her throat stopped her. She thought of other things to tell him.

"Julia's getting married in December. I'll bring you a photo of my dress next time. I think you'll like it. I could take a picture of Hercules for you and bring that, too."

She got up and moved to the other side of his bed, jingling her bangles as she did, hoping against hope that the sound would trigger a memory, pierce through the fog of the coma. She couldn't be sure, but it seemed as though his eyes moved behind their lids, following her. When she walked back, his head turned slightly. She cradled his hand in hers once more. This time, there was a slight squeeze.

His body began to shake uncontrollably and his eyelids fluttered wildly, just as the needle on the machine went haywire. A machine began to beep loudly. He'd responded to her! Nurses ran, shoving her aside. With a swish of the curtains, she was shut out. Frantic, she hovered. He'd heard her bangles. He wanted her there. Why had they ejected her? Seconds dragged until eventually the curtains were opened and she stepped forward. His body was motionless. His eyes no longer seemed to follow her when she moved. There was no pressure from his hand. He wasn't responding to her voice. He seemed sedated.

"He opened his eyes for a second," a nurse remarked casually.

She wasn't talking to Deborah. No one seemed to notice her. But she knew. From deep within his coma, Chris had responded to her.

ooo

"Sorry, darling. I just can't. Seeing Dad like that, I can't." Mum's hand grasped her wrist.

"I know. I want to stay longer this time. Could you fetch me later?"

She waited for the car to pull away before making her way to the ward. The nurses no longer questioned her, and she passed the beds of people who were becoming familiar to her. The woman who had been bandaged from the waist down had opened her eyes, and the little boy at the far end was propped up with cushions.

Chris' hair was creeping over his eyes, and she brushed it away with her fingers. She chatted about all the people he knew, Boetie's new bakkie and Julia's drama over the wedding flowers. She told him about *Panache* and the Design Indaba coming up. When she ran out of steam, the ward was very quiet, with only the sucking of ventilators and the rhythmic beep of monitors to break the silence.

Reaching into her bag, she retrieved slightly dog-eared pictures of herself and one of Hercules. She cleared a spot on his credenza and stopped. Behind the water glass, someone —presumably Katie—had placed a picture of herself. The air was sucked from her lungs. It was framed in sparkly glass beads. It was glamorous. She turned it face down, causing a momentary clatter in the silent room, and smoothed the turned-up edges of her little photos as best she could.

The sun melted into the indigo sky. Jacaranda blossoms still carpeted the lawn below. Deborah leant out of the window to look at the row of purple trees stretching towards the entrance. She blew out the stale hospital air and inhaled the pungent smell of damp red earth. One last flash of lightning lit the evening sky, and a distant rumble of thunder announced the passing of the storm. Her body ached with nostalgia for this feel of the Highveld. She hadn't realised that she missed it. She heard one of the nurses behind her, checking Chris' drip and straightening his sheet before joining Deborah at the window.

"He likes it when you come." It was the plump one, with the button nose.

"Really?"

The nurse smiled. "Rerig."

Deborah moved from one side of the bed to the other as she spoke to him, now certain that Chris' eyes moved. He knew she was there. She could feel it. She placed her shell necklace on the edge of his pillow, right next to his head. Perhaps it could trigger something.

She hadn't heard footsteps, but suddenly a presence made her look up and meet deep, dark eyes. They belonged to a distraught young man. She had seen him before, visiting the woman in the next bed.

He stretched out his hand. "Ek's Tiaan."

Deborah took it. "Deborah."

"Jou man gaan lewe. Hy's 'n vegter," he said with certainty.

Deborah looked across at the next bed. Bandages turbaned the woman's head, making her appear even tinier than she was. The machine's needle was flickering, ever so slightly. Her chest barely moved, and it was obvious to Deborah that there was very little life left in her fragile body. She was fading.

Deborah met Tiaan's eyes. They were brimming over with tears, and she reached to touch his shoulder. She said nothing. There was nothing to say. She left her hand where it was, as his shoulders shook and he struggled to regain his composure.

"Ek kannie."

Deborah felt her throat tighten.

"The baby. Ons het 'n baba ..."

She pulled a chair closer, and then crouched beside him as he held onto her hand.

"Sonja's familie. Hulle verstaan nie. I can't talk to—"

Deborah looked through the doorway and saw the family huddled together on the bench outside. She nodded her understanding and waited for him to go on.

"Sonja ... sy is my lewe ..."

Deborah looked up at the machine. The needle was barely moving at all. Tiaan met her eyes once more. "Ek moet vir hom sorg. But how can I if Sonja ..."

"He's yours. You love him, that's what's important. You will find a way, Tiaan."

He held out his hands to her and closed his eyes as he murmured a prayer. When he finished, an unusual calm descended in her heart.

Deborah looked at Tiaan's wife and then at Chris. She could surmise which side of the political divide they were on, but she could also be totally wrong. It didn't matter, anyway. In this ward, it was no longer relevant what ideology you were fighting for or which side of the political struggle you were on. This struggle was a great leveller—life or death.

When it was time for Deborah to go, she turned to Tiaan. "I'm so sorry."

He shook his head quickly. His grief was beyond words now. She touched his shoulder, and he put his hand over hers for a moment. Then he got up, leant over his wife and buried his head in her neck.

The bed next to Chris' was empty the following evening.

○○○

The plane to Cape Town took off on time, and Deborah pushed her face against the window to take in the last sights of the Highveld. The smell of burnt grass still filled her nostrils, and she watched the ground grow smaller and smaller as clouds surrounded the plane. Lightning zigzagged across her vision, and then the plane levelled out.

Her total despair had been replaced by a thread of hope. Chris was alive. Once the brain swelling reduces, the doctors could say more. She'd give up her job, move back to Pretoria, somewhere close to the hospital while he recovered. Her mind was spinning, and she pushed back the niggling fears. The seat belt sign pinged and went dark. People were getting up, and the drinks trolley was being manoeuvred into position.

"Would you like a glass of champagne, young lady?" The silver-haired man from the seat behind was standing beside her, smiling and indicating the drinks trolley.

"No thanks, I—"

His face looked very familiar. She recognised him, but couldn't quite place him. He gave her a wink. "I hope my tango partner is still dancing."

Of course! She should have remembered him straight away. "Were you up here to dance or something?"

"Or something," he offered and then added, "Human rights conference. I presented a paper. I'm Robert, by the way."

He stepped out of the aisle to avoid the trolley and crouched beside her. "Tell me about you. Have you been here for work?"

Deborah shook her head. He waited for her to continue, and she found herself telling him all about Chris, the accident, her hopes and fears. She could feel his concern, and his eyes never left hers. She stopped herself from telling him about Katie. That would be too much.

The plane began to dip for the descent, and she fastened her seat belt automatically. He slipped back into his own seat, and as the plane touched down, the seriousness of Chris' injuries began to sink in. She put a hand over her mouth as the thought took hold in her mind. What if he never, ever woke up?

ooo

Deborah snatched her suitcase off the pile and waved at Robert. She glanced into the waiting crowd for Julia. She couldn't spot her, but she'd be there with Boetie. She turned towards the entrance. People milled around her, and she felt herself being edged towards a wall. She looked up into a pair of strangely familiar steely eyes, and fear rippled through her in an instant. A tall man in a safari suit took her by the elbow and forcibly led her to the side.

"Hey! Let me go!" She pushed against him.

The grip on her elbow tightened.

"We just want to ask you a few questions, Deborah."

She was desperate to extricate herself, but the moustached man, the one in a sports jacket, opened the door to a small dark room, and she felt her legs being propelled forward.

"My friends are waiting."

"Sit."

When she hesitated, her shoulders were pushed down hard and she stumbled onto a wooden stool. There was a table in front of her. A pen and some paper were pushed towards her. The safari-jacketed man backed away and leant against the wall, leaving his companion to sit across the table.

"Cigarette?" He held out a packet of Benson and Hedges and shook the packet to release one. "We haven't spoken for a while, have we?"

Deborah shook her head.

"You don't have to be afraid, Deborah."

Drops of perspiration trickled into her neck as she leant towards the match. She steadied her hand and inhaled deeply.

"We just want you to answer some more simple questions. Okay?"

"Yes," Deborah whispered.

"Is Christopher Jarvis still your boyfriend?"

"Yes."

A thin smile played at her interrogator's mouth. "Where is he now?"

She stared at the wall in front of her.

"C'mon, Pixie. Make this easy for yourself."

The stool wobbled and she re-adjusted her position. How did he know Chris' nickname for her? The hairs on her neck bristled.

"How do you know? How dare you call me that."

His moustache came closer and she could smell sour beer on his breath. "You've just seen him, haven't you?"

She looked down at her lap. If he knew, why was he asking her? She nodded helplessly.

"He's been involved in an accident? A little problem with the car, I believe," the other man added.

"Yes, he has. I— Who are you?!"

She felt panic rising in her chest. Her questioner fingered his belt buckle, and she swallowed abruptly.

"You should tell us everything you know about Mr Jarvis and his friends, Deborah."

"I really don't know anything. Please let me go." Deborah willed Julia to come looking for her.

"You could tell us a little about Mr Jarvis' comrades. You must know them, of course."

The tall one stepped closer, towering over her now.

"I don't. I mean I don't know his academic—"

Sports jacket interjected. "C'mon. Mr Jarvis must have spoken about these friends of his? He must've mentioned their names. Even in some pillow talk. Just give us their names and—"

Deborah shook her head emphatically. "I don't. I really have no idea who he knows."

The tall one pulled Chris' books out of his briefcase. Clearly she and Julia had not buried them carefully enough. Her heart was racing. She tried to compose herself.

"But you do know about these. They belong to Mr Jarvis." He thrust the books at her. "Or perhaps his horse has become an avid reader?" The other man guffawed at his joke.

"Do you know what they are?"

She hesitated for less than a second. "Yes. I know."

The man's shoulders stiffened and his eyes froze. "And you know they are banned material?"

She did. She would take the rap for it. She'd say they were hers, not Chris'. She'd lent them to him. She was not about to throw him to the wolves. Her love for him was stronger than anything they could do to her.

"I'm a patient man, Deborah, but my hand is itching."

Deborah clutched the stool. This was getting worse by the minute. She could feel her breath quickening. Sweat poured off her, and she flicked her hair away from her face. *Don't give in,* she repeated to herself.

He got up abruptly and shoved the pen and paper at her.

"You've got fifteen minutes. Write down everything you know about Christopher Jarvis. We'll leave you to think carefully. When we come back, there'd better be a lot of words on this page."

"But my friends—"

"Will wait."

The two men glided through the door and she heard the key turn.

Sweat pooled in her neck and her hands stuck to her jeans. Her breath was rasping and she looked around the tiny grey room for a window. There wasn't one. Panic rose up in her throat. She couldn't do this. It had to be a nightmare. She concentrated on breathing. Eight breaths in, eight breaths out. Slowly, slowly. She would do this for Chris. She'd be strong for him. For his sake, she'd get a grip on herself.

She picked up the pen and wrote *Deborah Morley* at the top of the page. Then she wrote about her own involvement in *The Struggle*:

1973 to 1975 – an active member of NUSAS. 1974 – attended a NUSAS conference in Hogsback. A volunteer literacy teacher, to small groups of local Grahamstown residents. 1975 – graduated with a degree in Political Science, from Rhodes University. Volunteer dancing teacher in Gugulethu, to small groups of teenagers, every second Saturday morning. A humanitarian and believer in love and respect. Strongly disagrees with the apartheid government. NOT a terrorist!

When she had scribbled down everything she could think of about herself, she wrote:

Christopher Jarvis – Deborah Morley's boyfriend.

She drew a squiggly line under it. She was wiser this time around. She would not write another word about him. Nothing she said would ever incriminate him in any way. He'd said he would always be a pacifist, and that was good enough for her. They could do their worst; she would never talk about him. When the door opened, she braced herself.

The safari-suit stepped forward and picked up the piece of paper. Deborah watched his face turn puce and his hand harden into a fist. He held the piece of paper out to his colleague and indicated the door. Deborah watched the key turn. She clutched the edge of the stool and closed her eyes against what was coming. One of the men pushed her across the table, jerked her jeans down to her knees and held her hands up behind her back. Deborah heard the belt swish as it was unbuckled. Her breath came in short sharp bursts now. She squeezed her eyelids tight and prayed for the strength to survive. A sudden frantic knocking at the door caused a scurry of activity around her and she found herself back on her feet.

"Open this door immediately," an unexpectedly familiar voice boomed from behind it.

Robert stepped into the room and flashed his card at the men, before taking Deborah by the arm.

"You don't need to answer anything."

He faced the interrogators. "I'm her attorney. This woman will be saying nothing more."

"You'll be hearing from us again, Mejuffrow," the moustached one warned, before they backed out of the room reluctantly. "Next time it won't only be a *pakslae*," he mumbled under his breath.

"Gentlemen."

Robert moved Deborah towards the entrance. She was afraid to look back immediately. By the time she did, the two men had disappeared.

"You okay?"

Her legs had turned to jelly and she squeaked, "How did you know?"

Robert pressed a card into her hand.

"You were in front of me. I saw the men grab you outside the room. When you didn't reappear, I decided to investigate."

She stopped for a moment and turned towards him.

"I don't know how to thank you."

"Keep in touch. I've a feeling you might need me."

He waved her next words away. "Give me a call."

A taxi was waiting for him and he sped off without a backward glance. Deborah looked at his embossed card —*Silverman, Jones and Golders. Robert Silverman, Human Rights Attorney*—before she slid it deeper into her pocket.

○○○

Julia dashed towards her. "We were so worried about you. Boetie was about to call the police and report a missing person. Where were you? Why did it take you so long to come out?"

Deborah pointed in the direction of the speeding taxi. "He came to my rescue. He's an attorney. I chatted with him on the plane."

Julia took her suitcase.

"You're not making sense. Who is he and why did he have to rescue you?"

The last thing Deborah wanted now was a conversation. She needed time to absorb what had happened; what had nearly happened. Julia prodded her in the side.

"A couple of SB men cornered me after I'd collected my suitcase. They'd been to the stables and dug up the books. They were interrogating me." She couldn't recognise her own voice, and she desperately needed to sit down.

"What? How could they have found the books? How closely are they watching you? Could they have followed us? Are we in some kind of danger?"

Deborah's legs buckled. She couldn't think anymore. "I'll tell you about it when we get home, Jules. I just need a few minutes to—"

Boetie ushered Julia into the front seat of the bakkie, took the suitcase, flung it into the back, and then hugged Deborah so tightly she could barely breathe. When he let go, she slid into the back seat and leant her head against the soft leather.

Before Julia could start up again, Boetie cut her off. "Los 'it, Jules. She can't talk now. Let's get her home first."

ooo

The moon lit up Lion's Head and there was no tablecloth this evening. The last of the daisies were closed for the night, and she could hardly wait for the day to end. She felt her head throbbing and lowered it into her hands. Julia turned towards her.

"You okay, Debs?"

Deborah murmured, "Just terrified out of my mind."

Julia glanced nervously at Boetie, but carried on anyway. "That attorney. Maybe you should contact him."

"I will. Actually, it's more about Chris, not me."

Boetie tapped his fingers on the steering wheel. "Did they hurt you, Debs?"

She didn't answer. It was no use talking about it. She needed to get home and sleep.

"Did they?" Boetie was working himself up. Things were bad enough without involving him in this. She stared out of the window.

"Debs?"

"I'm okay, Boetie. Really."

Boetie banged the wheel with his hand. "I knew it. Bastards! Someone's going to die for this!"

○○○

"So how is Chris?" Julia passed Boetie a lit cigarette and looked back at Deborah.

"He's still in a coma, but the nurses say it's lifting. He's—"

Boetie looked at her in the rearview mirror. "Is he going to be okay?"

Deborah hesitated for a moment. "I don't know. It's too soon to say if he'll come out of it properly."

Julia seemed to mull over this now and Deborah looked up into Boetie's eyes in the mirror. "Did you talk to him? I've heard about coma patients responding to voices and music and—"

Deborah smiled. "Oh yes. I spoke about everything I could think of. Hercules, our walks, you guys. Just everything."

Julia looked straight ahead. "Did you ask him about Katie?"

Deborah felt herself bristle. "No, I didn't ask him about Katie. He's in a coma. How could I do that?"

Boetie's eyes jerked back to the rearview mirror.

"She probably hasn't been there yet. After all, she did say she'd postpone."

A flash of anger shot through her and she leant forward in her seat. "She's been there. There's a photo of her next to his bed."

Julia sat bolt upright. "I hope you smashed it."

"No, I didn't smash it. I turned it face down."

Boetie turned into their road and ramped the pavement. Julia jiggled the key until the door opened. She began warming up the soup while Deborah deposited her suitcase in her room.

She pulled her legs up and warmed her hands on the bowl. Boetie shifted her over and put the fresh baguette on the table. Silence fell over the table as they slurped at the butternut, which was thick and hot. Deborah's thoughts tumbled over each other, and she reached for her cigarettes. As she leant forward to offer them around, Julia picked up the conversation about Chris.

"So how was he injured?"

Deborah inhaled deeply before she answered. "Apparently, it's a head injury."

Julia drew a deep breath and Boetie put his arm around Deborah.

"No, but I think the main problem is his brain's all swollen. I think it just needs time to recover. I know he's aware, because he responded to me."

The phone rang then, hard and insistent. Julia rose to answer it and called down the passage, "It's for you, Debs."

A vaguely familiar voice echoed down the receiver. "Deborah? This is Katie. I phoned to find out how your visit was and to tell you that I'll be visiting Chris next weekend. I—"

Deborah slammed the phone down before she could finish her next sentence.

ooo

A bunch of flowers on her desk welcomed her back to work. The card was from everyone, but Deborah recognised Annie's spidery writing. Trust her to organise this.

She buried her nose in the posy and inhaled the rose scent. Gloria Fey was busy briefing the *Panache* team, but Deborah could sense they'd all been waiting for her.

"Welcome back, Deborah. Very sorry to hear about your friend's accident. If there is anything we can do, please say."

Gloria paused and allowed the rest of the team to chat with her before she resumed the meeting. Her new colleague, Shirley, was the first to step towards her.

"Is your boyfriend going to be okay?"

"I don't know, I—"

"Probably too soon to—" Shirley spoke over her.

Deborah looked around and noted the pitying looks and awkward silence. She took the folder from Gloria, who swiftly moved on with the briefing. Deborah returned her smile.

"The Modern Living expo … Take a few minutes to read up on it, and then Shirley will be whisking you off to the show. I want details of the stalls, fabulous pics and the absolute must-sees. Get all the samples on offer and test the edibles, too. I want our readers to have a complete feast. Got it?"

Gloria turned on her stilettos. "Oh, and have the story on my desk by five this afternoon."

"Right. It will be. I—"

Gloria had already vanished into the next room. "Come on. Grab your jacket. We'll work out the details as we go along."

Shirley was holding the door. Deborah followed her to the lift. Her heart wasn't in this, but she had to keep going. She checked for her pen and notebook. If she could just get through the day, she could run for the early train and get home to phone the hospital. Hopefully the matron would have more news.

"Listen, I'm really sorry to hear about—"

"Thanks." Deborah wasn't keen to discuss it. It was easier to maintain her composure if people weren't too kind.

"Just shout if I can help in any way."

"I will." She could feel that Shirley had something else to say and waited for it to come.

"I'm not sure if I should tell you this, but the SB guys came looking for you while you were away."

Deborah felt the heat in her face. She tried to appear neutral, but her stomach somersaulted. "What did they want?"

"Don't know."

"Who did they speak to?"

"To Gloria. She wasn't happy about it, hey. She gave them a mouthful. Told them they were welcome to search the office, but clearly they'd come to the wrong place. What did they expect to find in the *Panache* section, anyway? Bombs?"

Deborah took a deep breath and moistened her lips. "I'm sure it was all a misunderstanding."

She could feel Shirley's eyes on her as she rummaged around in her bag for her cigarettes. She slid one out, before offering the pack to Shirley.

"Thanks."

Grateful for the distraction, she lit Shirley's first. "I'm not going to be great company today. Sorry."

Shirley took a drag of her cig. "No, no. Don't apologise. I totally understand. Really."

They walked in silence for a bit and then Shirley said, "Oh by the way, Annie phoned earlier. I think she's really worried about you. She wants a bunch of us to meet for drinks after work. Charlie will be there, too. He's keen."

It took Deborah a second to answer. "Not this evening, thanks. I've got something urgent to do."

○○○

She held her breath as the phone rang. It felt a bit like Russian roulette. The news was always so unpredictable. "This is Deborah speaking. Um, Chris Jarvis, I'd like to know his condition."

The matron hesitated for a moment and then replied. "Yes. He came out of the coma a few days ago."

Deborah let out a triumphant "Yes! Please tell him I'll be in Pretoria by Friday. I'll—"

"Wait a moment. Mr Jarvis has requested no visitors."

She swallowed hard. This had to be a mistake. "But I'm his girl—"

The matron interrupted her. "Can you give me your full name, please?"

"Deborah Morley."

"Deborah, there is a letter for you. He's asked that you wait for it to arrive."

Her mouth opened and closed, but no words came.

"Miss Morley?"

The frog in her throat shifted and she managed, "I'm still here."

There was an audible deep breath. "I'm sorry, but Mr Jarvis was very insistent about this. He does not wish to see anyone at the moment."

The matron was muddling her up with someone else, of course. Chris would never have meant her. It couldn't be true. "But I'm sure he—"

The firm tone cut her off mid-sentence. "Please. It's important that we respect our patients' wishes. I'm sure that if he changes his mind, he'll be in contact."

Deborah put the receiver down. Her fingers felt numb and she was unsteady on her feet. It must be a mistake. Chris would never— Why would he not want to see her ... unless this was about Katie?

She made her way to the back door and pushed it open. Bob rushed out to chase the last of the Cape white-eyes and then joined her on the step. A slipper of a moon appeared. A single star lit up the heavens. Others would appear soon. How Chris loved the night sky. He'd lie on the grass with her head on his chest and look at the stars. He'd talk about life, the farm and how simple things could be. That's when she felt closest to him. When all was stripped away, his soul reached out to hers. He'd wrap himself around her, as if he was absorbing her into his own body, as if she were the missing piece.

And now this. This phone call didn't make any sense. If only she could speak to him. If they could talk, then she'd be able to sort it all out with him.

○ ○ ○

"Letter for you." Julia dropped the post in her lap as she walked past. "From Chris? It's postmarked Pretoria."

She watched Julia pulling an apron over her head. "Hope you like spicy fish cakes, because that's what I'm making."

Deborah stared at the envelope. The smell of chopped onions, chilli and garlic began to waft into the room.

"What's he say? Isn't it great that he can communicate now? By the way, Boetie's rewiring the neighbour's house. He'll pop in afterwards and join us for supper. Will you lay the counter when you have a moment?"

She couldn't answer. The seconds ticked by. While the envelope lay in her lap, unopened, everything would be all right. Everything would stay the same. Chris would be on the road to recovery. He'd be dying to see her, and they would be on the road to their life together.

"You okay, Debs?" Julia looked up from her chopping board. Deborah looked down quickly and slid the letter opener under the flap. The hospital stamp confirmed that it was from Chris. It didn't look like his writing, though. She unfolded it and began to read.

My dearest Pixie,
I know you will be surprised by this letter. Please forgive me.
The thing is that I don't love you anymore. I can't pretend otherwise. I know this will hurt you, but it's best we make a clean break. It is over between us. I want you to walk away and live your own life now. I'm setting you free to pick up your life and carry on. You have so much life in you and I want you to be happy with someone who can love you the way you should be loved.
You'll make something of your life. I know you will.
Make me proud.
Chris x

Deborah read the words feverishly. It couldn't be true. She knew he loved her. She didn't want to be free. She wanted to get on the next plane. Be at his side. Help him heal and get back to his normal life. He *was* her life. She couldn't bear it. She'd write back. Plead with him. Make him understand what he meant to her.

The words blurred as she read them again and again, trying to make them different, interpreting them another way. She dropped back into the sofa.

"Debs?"

"It can't be true. I'm sure it's not true, Jules. It just can't be." Julia was beside her now, tugging the letter from between her fingers.

"Oh my goodness." She reached for Deborah's hand. "I don't know what to say."

Deborah stretched for the half-empty packet of cigarettes, and Julia took them out of her hand. She lit two in rapid succession.

"I'm so sorry. I wish I could …"

The floors creaked under army boots, and Boetie's gruff voice echoed down the passage. "Yahoo. Anybody home?"

He stopped abruptly when he saw them, took two big strides towards Deborah and engulfed her in his arms. "Wat's fout, meisiekind?"

She buried her head in his chest and sobbed as if her life was over.

ooo

"Maybe you should just go and see him again. Find out from the horse's mouth."

Boetie glanced at Deborah as he folded the serviettes and placed them on the counter that he was laying for supper. He put the wine bottle between his knees and manipulated the opener. Julia snipped parsley and chives over the fish cakes and tossed the salad.

Julia's forehead creased into a frown before she spoke. "Good idea. I think he owes you a lot more than just a letter. Do you think he's found—?"

Boetie interrupted her mid-sentence. "Who the hell does he think he is? You've been visiting him every second weekend, flying up to Jo'burg, spending hours and hours at his bedside. What is this?"

Julia wasn't going to be fobbed off that easily. She was working herself into a frenzy now. "Is this about that other girl, what's her name again?"

Deborah shook her head firmly. "I don't think so. Maybe it is. I don't really know." She wanted to be angry with Chris. She wanted to slap him until he told her what was really going on. But he was still recovering, and it would be a long time before they could have that kind of encounter. She'd have to wait until he'd recovered fully.

Deborah busied herself arranging the Shasta daisies in a vase and then delved into the bottom drawer for serving spoons. She lit a candle and Boetie flicked the tape deck on. "Stairway to Heaven" drifted into the room. Julia glanced across at her as she took her place beside Boetie. She said nothing.

Boetie reached over and patted her hand. "But seriously, you should book a flight for this coming weekend. Praat met die man. That's the only way you're going to find out what he's really thinking."

Deborah shrugged her shoulders. "I don't want to beg. Maybe he really doesn't love me anymore. If he wants Katie, well then, I'll step aside."

Boetie slammed his knife and fork down. "Ag, nee, man. Chris needs to look you in the eyes and say what he wants to say. You deserve that at the very least. If he wasn't injured, I might injure him myself."

Deborah frowned, but nodded in agreement. He was right. She needed to see him. Sort this out. Maybe when he saw her, when he saw how much she loved him, he'd realise how much he really felt about her. She'd answer his letter. Often her thoughts flowed better when she wrote them down. She could read it to him.

"Do you think this really could be about Katie? Maybe he does ..." She needed the reassurance.

Boetie was adamant. "Nee, man. Forget her. She's not important, Debs. He just needs to get his head right."

Julia cleared her throat. "Look, I don't think we can just rule her out. We don't know what was really going on."

"Nonsense, man. Sy was net 'n stukkie, a piece of fluff on the side."

Boetie put his arm around Deborah, as Julia shook her head. "You can't say that for sure, Boetie."

He waved an arm at her, but she was not to be diverted. "I'm just trying to be realistic here. We don't know what was going on. Clearly Chris is a dark horse, so we can't presume."

Deborah could see where this was going. She couldn't bear a character assassination of Chris now. She didn't want this discussion to gain any more momentum.

"I'll book a flight first thing tomorrow morning."

○○○

Waiting for the lift to his floor, Deborah read through her letter one more time, just in case she'd left something out.

My dearest Chris,

I am heartbroken by your words and am hoping that you didn't really mean what you said. I want to be by your side. I want to help you recover. You are my whole world. When you stepped into the common room, into my life, it was as if the missing piece of the jigsaw puzzle had slipped into place. It's not possible to go back to life before you. You are my North Star.

It's my turn now, to offer you strength.

Please don't push me away. I'm begging you.

Forever,

Pixie x

She folded it before she stepped into the lift and pressed "3." She would read it to Chris as soon as she got to his bedside. Surely he'd understand. He'd reconsider. She'd persuade him not to be rash.

The ICU matron stopped her as she reached the entrance.

"Mr Jarvis has been moved to the High Care Unit now, just around the corner. I think he doesn't—"

Deborah got to the unit just as the doors were being opened.

"You've come to see?" the matron asked.

"Chris. Chris Jarvis."

"And you are?"

"Deborah. Deborah Morley."

"He is not accepting visitors today, my dear."

"But I've come all the way from Cape Town. Surely I can."

The matron shook her head at her.

Deborah stared at her in disbelief. What the hell was going on? This was ridiculous.

She could see Chris from the entrance. He was in the corner at the far end of the ward. A young nurse was with him and she looked to be asking him a question. A lump formed in Deborah's throat as she saw him shaking his head.

Deborah snatched her bag off the counter, tramped back to the chair outside the unit and put her head in her hands. It was unbearable. Grief and frustration flooded through her. She dug for her cigarettes and lit one shakily. She'd wait. There was no way she was going to come all this way and not see him. She'd wait as long as it took. The nurse glanced at her every now and again and shook her head at the cigarette, but didn't approach her. Deborah took another deep drag and then stubbed it out. After what seemed like forever the nurse came over to her.

"Perhaps he'll see visitors tomorrow, when he's feeling a little better."

Deborah pleaded with her again. "Can't I just go in for a few minutes? Please? When he sees me, he'll—"

"Sorry. I can't allow that."

Deborah held her gaze for a few more seconds. She had kind eyes. But she wasn't going to budge. Eventually Deborah held the envelope out to her and she took it. "Please give it to Chris then."

"Come back tomorrow. I'm sure he'll see you then."

Deborah shook her head dejectedly. "I'll be on a plane tonight. This was my only chance."

She watched the nurse make her way to Chris' bed. His face was turned towards the window. She put the letter on his bedside table, under the water glass and said something to him. Deborah got up to leave. She looked into the ward, hoping that he'd change his mind and turn towards her. But his head didn't move. Maybe she should push past the matron to his bedside. He'd just have to see her, whether he wanted to or not. She stared at the matron and felt her hands clenching into fists of frustration.

"Don't force it. He's not ready to see anyone today. You need to respect that." The sturdy matron held her in a steely gaze. It was no use. She'd probably rugby tackle her if she made a dash for him. She peered in one more time. Chris was still facing the window, clearly determined not to look at her.

Her knees were hardly able to carry her as she made her way to the lift. She pressed "ground." When the doors opened, she turned to face the long corridor. Appearing around the corner and clearly making her way towards the High Care Unit was a woman with loose black locks and a velvet hold-all over her shoulder. She recognised the cocky way she held her head. It was Katie.

○○○

The lift pinged and the doors slid open. Deborah stepped out into the entrance hall. Her heart was racing and she felt dizzy. Should she go back up? Confront the woman? How dare she just arrive here? The arrangement was that she'd check first. But obviously she was used to pushing other people out of her way. Actually no. She'd wait here. Katie would also have to accept that he wasn't seeing anyone. They were in the same boat.

Deborah stepped outside and found a bench under the big oak tree in the garden. She'd be able to see Katie from there when she came down. She lit a cigarette and kept her eye on the entrance.

It'd be easy to slip away quickly, as soon as she'd seen her. She tried to focus on the garden. There were so many birds. She really should learn to identify them. It always struck her that Pretoria had the most amazing birdlife. The jacarandas were in full bloom now, and the purple haze along the path was spectacular. Her watch ticked over. Ten minutes. Katie was probably still arguing with the matron. Well, good luck to her. All her cockiness wouldn't help her now.

She walked over to the duck pond and watched the ducklings plunging their heads into the water, showing off their fluffy yellow tutus. Some of the older males still had their tail feathers curled up, even though mating season appeared to be over. A bullfrog croaked from behind a rock, and Deborah leant forward to try and spot him.

She made her way back to the bench and looked at her watch again. Half an hour. The bitch must have talked her way into the ward. She paced the lawn and tried to breathe normally. This was a nightmare. Should she go back up? No. That would be stupid. Another minute ticked by. No sign of her. This was so unfair. She screamed silently into her clenched fists, walked back to the entrance and pressed the lift button. Then she turned abruptly and walked back to the garden.

What if Chris had chosen to see Katie, but not her? Maybe he was feeling a little better already. What if Chris really was in love with Katie? Nausea overtook her as she allowed the possibility to penetrate her thoughts. What if the unthinkable had happened and Chris had stopped loving her? Her mum pulled up as Deborah spotted Katie walking away from the entrance.

ooo

The carriage pinged and Deborah pushed it back and typed furiously. Her African lamps story was developing nicely and she was keen to finish it. The Design Indaba was exciting, and she was hoping to have at least three stories in the spread. She hadn't taken her normal coffee break. It was easier to bury herself in work. It was becoming increasingly difficult to join in the office chitchat. Her heart wasn't in it anymore. It was almost as if she was marooned on a little island and was communicating from afar. She was in a lively office, surrounded by great colleagues, and yet she'd never felt lonelier in her whole life.

"Can I see you for a moment, Deborah?"

Deborah looked up from her typewriter into Gloria Fey's serious face. She pushed her chair back and followed Gloria to her desk. Was she in some kind of trouble? Her gut told her she was and she squared her shoulders.

"Have a seat." Her boss indicated a chair, but dived straight in before Deborah could sit.

"Deborah, this is rather awkward, but I need to ask you why the SB has been snooping around our offices. Are you involved in something that I should know about? Is there anything you need to tell me?"

The questions took her by surprise and Deborah hesitated before she asked, "What do you mean?"

When Gloria didn't respond, she felt an unexpected surge of indignation coming up. "I don't have anything to tell you. Not that I can think of, anyway."

Gloria raised an eyebrow as she uncrossed her arms and then smiled tightly. "I'm not accusing you of anything, Deborah.

I just need to know what's going on. Is there anything at all that I should know about?"

Deborah shook her head adamantly. "I'm not involved in anything illegal."

Gloria kept her eyes pinned on her. "Could this be related to your boyfriend?"

Deborah twisted the pen in her hand as she answered quickly. "Chris is still in hospital, really badly injured. I don't think—"

Gloria leant back in her chair and lifted her pen to her mouth. "Okay, I understand that. Your friend Annie filled us in a little while you were away. I'm really sorry about it. Am I right in thinking that Chris was quite involved in student politics at some stage, or am I way off the mark?"

The words tumbled out now, as Deborah tried to explain herself. "No, you're not. I don't know much about it, though. He never spoke about these things to me. I really don't know any details of what he was involved in. I do know he's a pacifist and would never do anything that went against his principles. I just wish the SB would leave us both alone."

Deborah glanced at the pen Gloria was clicking. "Why do you think the SB is asking about you?"

"I suppose because I'm Chris' girlfriend."

Now the pen was back on the desk and Gloria had folded her arms. "Have you done anything, anything at all, to make them suspicious?"

"Well, maybe."

Gloria was leaning towards her now. "Maybe what?"

"I hid some of Chris' political books in his horse's stable. I was worried that the SB would find them. And then, of course, they did."

"Where exactly?"

"I'd buried them in the corner." Now Gloria was right in her space and Deborah shifted uncomfortably. "They confronted me about the books at the airport."

"What?"

Gloria's raised eyebrows spurred her on.

"Another passenger, a Human Rights lawyer, came to my rescue and stopped them from harassing me."

She'd said enough and reached for her notebook. Gloria looked at her intently until she blurted out the rest.

"The SB has been parked outside our cottage for two days now. I don't know what to do about it." She could hear a tremble in her voice.

Gloria's face softened a little. "Have you told me everything now? I can only help you if I have the full story."

Deborah didn't drop her eyes. "Yes. Yes, I've told you everything."

She felt Gloria summing her up carefully before she nodded. Deborah hoped she had said enough. She did know that Chris was involved in something, but she never knew exactly what. It was the truth.

"In that case, we'll just have to discourage these men from snooping around, where there is nothing to find."

Thank goodness. For a minute she'd thought Gloria was going to tell her she was causing too much havoc on *Panache*. Perhaps she'd have her sent back to the main section. She wasn't sure she would survive that. This job was her lifeline; her only link with the ordinary world right now.

"Your last story was good. I'm impressed. Now get moving on the follow-up."

Deborah smiled cautiously, stood, and stepped away from her chair.

"One more thing, Deborah."

Deborah hovered and then sat down again.

"I know you have an awful lot to cope with at the moment, so what I'm going to say is for your own good."

Oh boy. She folded her arms and met Gloria's intense stare.

"You are a very intelligent young lady, and your work so far impresses me."

"Thank you, I—"

"But it's time you stood on your own two feet. I want to see you develop. Your confidence needs to match your ability. I want you to shrug off the girlie-ness, become the strong, independent woman you can be. There's no need for you to stay in the background and be someone's 'little woman.' From this moment on I want you to stand up for yourself and fulfil all of your potential, as a journalist and as a person. Okay?"

Deborah felt the colour rush to her cheeks but held Gloria's gaze, nonetheless.

"Mull over what I've said. Come back and argue with me if you like, but know that you are anyone's equal. You got me?"

Deborah nodded and was about to leave when Gloria added, "As long as you are perfectly honest with me, I'll have your back."

"Thank you. I really appreciate it."

Gloria was already focussing on the latest photographs of the Design Indaba and didn't look up.

Deborah avoided any small talk on her way back to her desk. She sat down to read what she'd typed. *African lamps, designed by Thabo Segedi, are the must-haves of the 1976 Design Indaba. Young Thabo says he is inspired by nature and the community around him. He sketches ordinary people, collecting water, gathering wood, going about their daily chores ...*

She recited her notes to herself and studied the photographs. This story was really important to her. It had to be brilliant.

Julia had offered to drive her to the stables after work, but she needed to polish this and put it on Gloria's desk before she left. Gloria's words had struck a chord. She had one shot at life, and she needed to grow up and grab it. She pushed all other thoughts away and began typing furiously.

○○○

White horses raced across the darkening sea and the apricot sun melted into the horizon. Swallows flew in formation, arriving in time for the summer. The wind pushed the car towards the mountain, and Julia had to steer hard to keep it steady.

Prins was waiting at the gate, twisting his hat. "More nooi. More nooi."

Deborah greeted him and waited for him to open up. But he didn't. He seemed to be stalling, and when she stepped towards him, he blurted out, "Die ander nooi. Hercules is met die ander nooi ..."

Deborah stared at him in disbelief. She waited for him to continue, but he seemed reluctant.

"When will they be back?" Julia asked impatiently.

Prins shook his head. He looked at the ground and shifted from one leg to the other.

Julia persisted. "What do you mean? Where have they gone?"

He looked across the valley and raised his hands helplessly. He avoided her eyes but didn't move from the gate. There was something he didn't want to tell her. Deborah looked at Hercules' stable. The door was closed. Something seemed different. She squinted her eyes. The plaque had been removed.

Finally, Prins met her eyes.

"Hercules is never coming back here?"

"Baie jammer, nooi."

Deborah handed the carrots to Prins and he bowed his head. "Die polisiemanne. Hulle het gekom. Baie questions gevra, nooi."

She stared at him. It all started to fall into place. He'd directed the men to Hercules' stable, to the buried books. Of course. They hadn't been followed. Prins was the missing link.

"What sort of questions, Prins?"

Prins turned his cap around and looked into the distance. "Ek het niks vir die polisiemanne gese nie, nooi."

She stared at the top of his head, but he wouldn't look up again.

Julia was rapping her fingers on the gate. "I don't know what's going on now, Debs."

Deborah turned and whispered, "I'll tell you in the car."

Then she reached out and touched Prins' shoulder. "It's okay. It wasn't your fault."

He looked up at her miserably and shook his head. He seemed about to say something more, but she didn't wait for his reply. She strode to the car, anxious to get away.

Julia was a few steps behind her, jogging to catch up. She was irritated and out of breath when she reached her.

"It's not okay, Debs. Why did you tell him it was okay?"

Deborah carried on walking until she reached Julia's Mazda. Then she simply climbed into the passenger seat. There wasn't anything else she could do or say.

ooo

Instead of heading back home, Julia turned into Victoria Street and made her way to Valley Road.

"Where are we going?" Deborah drummed the dashboard anxiously.

"So, do you want to just give up?" Julia's jaw was set determinedly.

"Of course not." Giving up had seemed like a viable option, if Deborah was being honest.

"Well then. Let's go."

Deborah lit two cigarettes and handed one to Julia. "Love you, Jules."

Julia blew a smoke ring. "Don't get soppy on me now. Look for stables."

Homesteads whizzed by and horses grazed on the long stretches of paddock all around them. This was horsey country, horses, chickens and fresh veg.

"Slow down a bit. There's one coming up on the right."

Julia screeched to a halt to allow a group of young riders to cross. They trotted in perfect alignment and turned down a narrow gravel path. Deborah squinted down the lane, as Julia edged the Mazda forward. Windy Stud swung on a rickety pole as the last rider closed the gate behind them. An old oak tree shaded the car and Deborah pushed the gate open. Horses drank from the trough against the fence. A piebald nuzzled a chocolate brown stallion, who swished away the flies gathering behind them.

"There's someone to ask."

Deborah was about to step forward when the black stallion reared up. The groom struggled to grab his reins as he bolted in protest. Three times the stallion managed to evade his capturer, but the fourth time he was outwitted. The groom got a firm grip on him and then brought his crop down hard on the stallion's rump, before mounting him bareback and galloping around the paddock a few times. Then he jumped off and led his charge into a stable.

"What are you waiting for?"

Julia's edginess prompted Deborah to squish her way across the muddy grass. The stallion was chomping hay while the groom brushed him down vigorously.

"Molo Sissie."

Deborah dropped her head as she returned the greeting.

"I'm looking for a brown stallion. He's probably new here. Hercules."

The groom shook his head slowly, swept his brush across the stallion's flank and then stood up from his stool.

"He has a white star on his forehead."

He walked ahead and then turned when Deborah didn't follow. "Come."

She faltered after him as he took her down the length of the stables. She read the names to herself as they went along. Peanut, Smokey, Heaven, The Raj, Prince of Tides, Rosie, Raka; the last stable had no name plaque. A chocolate brown tail swished gently. Hercules? He was the height. Muscles rippled under his chocolate brown coat. Her heart skipped a beat.

"Hercules?"

The groom opened the stable door and led him out. His head was still dipped and she waited for him to lift it. She willed him to have a white star on his forehead and held her breath as his gentle brown eyes met hers. It wasn't there.

○○○

Julie reversed along the gravel path. Deborah struggled to regain her composure. It was no use. They weren't going to find Hercules. He'd been spirited away.

"Earth to Deborah. Hello!" Julia patted her arm. "Right or left?"

She wanted to go home. This was a goose chase. It was useless. "Can't we just go home?"

The death stare answered her question.

"Okay, right."

There was a narrow road across the Disa River Bridge. They could veer towards the village. Deborah remembered another stable about a block down from Victoria Street. Eagle's Place, Eagle's Nest, Eagle's something. The entrance was hidden down a sandy road on the right.

"Slowly, Jules. It's somewhere around here."

She scanned all the entrances for names. Most of the plaques were hidden under overgrown hedges. A new wooden gate caught her eye, and she strained to read the brass plaque.

"That's it. Eagle's Nest. We're at the right place."

Julie indicated, and then swerved in front of an oncoming bakkie. The driver braked hard and sat on his hooter. "Bloody women drivers," he yelled.

Deborah mouthed a "sorry," and Julia shot him a middle finger.

The Mazda churned dust up onto the windscreen and Julia geared down to second. Children appeared from nowhere and ran next to the car. They crisscrossed over the path. A tutu-ed purple fairy patted the bonnet cheekily.

"Where are the horses?"

Deborah handed over the bag of apples she'd brought and watched faces light up as the children bit into them. Fingers pointed ahead and the stables came into view. Julia ground to a halt under the willow tree.

The children hovered until a groom ducked his head as he emerged from one of the stables.

"Hamba," he bellowed and they scattered, except for three brave souls who stuck out their tongues. They bolted when he touched his horse whip. "Not so brave now, hey?" he teased and mock charged them.

"I'm looking for a stallion. A big brown one. He has a white star on his forehead. Hercules?"

The groom led her along the stables. She peeped into each one, but she knew he wasn't there. It was just no use.

"Thank you very much."

The groom shook his head in sympathy. "Eish. I'm very sorry, Sissie."

Her takkies crunched the peach-pipped pathway as she slunk back to the car.

Julia was leaning against the bonnet, inhaling her last drag. "No luck?"

Deborah flopped into the passenger seat and Julia turned the ignition.

The children re-appeared and skipped around the car, waiting for it to move. Just as Julia pulled away, one of the children called out, "Look."

The groom was striding towards them and Deborah wound her window down.

"I'm thinking. There's a new horse on the farm down there."

He pointed towards Victoria Street, waved away the tip Deborah offered, and barked at the children as he strode back to the stables.

Deborah pulled her seatbelt over and clicked it in. She stared into the distance and wished Julia would just drive home. This was going to be another goose chase.

"The Stables" was carved into the gate. Julia ramped the sidewalk and turned off the engine.

"Go, girl. I'll wait here."

Deborah parted the rambling honeysuckle and thrust it open. The sun was already dipping towards the mountain, and a sea breeze chilled the air. A rooster was heralding the evening and a few chicks scratched in the dust, next to their black and caramel mother. There was no one around to ask. The horses were still grazing in the paddocks. Surely someone would come to put them in their stables for the night?

Deborah ambled to the first fence. A dappled pony came to sniff her hand, and she stroked its velvety muzzle.

"Is Hercules here?" she whispered into her ear and the pony whinnied back encouragement. The second paddock was fuller and Deborah perused the horses. A heavily pregnant white mare eyed her jadedly. Some mottled ponies nibbled each other's necks. Two dark stallions reared up at each other, and their manes lifted in the breeze as they neighed territorially. They were beautiful creatures, all of them. But there was no Hercules.

She orbited the area one more time, stroked the resident tabby cat and peered into each stable. Then she headed back to the car.

"No luck?" Julia called as she started the engine. Deborah slammed her door and accepted a cigarette. She inhaled deeply, as Julia pulled off the kerb, turned into Hout Bay Main Road and changed into second gear.

ooo

Boetie was leaning against the gate when Julia pulled up. "About bloody time. I thought you girls had left the country!"

He took the key, jiggled the rusty doorknob and mumbled about fetching some oil. Bob raced out onto the grass and watered the rosebush, before he knocked Deborah off her feet.

"Hope you brought some wine, because we really need some after all that."

Julia peeped into his shopping bag and pulled out the cold KWV Riesling.

"So what's up then?" Boetie held the bottle between his knees and manoeuvred the opener.

"We checked all the stables in Hout Bay, but we can't find Hercules." Julia held out her glass.

"Ag, I'm sure he's fine, man. A horse doesn't just disappear." He patted Deborah's shoulder.

"I have to find him. I just have to." Deborah buried her face in a cushion. She'd been keeping her emotions in check, but now they rippled to the surface.

"Why're you so worried, Debs? I'm sure he's okay, man."

"I promised Chris I'd make sure he was safe. I want him to know that Hercules is fine." She held her hand out for a glass of wine. "Do you think maybe the police had—"

Julia stubbed out her cigarette. "Now you're being a bit ridiculous, Debs. What would the police want with Chris' horse?"

She took a gulp of her wine. Chris needed to have Hercules safely in a stable. Hercules should be ready for him. When he'd recovered enough, he'd—

"I promised him I'd see that that Hercules was okay."

Boetie grabbed some paper and rummaged in the kitchen drawer for a pen. "So where did you look today then? Did you find all the stables?"

"Windy Stud was definitely one of them. I'm trying to remember. Do you know the other names, Jules?"

Julia closed her eyes and put her hand on her forehead. "One had something to do with eagles. Eagle's Place, Eagle's Rest ..."

"That's it. Eagle's Nest."

Boetie scribbled the names down and ticked them off.

"Isn't there another one around there, too? It's got a simple name. Something like ..."

"The Stables."

Chris had often spoken about The Stables. Deborah had been so sure Hercules would be there. Julia was staring out of the window. Her eyebrows formed a crease at the top of her nose.

"Debs, are you saying that Hercules is tied up to Chris' recovery in some way? Is that what you're thinking?"

"I'm not sure."

"Do you think that, Debs?" Boetie topped off the glasses.

"Maybe. I don't know. I just know that I have to tell him Hercules is safe. He needs that. He is hearing whatever I tell him. No matter what anyone says, I can feel it. He responds whenever I talk about Hercules."

"Okay, that settles it then." Julia opened a packet of noodles and handed her the cheese grater. "We're going back to Hout Bay, first thing tomorrow morning."

ooo

Julia slowed down as she turned into Valley Road. "Don't get your hopes up too much. We'll try our best to find him. That's all we can do."

Deborah looked right and left. She scrutinized every horse and rider. When a group of children appeared from one of the side roads, Julia stopped so that she could make sure Hercules wasn't among them. Riders emerged from the farms on either side, and some headed towards the path along the Disa River. Others trotted along Valley Road until they reached the stop sign at the end. There were more paths off Victoria Street. A few riders were clearly heading towards the beach.

At the World of Birds, Julia did a U-turn. "There aren't any more stables after this." She went back down the road and Deborah peered into every property. It was impossible. They'd never find him. "Should we check the beach?" Julia turned back into Victoria Street and then headed towards the beach.

Deborah kicked her sandals off and allowed the shallow waves to tickle her legs. She watched a group of horses enjoying the water. A few Jack Russells barked around them, but they didn't seem to be bothered. Seagulls swooped for breakfast, and in the distance she could see dolphins diving in the waves. Surfers waited farther back, and glints of yellow and magenta boards broke the cobalt blue water. She lifted her face to the salty spray and turned to look at the horses again.

The Stables. She'd heard Chris use that name often. She knew Hercules wasn't there. It was probably a waste of time, but she needed to go back one more time. "Do you think we could drive back past The Stables?"

Julia jiggled her car keys in the air. "Sure. It's almost on our way home anyway."

Valley Road was alive with horses now. Everyone seemed to be either on their way back, or else just setting out for a ride. Deborah scoured each group for a chocolate brown stallion. They crept along until they reached The Stables. "Go in and have another look. I'll wait."

Deborah squelched through the mud. She walked along the stables and checked the names once more. No Hercules on any of the plaques. The few horses left in the paddocks were munching at hay troughs. There were no big chocolate horses among them. All the grooms seemed to be on a break. The place was pretty deserted. She leant against one of the jumps. There was just no way she'd ever find Hercules. The wind was coming up, and she twisted her hair into a bun. Mud clung to her toes as her sandals disappeared into it. She held her feet under an outside tap before she climbed into the car.

"No luck?" Julia held out a lit cigarette and she took a deep drag. "I'm sorry, Debs."

When they reached the World of Birds, Julia swung the car around. She sped up now. "We gave it our best shot. Don't be too hard on yourself."

Deborah stared at the road ahead. A trickle of riders was still heading out, but it had slowed down now. People were getting ready for work, and horses were being led to the paddocks for the morning. Soon Valley Road would be empty, except for the odd car here and there.

In the far distance she could see a figure leading a huge horse along the footpath. He was heading in their direction. "Can we stop for a minute?" They were still far away, but when Julia pulled over, Deborah got out of the car. The pair walked steadily towards them. Julia had climbed out now and was at her side. She couldn't make out the horse's colour yet, but as they drew closer, she could see he was dark. Another block or two and she'd be able to see properly.

"Do you think it could be him?"

"I don't know yet. But I'd like to wait."

They were three blocks away. The horse was definitely brown. She held her breath. Another few minutes ticked by, and the groom stopped to make sure there were no cars pulling out of the little side road. Then he led his charge across. They were two blocks away. It was chocolate brown. And a stallion for sure. His head was down and Deborah willed him to lift it up. They were on the last block now. Deborah felt Julia squeezing her arm tightly. The groom was saying something, and as they came even closer, the stallion lifted his head. The white star on his forehead came into focus. His ears pricked up and he quickened his pace. The groom held the reins back as Deborah ran forward and flung her arms around his neck.

"Hercules," she whispered into his mane.

ooo

"The dark-haired Sissie brought him." The groom indicated the edge of his shoulder. "Small like this."

Deborah followed him to the stables and passed him the brushes, while he began the grooming session. Hercules' head was deep in the hay, and he pawed the ground with his hoof.

"He knows you, Sissie."

Deborah didn't trust herself to speak. Instead she stroked Hercules' mane. The groom leant over and grabbed a bunch of carrots from a nearby bucket. He broke one off and handed it to Deborah.

"He loves them."

Deborah flattened her palm and held it up to Hercules, who had already smelt it. He chomped it off her palm.

"When did he come?"

She watched the groom counting back the days. "Last week. The small Sissie brought him."

Deborah hesitated before she tried again. "Can you remember her name?"

The groom frowned in concentration then shook his head sadly. "Sorry."

She had to have her name. "Was it a short or a long name?"

"Short. It was a white person's name," he said sheepishly.

It was a long shot, but she had to try. "Katie? Was it Katie?"

A broad smile lit up his face. "Katie. She is the new owner of Hercules."

ooo

Deborah watered the Shasta daisies at the kitchen door. They were looking green and lush. Hopefully they'd burst into flower by Christmastime. She gave the hydrangea bush an extra slosh. Maybe this time she'd manage to grow one successfully. They always seemed to die on her.

Her mind wandered as she pulled up weeds and tidied the beds. How had Katie become the new owner of Hercules? Had Chris given him to her? Had she managed to buy him? She'd really like an answer. There were so many things she'd like answers to. She emptied the watering can over the patch of grass and pulled the door closed behind her. The sound of Julia's sewing machine whirring away in the lounge lured her there, and she pushed Bob off an armchair. A car pulled up outside and she peeped through the stained glass window.

"They're back."

Terror rippled down her spine and her heart clambered against her chest. She pulled her jersey around her shoulders. Julia finished off a seam before looking up.

"Who is?"

"The SB men. They were there earlier, too."

Deborah felt sure they were just trying to intimidate her. What more could they possibly want? They knew Chris was in hospital, seriously injured. Didn't they have any compassion? She fluctuated between wanting to barge out and confront them or just curl up in a ball under her bed until they gave up on her. She shuddered at the memory of the slap. The sound of the belt swishing back, in the dark, windowless room made her shut her eyes. Thank goodness for her tango dancer. She didn't want to even think about what could have happened. She had been a hair's breath away from …

"Phone your tango guy."

Deborah stared at her. Julia measured the silk fabric. "Really, why don't you phone him? He did say he'd help."

She watched Julia manoeuvre the material beneath the foot. There was no way in hell she could design and make her own wedding dress—if she ever needed one. She felt around in her bag and pulled out the card. Robert Silverman.

"Debs, I'm serious. This is frightening stuff. Just phone him. Now."

"The SB would have detained me by now, if they were serious. I don't think—"

"Well, I do. Pick up that phone. Please."

Deborah took a step towards the phone and then turned back to say something. Julia shouted now, "People disappear into detention for months. I don't want that to happen to you. Pick up the bloody phone, Debs!"

The call was answered on the second ring, but Robert was in court. She left her number, just in case. He'd probably never call back, but still.

"What did he say?" Julia was tapping her foot anxiously.

"Not there. He'll phone back."

Julia's anxiety was contagious and Deborah's stomach twisted into a knot.

"Geez, Debs, what if he doesn't?"

"I don't know. I really don't know."

She peeped out again and willed the car to pull away. If they would just leave now, there'd be a chance that Robert Silverman would phone back, before they returned.

Julia was making her way down the passage. "I'm phoning Boetie. He must come. There's safety in numbers."

By six o'clock the car had disappeared, and Boetie was opening a bottle of Robertson's Shiraz.

"Thank the Pope," Deborah muttered and meandered to the kitchen.

"I'll cook tonight, Jules."

"Miracles never cease. What are we having?"

"Curry à la Deborah."

Julia threw her eyes upward. "Isn't that what she cooked last time?"

"It was good. I'm quite happy to eat that. Go for it, Debs." Boetie handed her a glass. She passed him a knife and some onions. Then she busied herself with her box of spices and checked that she had all the important ones. She began peeling potatoes rapidly, while the lamb knuckles soaked up the marinade. *Just don't think. Switch off Deborah*, she told herself again and again.

The car was gone. She could breathe. But she knew it would return.

oOo

By six o'clock the next day, the car was back. Deborah clicked her tongue as she opened the door for Bob and he lifted his leg on the rosebush before barking. Deborah stared for a moment, but the two men kept their eyes forward.

"Phone for you, Debs," Julia called from the passage. She mouthed "a man."

"Deborah Morley?" She recognised his voice immediately.

"Mr Silverman?"

"Robert. Just Robert. How can I be of assistance?"

Deborah peered through the window. "There's a car parked outside our cottage. It's been there every afternoon this week. We're being watched."

"Describe it to me."

"Black BMW, dark windows, a silver stripe along the mudguard."

"Good girl. Now the number plate. Can you see it clearly enough to read it out?"

She squinted through the curtain and read it out to him. "CY 008 2248."

"Got it. Give me your address and a landmark."

She repeated her address and added, "Just behind the Rosebank Station."

"Sit tight. I'll be there in half an hour."

ooo

"I think you'd better tell me everything."

Robert Silverman stirred cream into his coffee. Julia got up to leave the room, but he waved her into her seat again.

"Stay. You can help fill in the details."

"What do you want to know?"

"Just start talking. What needs to be said will be said."

He took out a notepad and a black Montblanc. "Tell me all about Chris. What does he do, what are his interests, where was he going to when … whatever you can think of about him."

"Tell him about the books," Julia prompted.

Deborah found herself re-telling the whole story, and this time she included Katie.

When she paused, Robert looked up from his pad. "I know this is hard for you, but could you tell me about his injuries —everything you know about them."

Julia refilled their cups.

Deborah coughed into her jersey.

"This is really important," he stressed.

She leant forward. "The driver lost control of the steering wheel on a sandy road. Chris was flung out and hit his head. He was in a coma for weeks, but he's out of the coma now, and he's going to be—"

He was scrutinizing her now.

"I think he's going to be fine."

Robert's eyes turned to Julia, who hesitated, then gave a quick nod. He scribbled a few more words before he snapped the notebook shut.

"Do you have any idea where Chris was going?"

Deborah looked directly at Robert. "No. No, I don't. He never told me."

He kept her gaze for a few seconds before he looked at Julia. "Anything else I should know?"

"Someone mentioned a loose steering wheel. I don't know if that means anything, but it just sounded suspicious." Julia shrugged as Robert opened his notebook again and made another note.

"If you remember anything else, anything at all, phone me."

The telephone. Deborah had almost forgotten about that. "I forgot to say. We think our phone is tapped."

"It probably is," he agreed instantly. "Anything else?"

She couldn't think of anything more. There was something bothering her, though. She had no idea how much this would all cost and how she could pay him.

"Um, there is one thing, Mr... Robert." Deborah noticed his cheek twitching slightly. "How much do I owe you for this? I don't—"

"Wednesday evenings. Every Wednesday evening. Tango nights. I need someone to partner the singles."

Julia leant forward. "You teach people the tango?"

Robert laughed and stood up. "I do indeed."

He shook Julia's hand and then turned to Deborah. "There are a couple of men parked outside, and I need to have a serious chat with them. You'll have to excuse me, ladies. I'll be in touch. I don't imagine you'll be seeing this car parked outside your cottage anymore, but if you do, I'm a phone call away."

"I don't know how to thank you."

Mr Robert Silverman patted her on the arm, pulled the door open and strolled over to the black BMW.

○○○

When the letter arrived, Deborah recognised the writing on the envelope. She hadn't dared hope he would reply. Perhaps he had changed his mind. The sudden knot in her stomach belied that, and she forced herself not to hope for too much.

My Pixie,
Thank you for your letter. I'm sorry I couldn't see you when you came to visit me. There was just too much to process and I needed time on my own.
I am finally being moved from the hospital to my parents' farm up in the North. You need to believe me when I say our relationship can never be the same again.
If, and only if, you can accept my offer of friendship, then I would like you to visit us.
Chris x

New hope flared in her heart. He did want to see her. For now, they could be just friends. She'd accept any conditions, just as long as she could see him.

Julia's key jangled in the door.

"It's open." Deborah waved the letter at her and patted the sofa. "He does want to see me. Oh, thank goodness. I'm so happy, I could burst."

Julia squinted at the letter and then read it aloud.

"What do you think, Jules?"

Julia's frown made her suck in her breath. "I think you need to hear what he is saying. It is over. You need to accept that first."

"I will. I will."

Julia reached for the cigarettes and slid two out. "No, seriously, my friend. You need to think this through before you go up and visit him."

Deborah took a deep drag of her cigarette. Chris was being totally honest. Could she accept a friendship? She didn't want to. She didn't know if she could. But she did want to see him, desperately.

"I need to see him."

Deborah watched her friend pouring them each a glass of wine. She could fly to Johannesburg and spend a night with her mum. There was a train up to Pietersburg. Perhaps Chris' dad could fetch her from there. She'd need to take a day or two off work. Gloria Fey would probably not like that, but perhaps she'd be empathetic. She'd just have to ask.

ooo

Chapter Fifteen

The train eased into Pietersburg Station. Deborah leant out of the window and looked around for Chris' father. She needn't have worried about not recognising him. A tall grey-haired man scanned the windows of the train. Her eyes met his and she felt as if she were looking into Chris' striking blue eyes. He walked alongside the train and took her suitcase as she stepped down onto the platform.

"You must be Deborah. Chris said I should look for the prettiest girl on the train." The resemblance was overwhelming. "At last we get to meet you. Welcome. My son is waiting for you." He shook her hand firmly.

"Mr Jarvis, you look just like your son."

"Speaking as his progenitor, I must say that the contrary is true: he looks just like me."

Deborah laughed and followed him to the bakkie. As she slid into the passenger seat he gestured at her slip slops. "Hope there are some *takkies* in that bag. You're going to come walking with me as soon as we've settled you in."

That wasn't what she'd planned to do. "Yes of course. I packed walking shoes."

The bakkie jolted over the sandy road. Deborah watched the rows of avocado trees whizz by. Dust shot up around the tyres, and she breathed in the country mix of fresh air and manure.

"Avos, pecans and some cattle. That's what we farm." Mr Jarvis slowed to let a goat cross the road.

"Chris told me you were a shy, quiet girl. Is that true?"

Deborah smiled awkwardly. "I used to be, not so much these days." It was true. The shyness she'd always had about her was dropping away, almost like an invisible cloak she no longer needed.

"Um, Mr Jarvis—"

He wagged a finger at her as he interrupted. "No Mr around here. Mickey's the name."

She tried again. "How is Chris?"

His eyes lost their sparkle for an instant. "We've got a long ways to go. A very long way, but he'll be fine. He will. We're all working really hard to make that happen."

He tightened his grip on the wheel and swerved to avoid two red hens. Silence settled and Deborah watched the sapphire sky. There were so many questions she'd wanted to ask. But there was time. She shouldn't rush things.

"You're going to cheer him up to no end. I can already feel that."

The bakkie slowed to a stop. Deborah took a moment to realise that she should jump out and open the farm gate. The bakkie edged past her and she swung the gate shut and clambered back in.

"You adapt to farm life easily, I see."

Deborah laughed. She had absolutely no intention of becoming a farmer's wife. She was going to become the best journalist she could possibly be. But still, Mickey's cheeky smile disarmed her. She could see where Chris got his charm. And his looks.

A woman stood in the doorway, her apron covered in flour. She wiped her hand on it before taking Deborah's hand.

"Hello, Mrs Jarvis."

Deborah felt the roughness of her skin. A black Alice band kept her curly hair away from her face. She smiled as the Rottweiler puppy, pressed up against her leg, licked her hand.

"Come in, come in. We don't stand on ceremony here."

Mickey led her to a bedroom at the end of the hall. "We'll sort out your bag and room in a moment. First things first."

When the wheelchair appeared in the doorframe, Deborah found herself struggling for air. She hadn't expected a wheelchair. She stretched her hand out and then dropped it to her side. But of course he would need to use a wheelchair until he'd recovered properly. He must get very tired.

Fear gripped her heart and she felt it pounding in her chest. What did she really know about his injuries? She had focussed only on the coma; had thought that, if only he would wake, everything would be fine. He would be back to his old self.

She met Chris' eyes. He was watching her intently, and pity was the last thing she wanted him to see. If he really looked at her, he'd see how much she loved him. When she looked at him she saw the reason for her existence. She'd do anything for him. The wheelchair didn't change that. She willed him to see it, to reconsider, to give her a chance.

When he smiled at her, she felt as if a reprieve were still possible. His eyes lit up his pale face and she crouched to hug him. His left arm seemed gripped in a kind of spasm, but slowly, his right arm moved towards her and his fingers entangled themselves in her hair. After a few seconds, she sat on the chair close by.

Mickey had turned away and was staring out of the window. He took a few seconds to regain his composure before he turned around.

"Welcome to the farm, Pixie." Chris was speaking slowly and with effort, but he was actually speaking. Deborah drew in a deep breath.

"Thank you. I'm really pleased to be here."

"How was your trip?"

"Fine. It was fine."

"My dad will show you the farm later. And the horses. I'm sure you'd like to see the horses." Chris gazed past her and out of the window towards the stables. His eyes darkened for a moment before he looked back at her.

"My mum sends her love. She always asks after you."

"Thank you. Same to her." He choked as he tried to swallow and Anna was at his side in an instant, holding a glass of water to his mouth. He took a few sips and cleared his throat.

"Speaking still tires him out a lot. He needs to get used to it," Mrs Jarvis explained. "You know, he—"

"Tell me all about Cape Town." Chris focussed on Deborah.

"I'm still in the cottage with Julia. She's preparing for the wedding, so there are bits of fabric and needles all over the place. Boetie pops in often and ends up staying for supper. Bob insists on his walk every evening. Not much has changed really."

"What about your job? What are you writing about now?"

"I'm with *Panache* permanently now. Fashion and lifestyle are what I do best, I think. At the moment, I'm covering a Design Indaba in the city." She was aware of her cheeks heating up as she anticipated Chris' disapproval. But he smiled encouragingly. Anna seemed to give Mickey a secret signal, because he stood abruptly and walked towards Deborah. "Let's get you settled in your room, young lady. Anna and Chris need to take care of a few things before lunch."

Deborah looked at Chris and he nodded. Mickey left her at the guest room, where she put her bag on the blue and white striped bedspread and patted the Rottweiler puppy that was shadowing her. She was about to explore the farmhouse when she noticed Mickey waiting in the passage.

"Takkies. We're going for a quick walk now."

The farm stretched out before them. Deborah watched the lambs skitter after one another. Speckled red and black hens dashed between the rows of trees to escape a strident rooster, who announced his intent unashamedly.

"How?" Deborah stopped. She didn't know how to ask him. "I mean, I just don't know anything about his injuries."

Mickey nodded and watched the hens scurry among the trees. "It's a head injury. A bit like suffering a stroke. His movements," Mickey ran a hand over his face, sniffed, and then continued, "... well, you saw him."

He turned and smiled at her. "But where there's life, as they say. We'll never give up on seeing him walk and—"

She returned his smile. Mickey pulled out his Leatherman to fix a small hole in the fence. "I hope my son has behaved like a gentleman towards you."

Deborah hesitated. "Sorry? I'm not sure what—"

"I didn't mean to embarrass you, my girl. But what with Katie arriving at his bedside, too, Anna and I were a bit puzzled by it all."

"I'm also a bit puzzled." She kept her eyes on the fence.

"Don't get me wrong. We knew all about you. Chris spoke about you all the time. Katie came as a bit of a surprise to us, I must say."

Deborah shifted the sand with her takkie. "Tell me about it," she mumbled.

She could feel Mr Jarvis' eyes sizing her up, but she didn't look at him. This was not the kind of conversation she felt comfortable about, especially not with Chris' father. "I'm just focussing on Chris' recovery now. I'd really like to be part of that if I can, Mr, I mean, Mickey."

"Your being here will help, I can assure you."

Mickey was pensive as they walked between the trees. Deborah chewed her lip and looked across the fields. The sun was bearing down on them. She watched the wisp of cloud disappear and listened to the crickets.

"Give him some time," Mickey said, without turning to look at her.

She shook her head. "I'm not sure. It's no use. He seems to have made up his mind."

Deborah watched the farm stretch out before her. She couldn't bring herself to look at Mickey. The sorrow in his eyes was a reflection of her own.

"She hasn't been here, you know."

Deborah didn't turn her head.

"Katie. He never invited her here. Only you."

"I didn't know."

"It's verby with her. It's over. Chris said so."

Deborah could feel her cheeks burning. She kept her eyes on the ground and tried to steady her breathing. She couldn't have this conversation. Not with Mickey, anyway.

Mickey swore at a herd of goats which had ended up on the wrong side of a fence. Chicks were scratching in the dust, mimicking the red hen, and the puppy began chasing them.

"Stay!"

The puppy stopped in mid-flight and crept back guiltily. Mickey patted his head. "Smart move."

Deborah threw her head back in laughter at the pup's miserable face.

"Your face lights up when you laugh. You should do it more often."

He was trying to make her feel at home. And she did. She could get used to a life like this. Perhaps being a farmer's wife wouldn't be so bad, after all. She envied Anna the simplicity. She imagined Chris and his siblings growing up here in the country.

Life seemed uncomplicated. It must have been special. The wide open spaces, the freedom, horses to ride.

Mickey broke into her reverie. "He loves you, you know."

The lump in her throat brought on a coughing fit. She tried to keep her eyes focussed ahead. Mickey slowed his pace. He seemed ready to say more, but then shook his head. Deborah followed him down the next row of trees. He was checking the avos as he went along. She stroked the puppy, who seemed to have adopted her.

"Mind the prickly pears."

Deborah watched in awe as he cut a pear loose, skinned it expertly and then handed it to her. The greenish flesh melted in her mouth as she bit into it, and she held one hand under it to catch the juice.

"Heavenly."

Mickey beamed at her. "Thought you'd like that."

He helped her over a fence and into another section. Then he pulled out a packet of Camels and popped one in his mouth. Just as he was about to light it, he turned to her. "You don't smoke, do you?"

She hesitated and he held out the packet. "Thanks."

She could feel him watching her as she took a drag and blew the smoke into the fresh country air. A storm cloud was forming and the sun dipped behind it. Mickey put his jacket over her shoulders.

"We'd better get back. Anna doesn't like anyone to be late for lunch."

ooo

The smell of roast chicken filled the house, and Mickey gestured Deborah to a seat at the table. Then he walked back down the passage to bring Chris. "He'll be doing this himself in no time." He manoeuvred the chair into position before taking his place at the head to carve the chicken. Anna served roast potatoes, pumpkin fritters, sweetened carrots, tiny green peas and a salad topped with avocados and pecans. Deborah brought a forkful up to her mouth and stopped mid-air when Anna bowed her head.

"For what we are about to receive, may the Lord make us truly grateful."

Anna cut up Chris' food into bite-size bits. Deborah wanted to say, "Stop that. Chris can do it," but the truth took her breath away. He couldn't. She felt herself go limp and could barely swallow a mouthful. She pushed the food around her plate and wondered how she was going to force it down. A picture of Chris on Hercules galloping along Noordhoek Beach flashed across her mind, and she swallowed hard before she met his eyes again. He looked embarrassed.

"Sorry, Mum. I wish—"

"Shush. Don't be silly, Chris. I don't mind doing it."

"I could do it." Anna's glare stopped Deborah from saying anymore. It wasn't her place. And yet she was overwhelmed with love for him, and all she wanted to do was take over, look after him. Mickey cleared his throat and winked at her as he directed a question at Chris.

"Did you know that your girlfriend smoked?"

"That's not really your business, Dad. She'll make up her own mind about when to stop."

Chris shot his father a look and Deborah coughed into her serviette. Anna began to serve seconds and Deborah declined politely. Every tick of the grandfather clock sounded loud and imposing. Time seemed to slow down, and the pudding spoon reminded her that lunch wasn't over yet. The south-facing room was dark, in stark contrast to the sunny farm. Deborah watched Chris' face turn towards the stables again, and the longing in his eyes brought another surge of heartache.

She tried to catch his attention and start up a conversation. "Should we play a little chess after lunch? I brought my set with me, in case you felt like—"

His eyes lit up and a gleam of the old Chris shone through. "I'd love that."

"I've taught myself a few more moves, so I might even be able to beat you this time."

"Not a snowball's chance in hell."

To hear him laugh again was worth all the awkwardness over lunch. Her heart skipped a beat as she looked into his twinkly eyes. He was still her Chris.

Mickey took a sip of beer and leant back in his chair. "You should stay a little longer. Chris is cheering up with you here."

When Anna began to clear the dishes, Deborah pushed her chair back. "May I help?"

Anna's eyes were soft now and a smile crept into the corners of her mouth. "Not this time. You sit and catch up with Chris."

Mickey piled the plates and followed Anna, closing the door firmly behind him. Deborah folded her serviette and glanced at Chris. She wondered what he was really thinking. Had he changed his mind about their relationship? He seemed more relaxed now. She studied his face. "Are you pleased I came?"

He moved his hand up to brush away some potato. "Yes. I'm pleased you came, Deborah, very pleased."

She shifted her seat closer and took his hand. "It's so good to see you, Chris. I—"

His frown made her withdraw her hand. "We are friends, right?"

Deborah hesitated for a second. "It isn't what I want."

The sparkle left his eyes, and Deborah watched the muscle in his jaw twitch. "We've been through this. You read my letter. You agreed to the conditions of the visit."

She should have stopped the conversation. She reached for the chess set and then blurted out, "I was hoping that in time— It's Kate, isn't it?"

His eyes flashed. "Katie's not even in the picture. She's long gone. That's unfair to say. I told you we couldn't be together and you said you agreed. We can't. I'll never be the same again."

Deborah reached for his hand, but he pulled it back. "I love you, Chris. I want you just the way you are. I—"

Now his voice boomed across the room and he strained his neck in the effort. "For heaven's sake. Don't you ever listen? I can't offer you anything. My body's buggered. All I've got is the partial use of one arm. I have no idea if I'll ever be able to walk again. I—"

He broke into a coughing fit. Deborah slapped him on the back.

"But your dad said you would. You're still recovering. In time you will, Chris. I'll help you, I'll—"

This time, his voice was almost a whisper. "Goddam it, Pix. You promised. My brain was fried on that road. There's a part of it that will never recover. It's gone, knocked out. Do you know what that means? I can't talk properly and maybe I'll never walk. Get that into your head."

Deborah shuddered. "I don't care about that, Chris. I love you! I want to be with you. Can't you get that into your head?"

"No. No, I can't. I don't want you to love me. I want you to live your own life. I can't be in a relationship with you. Can't you see? It's killing me to see you there, as if nothing has changed. I can't even manage my own life."

Deborah looked out at the stables. She swallowed hard and pressed her palms against her eyes. Try as she might, she couldn't stop tears from trickling down her cheeks and she swiped at them angrily. She felt his fingers reaching for her hand, but she didn't respond.

Mickey pushed the kitchen door open with his hip, balancing a tray of jelly and custard. Deborah jumped up to help. They must have heard the argument from the kitchen. She tried her best to be cheerful.

"My favourite pudding." She put the bowls on the table.

"Phew. I'm pleased I got that one right." The tension in Mickey's jaw relaxed.

Cool jelly and custard slid down her throat, and this time she accepted a second helping. Mickey chatted and Anna fussed over Chris. Deborah dug deep to regain her composure. By the time Anna and Mickey cleared the table and disappeared into the kitchen, Deborah could meet Chris' eyes again. This time she allowed him to take her hand.

"Can we be friends?" he asked.

When she didn't reply, he squeezed her hand.

"If that's what you want." She followed his eyes to the dresser.

"Pick it up." The parcel felt soft and she pulled at the ribbon. "It's for your birthday. Promise you won't open it before."

She looked at him for a few seconds. She imagined him in the fields, riding his horse across the acres, leaving his muddied boots on the stoep as he entered the house. He was made for this farm. She remembered the sangoma's prophecy. Chris would have been the only one of his siblings to seek out the farm's sangoma under the star-filled night sky. He listened to his predictions, instead of pooh-poohing them as primitive folklore.

She could picture him leaving for university and hitching home every vac, instead of catching the train like everyone else. He always longed for the break. It was as if his soul needed to be here in order to rejuvenate. The brick-red soil of this African farm was in his blood. It gave him the energy he needed for The Struggle, for politics and city life. The farm had formed him, probably more than anything else in his life. He belonged here.

Then the penny finally dropped. Chris was never going to leave the farm again. He was never going to walk again. More than that, he would need help with the simplest details of his life. He didn't want her to be part of that. He would hate it. He would resent her for seeing him in that state. He would prefer not to have her at all. He was sending her away, and it was unlikely that she'd ever come back. He was staring at her, but she turned her head towards the window.

"Debs?"

"I promise."

ooo

The ringing was dead on-cue. Deborah scrambled for her watch and switched on her bedside lamp. One a.m. "Where am I?" It took her a second to register. She was back in the cottage. She ran for the phone and listened to the heavy breathing. She banged the receiver down and made her way back to bed. If the SB had wanted to remind her they were still stalking her, then they had done that. She'd left the receiver off the hook some nights and on others, tried to ignore it; but if she didn't pick up, the caller simply rang again and again until she answered.

A pang of loneliness washed over her. She missed Chris so much, it hurt physically. After shivering for a while, she tiptoed to the kitchen to make some tea.

When six o'clock came, she dragged herself to the shower and let the stream of water revive her. What more did they want from her? She couldn't be useful to them.

Julia called from her bedroom, "Shall we try and get our number changed?"

Later, when Boetie popped in for coffee after work, he examined the phone. "Let me see what I can do. Maybe I can block that caller somehow. I'll come and fiddle with it as soon as I have a gap."

"Why don't you ask your tango man on Wednesday? He'll have a good idea," Julia suggested.

Deborah shook her head. She couldn't keep asking Robert Silverman to rescue her. He'd already helped so much. She was pretty sure it was one of the SB men. They wanted her to know she was still on their radar. As long as she stayed in Cape Town, she'd have them breathing down her neck. Julia was getting married soon, and she'd have to go to the wedding alone. The cottage was on the market. She needed to find new digs, start all over again, this time without Chris.

Maybe it was time to go away, leave Cape Town for a bit. She was in a rut. The persistent phone calls were like a constantly dripping tap. Chris' absence had left a huge hole. On some mornings, she'd force her limbs out of bed and hope that the hot shower would inject energy into her. She'd climb into whatever clothes hung over her chair and scoop her knotty hair up into a ponytail. The dark rings under her eyes were attracting comments from friends. She had taken no notice until an unexpected glance at a dishevelled reflection in a shop window had shocked her. It had taken a second to register that she was looking at herself. She didn't look like that. She couldn't look like that.

ooo

"I've decided to go away."

Gloria Fey shifted the papers on her desk and looked up at Deborah blankly. "Take a seat, young lady." She bit the end of her pencil and raised an eyebrow.

"I need to get away from everything. At least for a while." Deborah interlaced her fingers on her lap.

Gloria pushed her glasses down to the tip of her nose and peered at Deborah. "Are you resigning?"

"Yes. Yes, I am."

Gloria got up and poured two cups of filter coffee. "Cream and sugar?"

Deborah nodded to both. She didn't usually take sugar, but suddenly it felt like a good idea. This wasn't coming across the way she'd planned it.

Gloria was sipping her coffee and fixing her full attention on her now.

"I don't really know what to say."

Gloria twiddled her pencil and gazed at Deborah. "Are you unhappy with us?"

Deborah sipped her coffee and declined the biscuit. She attempted a smile but knew her eyes were giving her away. "No. No, I'm happy. It's just that—"

She looked at Gloria hopefully. Gloria merely nodded. Deborah straightened her back and launched in. "After Chris' accident and everything. I need to go somewhere new. I need to unscramble my life, find out who I am and where the hell I'm going."

Now a hint of a smile crossed Gloria's face. "I'm beginning to understand. Go on."

Deborah took a deep breath. "I just need to go away."

"Perhaps you do."

Deborah peered at her as she drank her lukewarm coffee.

"How about sleeping on this for a week or so? Mull over your idea some more and then come back to me. We'll talk about it again. What do you think?"

Relief flooded through her and she leant towards Gloria. "I'd like that. I don't think I'll change my mind, but yes, I'll mull over it."

Gloria stood up abruptly, flashed a smile and put out her hand. "That's settled then. We'll talk in a week or two."

She was being dismissed. "Thank you so much. I really—"

"I'm seeing your progress and I like it. Don't rush into a decision just yet. Okay?"

Deborah pushed her chair back and wound her way to her own desk. She'd hardly slept the night before, and now she'd done it. Yes.

Her phone was ringing off the hook and she snatched it up. "The intrepid traveller here," she said on impulse.

There was a hum on the line and then Charlie said, "Still on for this evening? Pig at six?"

"Yes. Yes, of course."

She could feel his hesitation. "Why the intrepid traveller?"

"Oh, just a whim. Nothing really." When there was no response, she added, "See you later."

ooo

The Pig was already in full swing when they got there. Charlie stood up and waved at her. He shifted over to make space on the bench between himself and Annie. Boetie was pouring the champagne, and he handed her the first flute. Julia smiled at her.

"Cold Duck's my absolute best. I hope you know that I dance on the table after two glasses."

Boetie raised his glass. "I'll hold you to that, birthday girl."

"You think I'm joking, hey?" Deborah swished her skirt at him and grabbed one of the roses to put between her teeth.

"I'm coming round tomorrow morning, to give you your birthday present."

The rose fell onto the table and Deborah put it back into the vase. "Oh? What is it, Boetie? Now you've got me all curious."

"Let's just say your phone is going to get a make over." He puffed out his chest and a grin spread across his face. He was up to something and Deborah prodded him in the ribs.

"What do you mean?"

"I think I've worked out how to short circuit a little something that doesn't belong there. It might just cut out those midnight calls."

She planted a kiss on his cheek before she took a gulp of her bubbly. "You'll be my hero forever if you manage to do that for me."

Boetie poured champagne into the rest of the flutes. "I wish that was really true."

Deborah was about to take another sip, when Julia opened the box she'd been carrying. She took out a huge chocolate cake, decorated with tiny gold roses and *Deborah* written in the middle. Twenty-five candles stood around the tray like torch-bearing guards.

"That's out of this world." She squeezed Julia's shoulder. "Thanks so much for spoiling me."

Boetie led the group into a loud, not quite in tune, "Happy Birthday," and Deborah took a deep breath to blow out the candles.

"Veels geluk, meisiekind." Boetie's bear hug lifted her off her feet, and the sound of clinking glasses competed with "Bye, Bye, Miss American Pie" belting from the speakers.

"Make a wish, my friend." Julia handed her a silver knife and she slid it down into the moist sponge. Her thoughts took her to Chris' bedside, and she wished for his recovery. She wished for a miracle, for him to wake up and be able to walk again. She wished she could wave a magic wand, and she wished for a radical change in her life. She felt Julia poking her in the ribs.

"Just one wish, otherwise it won't come true."

"I wish for you all to be my friends forever." She looked around at her circle of amazing people.

The flutes were raised and Charlie made the toast. "To Deborah. Stay just the way you are. We wouldn't change a thing. Happy Birthday."

Glasses clinked and Deborah took a slug of her champagne. Her friends were waiting, and she didn't know how to start.

Boetie tapped his glass and winked at her. "Say something, meisie."

"Thank you so much for being here with me. This is really special. I don't know what I'd do without you all in my life, and I hope you'll still be here when I get back."

The smiles surrounding her dropped away. She hadn't intended to drop a bomb like that. She'd meant to thank everyone, talk about the wonderful times they'd had together, eventually ease into the news of her leaving. She searched for Julia's face.

"After the wedding, that is." All her friends still looked astonished. "I'll come back," she offered as an apology.

The questions overwhelmed her.

"What do you mean?"

"But where are you going to?"

"How long will you be away for?"

Charlie interrupted the bombardment by jumping up on the bench and clinking a glass. "To old friends and new beginnings. To treasuring the times together and embracing change. Wherever you plan to go, we wish you well. And yes, some of us will be here when you get back."

The mood reverted and Rodriguez' sexy voice singing "Sugarman" eased the crowd into a rhythmic sway.

"You could have knocked me down with a feather, girl." Annie punched her arm.

"Sorry. It wasn't meant to."

"I'm dying to know what you're planning. Where *are* you going?" Annie ran her fingers through her new violet fringe and pulled out her box of cigarettes. Boetie put his hand on her neck and shook his head, as Julia wedged herself between them.

"Jy's full of surprises, meisie."

"You'll definitely still be my bridesmaid, hey?"

Deborah laughed and held out her glass for Charlie to fill. "I love you guys."

"Last round, anyone?" Charlie shouted over the hubbub. The Pig was filling up rapidly, and Deborah accepted Happy Birthday wishes from random strangers pushing past and spilling beer as they went.

"Deborah, my friend, your lift is now leaving." Julia gathered the tray of cake and the flowers. Boetie got up to follow her, and Deborah looked around for Charlie.

"Would you mind giving me a lift a little later?"

Charlie patted the space next to him on the bench and swung his leg over so that he could face Deborah. "I couldn't think of anything I'd look forward to more."

Julia waved as she pushed through the swing doors. "Great. I'm not waiting up for you, though."

Deborah put her box of cigarettes on the table.

"Coffee, birthday girl? What about an Irish coffee?"

"Oh, yes, please." Irish coffee was her favourite treat. She lit a cigarette as Charlie gestured to a waiter.

"So?"

She blew a smoke ring and smiled at him. "So what?" She could see a thousand questions coming her way and she laughed.

"What's this all about? When did you decide to do this? When do you leave? Are you coming back?"

Deborah took another deep drag before she answered him. "I don't know yet."

She felt an unexpected lurch in her stomach as he shifted closer. "That's it? Four words to answer all my questions?"

"I'll come back, one day," she offered.

"Hmmm. Time is of the essence then."

She looked at him quizzically.

He was being his usual cryptic self, and she wasn't sure if he was saying what she thought he might be.

"Time for what?"

Charlie tickled the palm of her hand. "To woo you, win you over."

She let him walk his fingers over her hand for a little longer, before she put it on her lap. "I'm not sure I'm worth the trouble."

Charlie handed her an Irish coffee, and she sipped the hot liquid through the thick cream. She was enjoying his company. He had been so great this evening. She admired the way he could think on his feet. He jumped in, took over when he needed to, smoothed over the cracks. He was really sophisticated. She wished she was half as smart as he was.

"I really like you, Charlie. You're the most dynamic person I've ever met. I could be in your company forever. It's just that I'm kind of mixed up at the moment, you know. I need some time."

Charlie leant forward and put his finger on her lips. "I've got time."

She studied him. His impish face was quite serious now, and she noticed his knee jumping up and down rapidly. An untamed curl was falling across his eyes, and she stopped herself from pushing it back.

"I can't promise anything."

He took the small parcel out of his jacket pocket and slid it over to her.

"What's this?"

"Open it."

She pulled the ribbon and carefully unwrapped the gold paper. Staring up at her from the wooden frame was the newspaper cutting of The Magpies. There she was, in the middle of the winning quartet, smiling at the press photographer. "How did you know about this? Where did you find it?"

"Boetie told me about your dance classes in the townships. I was impressed, so I did a little research. I'm a newspaperman, in case you'd forgotten."

She pressed the framed cutting against her heart and reached up to peck Charlie on the cheek. He turned his face in time to receive it on his lips. Deborah pulled back quickly and he put his hands on her shoulders.

"If you think I'm going to just let you disappear from my life, you'd better think again. I'm tenacious enough to hang in there. I'll wait until you've travelled the world and you're ready to come home. It'll be a pain in the butt, but I'll do it."

"It might take me a long, long time to do all the travelling I need to do, Charlie."

○○○

Julia had left the passage light on. Deborah tiptoed into her room. It had been a magical night, and her heart was bursting with gratitude. She would never have survived the year without her friends. So much had happened. Her life had been turned upside down. She'd been jolted out of her little world and catapulted into the big wide one. There had been times when she couldn't cope. But she had. Some hidden strength had emerged from deep within.

The phone rang on the dot of midnight and she dashed into the passage. "Deborah doesn't live here anymore," she whispered into the receiver, before she slammed it down hard.

The moon shone in through her window and a breeze shifted her curtains. Chris' present beckoned from her bedside table. She'd left it for last and now the ribbon fell away. She parted the tissue paper to pick up the African print fabric. It was a circular skirt, in her favourite shades of green. Beneath it she spotted the card nestling in the folds. Tears blurred the words as she read it and Bob pushed a wet nose into her thigh.

She leant out of the window and looked up at the stars. The Milky Way was easy to spot, but her eyes clouded over again before she could make out Orion's Belt. She climbed into bed and read the card one last time …

For my pixie girl,
Just a little something to remind you, that wherever you end up in the world, you are an African.
Hamba Kahle my friend.
In my heart forever,
Chris.
P S Remember to look up at the night sky.

○○○

Chapter Sixteen

The train glided into Venice Station. Deborah put her backpack down so that she could wriggle into it easily. A barefoot girl in a gypsy skirt scooped it up, jumped off the train and then held it out to her as she dismounted.

"That's so kind of you," Deborah began.

"Two lira."

Deborah shook her head and held out her hand for the backpack.

The girl clutched it against herself. "Pay."

There was no use arguing. Deborah handed over the money and the smile returned immediately. Damn. She wasn't used to this. Cape Town beggars were polite, funny even.

A wave of homesickness seeped in again. Julia and Boetie would be on their way to Hermanus. She wondered how Chris was really coping. She smiled at Charlie's sweet postcard and missed him more than expected.

The throng of people jostled her along. Many of them were heading for the Grand Canal, so it was easy to find.

"Vaporetti?" she asked the woman walking next to her.

"There." The woman pointed at the jetty.

Deborah walked towards the ticket machine, slotted the liras in and took her ticket.

"San Silvestro?"

The conductor snatched her ticket and then threw it back at her. "Off!" He pointed back to the jetty.

"But why?"

He shook his head angrily. "Pronto, Pronto!" He bellowed at the passengers crowding the entrance and gesticulated towards the seats inside the boat.

Deborah watched the boat pull away without her. Now what?

An elderly gentleman walked towards her and pointed towards the ticket machine. "Validate, validate," he repeated.

"Oh. Thank you very much."

"Beeeg fine." He showed her with his outstretched arms.

When the next boat arrived, Deborah was the first to jump aboard. She flashed her ticket and asked, "San Silvestro?"

The conductor shouted "Pronto" at her and she edged her way to the other side. If she was on the wrong boat, then so be it. She read the names of each stop and watched as people got off and others swarmed on. Ahead looked like a bridge. Of course. Rialto Bridge. She could jump off there. She'd find her way to San Silvestro. It was close enough.

"Wrong ticket." The conductor bellowed at her. She looked down at her ticket. It was validated and for the right route. Even if she was going in the wrong direction, the ticket was still valid.

She hesitated for a moment and then raised her voice. "It's right. I have the right ticket."

"No, no." The man wagged his finger at her.

She stood her ground. "Yes. It is correct. I'm sure it is."

At the next stop he waved her off. "No. I'm not getting off. I have a ticket and I'm going as far as Rialto."

He frowned and then shrugged his shoulders. "Okay, okay." She held his gaze. "Okay, okay." He turned away first and she felt a little bubble of pride coming up in her chest. She'd stood up to someone.

"Not bad, Deborah," she murmured to herself. It was a feeling she wasn't familiar with. But it felt good, really good.

ooo

She'd had an exciting time travelling all over: UK, Spain, Portugal, France, Germany, Switzerland, Austria, and now Italy. She'd absorbed the art, the music, the culture, street theatre and late night pub crawling. She'd even been lucky enough to see Nureyev perform *Afternoon of a Fawn* at Covent Garden. She'd learnt so much and there was a still lot more, but it was time to go home.

She was a visitor in Europe, but she belonged in Africa. Chris was right. She was African in her heart and soul. She understood the way things worked there, what made people tick. The sounds of the wild stirred her being. Drumming in the far distance called to her spirit. The red earth grounded her. Lightning flashing across a star-studded sky sent shivers of life through her. Campfires in the bush; thorn trees and quivers; leopard prints outside a makeshift tent; the sound of lions calling in the far distance; dramatic cliffs dropping into a cerulean ocean, where seagulls swooped for fish and dolphins and whales were common sights.

She missed all of it desperately. Africa was in her blood, and the longing in her heart was growing stronger with each day that passed. She could go home and help, not in the way Chris had been helping, but in her own way. She'd learnt so much from him, and she'd never forget that. But this was her journey now and it was time to start it. She needed to go and be the best person she could possibly be. After Venice, she'd be on her way.

People surged forward. She allowed the crowd to jolt her back into the moment and move her along. She was here, in magical Venice, and she needed to make the most of the last few days.

There it was in front of her. The famous bridge over the Grande Canale, swarming with people. She hugged the pier and took in the flickering candles on starched linen tablecloths, casting a warm glow across the water. Bellini glasses were clinked and snippets of Italian caught the breeze. Passing shop windows displayed masks, glass jewellery, silk scarves, crafted leather shoes and bags. Chic Venetian women linked arms with dapper Italian men.

By the time Deborah reached the bridge, she was mesmerized. She stopped in the middle to survey Venice stretching on either side. Water lapped at the edges of majestic palazzos, famous art galleries, museums and churches. She was surrounded by mystery and subterfuge. She imagined the masked balls, velvet gowns, clandestine lovers. A crescent moon sparkled on the water as gondoliers serenaded their passengers, ferrying them to candlelight dinners on the water's edge.

A pram jammed into her leg and she stepped back to allow the young mother to squeeze past her. Children zigzagged through the crowd, and a red balloon bobbed above the heads. It seemed to be coming her way, and as it got closer, she saw a golden "D" had been painted on it. How funny. A good omen?

The balloon's owner was coming into view. His blonde curls were hiding his face and she watched him moving closer. The way he bounced along reminded her of someone. Strange, the bird on his t-shirt looked a lot like a hadeda. He was waving now and walking fast. He looked like—it was impossible. Never in a million years could that be Charlie making his way across the bridge, towards her.

ooo

22981251R00119

Printed in Poland
by Amazon Fulfillment
Poland Sp. z o.o., Wrocław